Em... ·guile.
She is the author of the Mrs Jeffries murder mystery
series, and has also written romance novels as Sarah
Temple and Young Adult novels as Cheryl Lanham.
She lives in Southern California.

Visit Emily Brightwell's website at
www.emilybrightwell.com

Mrs Jeffries Sweeps the Chimney

Emily Brightwell

CONSTABLE

CONSTABLE

First published in the US in 2004 by The Berkley Publishing Group,
an imprint of Penguin Group (USA) Inc.

This edition published in Great Britain in 2018 by Constable

1 3 5 7 9 10 8 6 4 2

A CIP catalogue record for this book
is available from the British Library.

ISBN 978-1-47212-568-2

Typeset in Bembo by TW Typesetting, Plymouth, Devon
Printed and bound in Great Britain by CPI Group (UK) Ltd, Croydon CR0 4YY
Papers used by Constable are from well-managed forests and
other responsible sources

MIX
Paper from
responsible sources
FSC® C104740

Constable
An imprint of
Little, Brown Book Group
Carmelite House
50 Victoria Embankment
London EC4Y 0DZ

An Hachette UK Company
www.hachette.co.uk

www.littlebrown.co.uk

CHAPTER ONE

The Reverend Jasper Claypool ran for his life. His legs ached, his lungs were on fire and his breathing was so loud he could no longer hear if there were footsteps pounding behind him. A thick fog had rolled in off the Thames, blanketing the area, and he could barely see three feet in front of him, but perhaps that was all to the good. Perhaps his pursuer couldn't see where he went. It didn't help that he had no idea where he was or in what direction lay help. Generally, though, he'd always thought the London docks fairly teemed with humanity; it had certainly looked that way when he had arrived that morning. But now that he needed someone, anyone, to help him, the place was utterly deserted.

Claypool skidded around the corner, almost lost his footing and then righted himself before his knees hit the cobblestones. In the distance, he could hear the tolling of a church bell for evensong. The Reverend Claypool was a genuinely religious man; he knew the ringing of the bells was a sign from God. 'Thank you, Lord,' he gasped as he turned in what he hoped was the direction of the church. He hurried across the empty

1

street and paused for a moment to get his bearings. But then he heard the thud of footsteps hot on his heels. The bells kept ringing, so he charged toward them, hoping that he had the strength to make it to safety. But he was seventy-five years old, and he knew he couldn't go much farther. There was a funny rushing sound in his ears, and his vision was starting to blur. 'Please, Lord, show me the way,' he prayed silently. God must have heard his plea, for just then the fog parted and the church came in sight. 'Thank you, Lord.' With renewed determination, he raced toward the dimly lighted building. He ran under the wooden eaves and grasped at the handle, but before he could yank the door open, a hand grabbed his arm and pulled him around. With ruthless efficiency, his assailant clutched Claypool and half-dragged, half-carried him around to the side of the building.

Jasper flailed his arms at his attacker, but to no avail. He was clasped around the neck and pulled, against his will, away from the certain safety of the church. He tried to scream, but he was so short of breath, he couldn't do more than whimper. When they turned the corner of the building, he was slammed up against the wall. He gasped in shock and opened his mouth in surprised horror. But just as the last peal of the bell sounded, his pursuer fired a small pistol directly into his forehead. Whether he wanted to or not, the Reverend Jasper Claypool had gone to meet his maker.

'I don't think I like this,' Wiggins muttered. He frowned at the letter in his hand and then shook his head.

'What's wrong?' Mrs Jeffries, the housekeeper to Inspector Gerald Witherspoon, asked. She was a plump woman of late middle age with a ready smile and a kind disposition. Her hair was dark auburn sprinkled with gray, her eyes were a deep brown color and her pale skin was dusted with faint freckles across her nose. She glanced at the footman as she reached for the teapot. It was rare for the lad to get a letter, rarer still for him to look so upset by the contents of said letter.

The household of Inspector Gerald Witherspoon was gathered at the kitchen table for afternoon tea. The last post had arrived, and with it, the footman's letter.

By this time, the others at the table had realized that something was wrong. Wiggins, who was naturally a good-natured chatterbox, had gone very quiet.

'Has the letter upset you, lad?' Smythe, the coachman, asked. Smythe was a big, brutal-looking man with black hair, harsh features and the kindest brown eyes in the world. He'd come to work for Inspector Witherspoon's late aunt, Euphemia Witherspoon, years earlier. When she'd died and left her nephew a house and a fortune, he'd stayed on to keep an eye out for the inspector. Then he'd stayed on for other, more personal reasons. He took a sip of his tea and watched the boy over the rim of his mug.

'It's not upset me,' Wiggins said quickly, as he swiped a lock of unruly brown hair off his forehead. He was a good-looking young man in his early twenties, with rounded cheeks, bright blue eyes and a ready smile, but he wasn't smiling now. 'It's just a bit of a bother, that's all.'

3

But everyone knew he wasn't being honest. They'd been together too long to be fooled by the lad's attempt at indifference. Mrs Goodge, the cook, glanced at Mrs Jeffries. She wasn't sure who should take the lead here. But the housekeeper, aware that the cook and the footman had become quite close over the last year, nodded her head slightly, indicating the cook should do as she thought best.

'Look, Wiggins,' Mrs Goodge said bluntly, 'we can all see something's got you in a bit of a state.' The cook was an elderly, portly woman with gray hair neatly tucked under a cook's cap, and spectacles that persisted in sliding down her nose. She had worked at some of the finest houses in all of England and had once thought she'd come down in the world by having to accept a position as the cook to a police inspector. But now she wouldn't leave the Witherspoon household even if she were offered the position as head cook at Buckingham Palace. For the first time in her long life, she felt she had a family and, more importantly, a real purpose in her life. 'There's no shame in being upset if you've had a bit of bad news.'

Wiggins looked down at the table. 'It's from my father's people. My grandfather is dyin' and 'e wants to meet me before he goes. He lives in a little village outside Colchester.'

No one knew what to say. Though the footman didn't often speak of his early life, everyone knew that the lad's mother had died when he was a boy. Her relatives had taken him in until he was old enough to go into service. None of them had ever heard Wiggins speak of his father or his father's family.

4

Betsy, the pretty blonde maid, finally broke the silence. 'Perhaps you ought to go,' she suggested. She didn't want to interfere, but she knew how much it would have meant to her to get a letter from a relative. Unfortunately, most of hers were dead. Now the people sitting around the table were her family. She glanced at Smythe, her fiancé, and saw him nod in agreement.

'Why?' Wiggins muttered. 'They didn't want to know me or me mam when I was little. They hated her for marryin' my father. I know that because I used to 'ear my Aunt Nancy and Uncle Severn squabblin' about 'avin' to feed me when I 'ad other relations with money. Aunt Nancy was my mother's sister; she took me in when Mam died. They could barely feed themselves, let alone have to feed me too. My father's people didn't want to know me. So why should I go see this old man now?'

'Maybe he's sorry,' Betsy said softly. 'Sometimes people do things in their life that they regret. Maybe he wants to make it up to you.'

'I don't want 'im to make anythin' up to me.' Wiggins shoved back from the table and leapt to his feet. The abrupt action spurred Fred, their black-and-brown mongrel dog, to leap up from his spot near the stove. As if sensing the boy's distress, he trotted over and butted his head against the lad's knee. Wiggins absently reached down to pet him. 'I just want 'im to leave me be.'

'Are you sure?' Mrs Jeffries asked calmly. 'Aren't you in the least bit curious about your grandfather?'

'Why should I be?' He pursed his lips and shook

his head. 'They've not been curious about me all these years.' A sheen of tears welled up in his eyes. 'When my father died, he wouldn't even let my mother bury him. I was just little, but I remember it. He come and took the body and wouldn't let her go to the funeral. I hate him for what he did, and I don't need 'im now. I've got me a real family. I've got you lot.' He blinked rapidly and looked down at Fred, averting his face while he got his feelings under control.

'Of course you do, lad,' Smythe said softly. 'And you know we'd do anything for you. But you might want to at least think about meetin' the old man. Not for his sake, but for yours. It's not like you to 'ave so much anger in ya.'

Wiggins looked up. 'I'm not angry, I just want 'im to leave me alone. I can't be runnin' off to Colchester at the drop of a 'at. I've got me duties 'ere to consider.'

Mrs Jeffries wasn't sure what to say. As Inspector Witherspoon had no more need of a footman than he did a hole in his head, the lad was exaggerating. Though in all fairness, Wiggins did his part in keeping the household running. 'I'm sure the inspector will be quite willing to do without your services for a few days. The rest of us can take over your responsibilities.'

'I'm not just talkin' about my household chores,' Wiggins protested. 'I'm talkin' about the other. You know what 'appens every time someone goes off. We get us a murder. Luty and Hatchet still 'aven't got over missin' the last one, and I don't want that to 'appen to me.'

'But we might not have one,' Betsy interjected. 'It's been very quiet lately.'

'That's what Luty and Hatchet thought before they went off for America,' Wiggins said. Luty Belle Crookshank and her butler, Hatchet, were good friends of the household of Upper Edmonton Gardens. Inspector Gerald Witherspoon was quite a fortunate man. He was not only rich, but he'd made a real name for himself as the best homicide investigator in the country. He'd solved every murder that he'd been given. What he didn't know was that it was his staff, along with their good friends, who supplied him with the clues he needed to crack the cases. 'The minute they was gone, we had that murder and they missed it all.'

'But they were gone for a long time,' Betsy argued. 'They went all the way to New York. You'd just be going to Colchester.'

'You could always come back if we had us one,' Smythe pointed out.

'There are telegrams,' Mrs Jeffries assured him. 'All you'd have to do is make sure we had your grandfather's address and we'd send for you immediately.'

'But I don't want to meet 'im,' Wiggins cried. ''E was horrible to my mother. She went to him when my father died, and the old man tossed her off his farm.'

'And maybe he bitterly regrets that action,' Mrs Goodge snapped. She glared at the footman. 'Now you listen to me, young man, I'm an old woman . . .' She broke off and raised her hand for silence as the others began to protest.

'You're all trying to be nice, but the truth is, I am old and there's no getting around that. But what I'm

7

ing to get the lad to understand is this; there are things I did in my life that I regret. Not many, but some. If I could have a chance to make up for some of the unkind things I did or said before I go to my final restin' place, I'd do it.'

'You think I ought to go?' Wiggins's shoulders slumped. He didn't look happy.

'I think you ought to give the old man a chance,' she replied. 'It's only a few hours' train ride to Colchester. It's not the ends of the earth.'

'What if he says bad things about my mother?' Wiggins dropped his gaze again and leaned down to pet Fred. 'What then, Mrs Goodge? I'd not like to be rude, but I couldn't stand for anyone to speak ill of me mam.'

'If he says one unkind word about her, then you tell the old fool that he's a scoundrel's arse and not worth a decent fellow's bother. Then you nip right back home,' the cook replied.

Wiggins lifted his head and broke into a grin. 'Cor blimey, Mrs Goodge, I didn't think you even knew words like that. All right, then, if the inspector gives me permission, I'll go.'

'Thank you, Mrs Jeffries.' Inspector Gerald Witherspoon took the glass of sherry from his housekeeper. He was a slender man in his mid-forties. He had thinning dark hair, a rather long, bony face, deep-set gray eyes and a mustache. He was a bit short-sighted, so he generally tried to remember to wear his spectacles. He had them on now. 'Do pour one for yourself,' he told her.

'I have, sir,' she replied. She took the chair opposite his. They were in the drawing room of Upper Edmonton Gardens. 'Are you sure you've no objection to Wiggins going off for a few days?' She'd already told him about the lad's grandfather.

'Of course not,' he said. 'He's right to go and see his father's people.'

'We had to talk him into it,' she said bluntly. 'If left to his own devices, I believe he'd have ignored the letter completely.'

'I'm glad he didn't,' Witherspoon replied. 'Er, do you happen to know why he's had so little contact with his family?'

'From what I gather,' she said, eyeing the oriental carpet on the floor, 'his father's family wasn't all too happy when Wiggins's parents married. They've a small farm outside Colchester. The village is called Langham. I believe his mother's people were very poor. When his father died, they were quite awful to his mother, and they didn't want anything to do with him.' She made a mental note to have the carpet cleaned. It was looking a bit tatty.

'Let's hope it all goes well for the boy.'

'He's taking the eight o'clock from Liverpool Street Station,' she said. She noticed the curtains were looking a bit dingy too.

'Tell him to stay as long as he likes, we can always manage. Uh, does he need any money for train fare?'

'No, sir, he's fine. He's quite a saver is our Wiggins. He did ask me to ask you to keep a sharp eye on Fred. He'll be a bit lonely without the boy.'

'Fred and I are great friends,' Witherspoon smiled

broadly. He loved the dog almost as much as the footman did. 'We'll do just fine.'

'Thank you, sir,' she said. 'Is anything interesting going on at the station, sir?' She and the inspector frequently talked about his work. As the widow of a Yorkshire police officer, she would naturally be interested in crime. More importantly, as the leader of their investigations on the inspector's behalf, she needed to know what was happening at any given moment.

'Not really,' he sighed. 'Just the usual; a few burglaries, an attempted suicide and some pickpockets. It's been very quiet. I hope it remains that way.'

'Yes, sir.' Mrs Jeffries hid her disappointment. 'I do believe we'd best get this rug cleaned, sir. Especially now that it's spring.' She glanced about the large room. 'Those curtains could do with a clean too. As a matter of fact, this floor of the house could use some new paint and wallpaper.'

Witherspoon gulped his sherry. The room looked fine to him, but then again, he'd no idea how to care for a large home. He'd been raised in far more modest circumstances. 'If you think it's necessary.'

'We've nothing else pressing.' She got to her feet. 'And the house hasn't had a good sprucing up for a long time. Tomorrow I'll see about getting the cleaners in, and we'll give the whole house a nice tidy up. Then I'll call the decorators.'

But the next morning Mrs Jeffries didn't even think about calling in cleaners or painters. A few minutes after they'd put Wiggins in a hansom for Liverpool Street Station, Constable Barnes knocked on their front door.

'Good morning, Mrs Jeffries.' He smiled politely as he stepped into the foyer. 'Sorry to pop in so early, but I must see the inspector.' The constable was a tall, craggy-faced man with a headful of iron-gray curly hair under his policeman's helmet. He'd worked with the inspector for a long time and knew the household very well.

'Of course, Constable,' Mrs Jeffries replied. She was delighted to see him. When Constable Barnes arrived this early in the morning, it generally meant one thing: they had a murder. 'Come into the dining room, Constable. The inspector is having his breakfast.' Mrs Jeffries ushered him down the hall and into the room. 'Inspector,' she said as they went inside. 'Constable Barnes has come to see you.'

'Good morning, sir,' Barnes bobbed his head politely.

'Good morning, Constable.' Witherspoon half rose and gestured toward the empty chair next to him. 'Do sit down. Have you eaten?'

'I have, sir,' Barnes replied as he took his seat. 'But I wouldn't say "no" to a cup of tea.'

'Of course, Constable.' Mrs Jeffries was already on her way to the mahogany sideboard where extra cups and plates were kept. She took her time opening the cupboard door so that she could hear what the constable had to say.

'There's been a murder, sir,' Barnes began, 'and the chief inspector wants you to take it.'

'Oh, dear.' Witherspoon shoved another bite of bacon into his mouth. 'Do we have an identification? Do we know who the victim is?' He'd always found that was a good place to start.

'Not really,' Barnes replied.

Mrs Jeffries took down a cup and saucer and closed the cupboard. Moving as slowly as she dared, she went to the table and reached for the teapot. She could only dawdle over this task for so long before it would become obvious she was trying to eavesdrop. If she had to, she could always listen out in the hall. She'd done that on more than one occasion.

'It's a bit of a strange one, sir,' Barnes continued. He nodded his thanks to the housekeeper as she handed him his tea. 'The victim was found propped up against the side of St Paul's Church over on Dock Street. It's just up from the London Docks. Luckily, the lads that did the findin' had the good sense not to move the body.'

'You mean it's still there?' Witherspoon asked.

'Yes, sir. Chief Inspector Barrows wanted you to have a look at the scene with the body intact.' Barnes broke into a grin. 'Looks like your methods are starting to have an impact, sir.'

'Er, yes. Well, like I always say, one can learn a lot about the murder if one has a chance to see the body before it's moved.' Witherspoon wasn't sure when he'd come up with this idea. He thought it might have been right from the very beginning of his career in homicide. He quickly shoveled the remainder of his breakfast into his mouth. 'Gracious, we'd better hurry then. Corpses do tend to draw a crowd, and that won't help the investigation any.'

'Not to worry, sir, the body is on the side of the chapel, and there's not much foot traffic in that area. The lads should be able to keep everyone back. We've

12

a few minutes. I've arranged for the district police surgeon to meet us there.'

As soon as the inspector and Barnes had gone, Mrs Jeffries flew down to the kitchen. Betsy was at the sink doing the breakfast dishes, and Smythe was sitting at the table with an old newspaper spread out in front of him, oiling the horse's harness. Mrs Goodge was at the other end of the long table rolling out pie crust.

'We've got us a murder,' Mrs Jeffries blurted out. 'And we've no time to lose.'

'Oh no,' Betsy wailed. 'Wiggins will have a right fit. He was afraid this was going to happen. He'll have to turn around and come right back as soon as he gets there.' She put the plate on the drying rack and wiped her hands on a dishtowel.

'Who died?' the cook asked. 'Anyone important?' Mrs Goodge did all of her investigating from the kitchen. She had a veritable army of informants that trooped through her domain on a daily basis: delivery boys, rag and bone sellers, fruit vendors, chimney sweeps, laundry maids and even the communal-garden caretakers. She plied them all with tea and pastries while squeezing every morsel of gossip about victims and suspects out of them. Naturally, the higher the victim was on London's social scale, the easier it was for her to get the information. In addition to the people who came through her kitchen, she also had a vast network of people from her former days of cooking in both London and the countryside.

'We don't know yet,' Mrs Jeffries replied. She told them what she'd heard from Constable Barnes.

'He and the inspector have just left.' She looked at Smythe.

He'd already put the cap on the oil and was now wrapping the harness in the paper. He pushed it to one side and got to his feet. 'Should I go get Luty and Hatchet?'

Mrs Jeffries hesitated. 'Not yet. We don't even have a name. But it would be useful for you to nip over to St Paul's Church and see what you can find out. If we're really lucky, we can get a nice start on this case.'

'I'll go along then.' He picked up the folded parcel and scooped up the can of oil. 'I'll try and get back with some information by teatime.'

'We'll have Luty and Hatchet here by then,' Mrs Jeffries replied. 'Maybe even Wiggins if we can get a telegram to him and he can get a train right back.'

'I don't think we ought to do that,' Mrs Goodge said softly. She looked at the housekeeper. 'I don't want to be oversteppin' my bounds here, but I think it will be good for the boy to get to know his father's people. I'd not realized how much bitterness he's got locked up inside him. That's not right. Wiggins is naturally a good lad; he shouldn't walk around with that kind of poison in his system.'

'But we promised him,' Mrs Jeffries reminded her.

'I know,' the cook replied. 'And we'll keep our promise, but as you said, we've not even got a name for our victim. I think we can wait a day or two before we send for him.'

'I agree,' Smythe said quietly. 'Wiggins should have a day or so with his people. They might have mis-treated 'is mother, and now they might want to make it

14

up to the lad. Everyone deserves a second chance.' He knew all about second chances. He felt he'd been given one in life with Betsy.

Mrs Jeffries looked doubtful. 'All right, if you both think so. But we must send him a telegram by tomorrow. I agree with all you've said, but we did make a promise.'

'We'll keep it,' Mrs Goodge said brusquely. 'Now, I'd best see what we've got in the dry larder. We're almost out of flour and sugar. I'll do up a list, Mrs Jeffries, and I'd be obliged if you could get it to the grocers right away. They can deliver by late this morning, and that'll give me time to get some baking done this afternoon. I've got to have things baked to feed my sources.'

'I'll take it right away, Mrs Goodge.' She turned to Betsy. 'Can you get over to Luty's and tell her and Hatchet to be here this afternoon for tea? If we're very lucky, we may actually know something useful by then.'

Betsy was already taking off her apron and heading for the coat tree. 'Of course. Thank goodness they're in town. Luty would have a stroke if they missed another case.'

'Luty,' Smythe exclaimed. He waited by the entrance to the hall for Betsy so they could walk out together. 'Hatchet's worse. He was so upset about missin' that last case I 'eard 'im tellin' Luty he wasn't ever goin' to leave London again.'

Despite the best efforts of the police, a small crowd had gathered in front of St Paul's Church. The constables had managed to keep everyone away from the corpse, but they looked extremely relieved when Witherspoon and Barnes arrived. 'He's over here, sir.' One of the constables pointed to the side of the building.

Witherspoon started in that direction just as a hansom pulled up and a man carrying a doctor's bag got out. 'It's the police surgeon, sir,' Barnes said. He broke into a grin. 'Gracious, sir, it's Dr Bosworth.'

Witherspoon stopped and waited for the doctor to catch up with them. 'Dr Bosworth, I didn't know you were the police surgeon for this district.'

Bosworth grinned and extended his hand. 'I was just appointed, Inspector.' He shook hands with Witherspoon and then shook with Barnes. 'Dr Niels retired and I applied for the post. Have you had a chance to examine the victim, gentlemen?'

'Not yet,' Witherspoon replied. They moved to the side of the building, and he cast a quick glance at the dead man. Witherspoon was very squeamish about corpses. But he knew his duty, so he steeled himself and moved closer to get a good look.

The body was propped up against the back wall with the legs sticking straight out like the poor fellow was just having a rest. His arms hung at his sides, and the hands were both balled into fists. He was dressed in a heavy black coat, which was unbuttoned, black wool trousers, a black vest, a white shirt and a clerical collar. His eyes were open and staring straight ahead. There was a neat, blood-encrusted hole in the center of his forehead.

'I don't suppose he's the vicar of this church?' Barnes knelt down next to the victim. He glanced up at the two police constables standing guard.

'No, sir, he's not. We checked that right away,' one of the constables replied.

'Who found the body?'

'I did, sir,' the second constable offered. He was a young man with pale blue eyes and a thin face. 'I spotted it this morning when I was making my rounds.'

'What made you look at the side?' Witherspoon asked. 'Sometimes vagrants sleep there, sir,' the constable replied.

'Have you searched his pockets?' Barnes asked.

'Yes, sir, they're empty. We think he might have been robbed.' He jerked his chin toward the church. 'We've sent PC Boyles to get the vicar. We're hoping he may know who the poor man is.'

'Good thinking.' Witherspoon swallowed heavily and then knelt down on the other side of the body. 'If this man is a clergyman, he might have been coming to visit the vicar.' That sounded logical. 'Dr Bosworth, could you come have a look, please. I'd like to get some idea of the time of death.'

Bosworth knelt down in front of the dead man, put his bag to one side and then touched the man's face. 'He's quite cold, I should say he's been dead at least twelve hours. Perhaps even more.' He touched the hand and pried at the fingers. 'Rigor has set in.'

'You think he was killed last night?' Witherspoon asked.

'It's hard to say exactly.' Bosworth pried at the fingers of the other hand, and this time a slip of paper fell out and landed on the grass. 'I was just trying to see how stiff the poor fellow was!'

Barnes grabbed the paper and handed it to the inspector. Just then, they heard footsteps and low muttered voices coming toward them. It was a police constable, and with him a short, very fat clergyman.

'Good day, sir.' The police constable stopped a few feet from them and nodded respectfully. 'I've brought Reverend Sanderson, sir. He's the vicar of St Paul's.'

Witherspoon and Barnes got to their feet. Bosworth continued examining the body. 'Good day, sir,' the inspector said. 'We're hoping you can help us.'

'I'll do my best, sir,' the vicar replied. He spoke to the inspector, but his eyes were on the corpse propped against his church. 'But I don't think I'm going to be of any use to you at all. I've no idea who this poor fellow might be.' He shook his head sympathetically. 'May God rest his soul.'

'Are you sure?' Barnes pressed. 'Would you like a closer look? Try imagining him without the hole in his forehead.'

The vicar leapt backward and shook his head vehemently. 'I've never seen him before, sir. I know a number of clergymen, sir, but I've never seen him before in my life.'

'So you've no idea why he was near your church?' Witherspoon persisted.

'None whatsoever.' Reverend Sanderson took a deep breath and then knelt down by the dead man. 'If he was coming to my church, he was coming as a stranger. But even a stranger deserves a prayer.' Without interrupting Bosworth, he quietly and fervently said a prayer over the dead man, and then he rose to his feet. 'I'll do anything I can to help find this poor man's killer,' he said. 'But unfortunately, I've no idea why he was killed here.'

They questioned the vicar until it became obvious he'd seen nothing, heard nothing and knew nothing. 'I'm terribly sorry, Inspector,' he finally said. 'But I simply have no idea about who this man is or why anyone would want to kill him. Now if you'll excuse me, I must contact the bishop immediately. Perhaps he can be of some use in this situation.'

'Bishop?' Witherspoon repeated. 'Oh yes, of course. He's wearing a collar.' He turned toward Constable Boyles and said, 'Go along with the reverend and see if the bishop has any ideas about who this fellow might be.'

The reverend didn't look pleased by this request, but he didn't object either. He was muttering to himself as the two of them went back toward the front of the church building.

The police ambulance pulled around the corner and halted in front of the church. It made an enormous racket as it trundled across the cobblestones. Dr Bosworth stood up and waved the attendants over. 'I can't tell any more until I get him back to the morgue and do the postmortem,' he told the inspector. 'I should have a report for you by tomorrow morning. I'll send it around to the station.'

'Thank you, Doctor,' Witherspoon said. 'We'd appreciate that.'

They loaded the body onto the stretcher and into

the van. Dr Bosworth waited till the doors closed and then turned to Witherspoon. 'If you don't mind my asking, what's on that slip of paper?'

Witherspoon had almost forgotten about it. He opened it up and read. 'It appears to be an address . . . yes, it is. It says Seven Dorland Place, Bermondsey.'

On the other side of the road, Smythe dodged behind a tree as the van emerged and pulled out into the traffic. He'd been keeping the large van between himself and the inspector since it had pulled up in front of the church. Now that it was gone, so was his hiding spot. Not that he'd been close enough to hear anything useful, but he'd seen the body. Apparently, someone didn't much like vicars. He stuck his head around the trunk for a quick peek and then just as quickly pulled back. Two police constables were crossing the road and heading his way, but they'd not spotted him. He moved from his hiding place and strolled over to stand in front of a tobacconist's. The policemen got close enough for him to hear.

'I'll start on this side of the road,' one of them said to the other. 'You take the other side and then we'll do the street across the way.'

They must be doing a house-to-house, hoping to find someone who'd heard or seen something. Fat chance of that happening, Smythe thought. In this neighborhood it was see no evil, hear no evil and speak no evil, especially to coppers. He waited till they'd gone past and then ducked back across the narrow road to the front of the church. Witherspoon and Barnes were walking away from the building, toward a hansom stand at the far end of the road. He took off after them.

Smythe made it just in time to see them getting into the one available hansom. He looked around, hoping to spot another cab. But the street, though crowded with traffic, was empty of public conveyances. 'Blast a Spaniard,' he muttered. He knew he should follow them. But the cab was already moving fast, so Smythe did the only thing he could in the circumstances. He started running.

He managed to keep the cab in sight for a good half a mile, but his legs were aching and his lungs were bursting. Just then, he spotted a cab pulling over to discharge a fare. Smythe leapt across the road and pointed to the inspector's hansom as it disappeared around the corner. 'Follow that cab,' he yelled at the driver as he jumped into the seat.

The driver cracked his whip and they pulled away. Smythe kept sticking his head out and giving the driver instructions. 'Don't get too close,' he called.

'Look, guv, I've been driving this cab for ten years, I know what I'm doin',' the driver retorted.

Smythe finally gave up and settled back in his seat. The driver did know what he was about; he kept the inspector's cab in sight without getting too close.

Finally, after what seemed like hours, the cab slowed and pulled over to the side of the road. 'Your cab's stopped just up the road in front of that dilapidated old cottage. Do you want out here?' the driver asked.

Smythe cautiously slipped out of the safety of his seat. Inspector Witherspoon and Barnes were both visible and walking up a short path to the front door of the cottage. They weren't even looking in his direction. He reached in his pocket and pulled out a handful of coins. 'This is fine,' he said as he reached up and handed the driver the fare. 'And this is for all your trouble.' He gave the fellow an extra ten shillings.

'Cor guv, this is a lot . . .'

'You earned it,' Smythe yelled as he dashed down the road. He looked about for a good hiding place in case the inspector or Barnes came back outside. He spotted an oak with a large-sized trunk just across the road from the cottage. Its roots were gnarled and it looked as if the ground around the base had sunk a goodly amount, but it would do in a pinch. Smythe looked about the area and noted that the cottage was the last in a row of tiny wooden houses. But the houses were all detached with scraggly lawns separating them from their neighbors. Across the road was a huge industrial building with a sign that read 'Claypool Manufacturing'.

He wondered if he ought to try to sneak up to the window to have a good look, but then he decided against it. If he was caught, there was no excuse he could give for being here. No, best he just duck behind the tree.

Inside the cottage, Witherspoon and Barnes stood in the center of the tiny sitting room. The cottage had been locked, but the slightest pressure on the door had popped it open. The room was covered in dust, cobwebs and dirt. It was empty save for a broken footstool and an armchair with all the stuffing pulled out. To the left of the entry was a small kitchen, also filthy, and to the right of the sitting room, a bedroom.

'What exactly are we looking for, sir?' Barnes asked.

Witherspoon hadn't a clue. 'I'm not sure. But our murder victim must have had this address in his hand for a reason.' He sighed. 'I suppose we'd best do a good search of the premises. Perhaps we should have brought some lads with us.'

'I think we can deal with it, sir,' Barnes replied briskly. 'I'll start with the bedroom if it's all the same to you.'

'I suppose I'd best begin in the kitchen,' the inspector murmured. They worked in silence for a few minutes, opening cupboards, checking floorboards and generally trying to find anything useful in the empty house. After exhausting every conceivable idea he had about where something could or couldn't be hidden, Witherspoon, brushing cobwebs off his bowler, went back to the sitting room. Barnes was on his knees looking at the fireplace. 'I take it you found nothing.'

'Nothing, sir.' Barnes got up. 'Just more dirt and spiders. If there is something here of interest, I certainly can't see it.'

'Me, either,' Witherspoon said. He put his bowler back on his head. 'I wonder why these cottages were abandoned? A bit of spit and polish and they could be quite nice.'

'They're condemned, sir,' Barnes replied, brushing the dust off his sleeves. 'There's a small sign at the top of the road. I think the ground must be shifting. Look.' He pointed toward the bricks in the fireplace. 'See how they're not in straight lines? That means the earth must be shifting underneath.'

Witherspoon ambled over to have a closer look. 'You're right, none of these lines are at all straight. I wonder how long it's been empty. Look, there are still ashes in the grate.'

Barnes laughed. 'I expect a few of our less fortunate friends have availed themselves of the place in the past few years. Mind you, though, I don't think the structure is all that secure.' He placed his hand against the mantel and pushed. It creaked loudly and something heavy dropped from the chimney.

'Gracious, it really is getting ready to collapse,' Witherspoon exclaimed. He looked down at the grate, expecting to see a clump of ash or a bundle of leaves. Instead, he gasped and leapt backward. 'Egads, Barnes, is that what I think it is?'

Barnes dropped to his knees and stared at the object. He shook his head. 'I'm afraid so, sir.' He ducked his head under the front of the fireplace so that he could stare up into the chimney proper.

'What are you doing?' the inspector asked. He got a hold of himself. This was rather surprising, but he'd seen worse.

'Seeing what else is up there, sir.' Barnes's voice was muffled. 'But it's too dark to see much of anything. There's a police constable on the main road. I'll nip up there and raise the alarm. We need a good lantern to see what's what.'

'Yes, I think that's an excellent idea.' Witherspoon looked down at the grate again. 'I suppose we ought to see if the rest of it is up there.'

Barnes crawled out from the fireplace. There were smudges of dirt on his cheeks and forehead. He took off his helmet and wiped his face. 'I expect so, sir,' he replied as he looked down at the object on the grate. 'Generally where there's a foot, there's a body.'

Witherspoon swallowed hard. Even though it wasn't

particularly disgusting, he couldn't take his eyes off the wretched thing. It was merely bones, darkened, of course, from being in the fireplace. But it was most definitely in the shape of a human foot.

CHAPTER TWO

'Blast a Spaniard,' Smythe muttered to himself as he saw another police constable enter number seven. 'What's goin' on in there?' Something important was happening at the cottage, and he knew he shouldn't leave until he found out what it was. On the other hand, he knew he should get back to Upper Edmonton Gardens by teatime. The others would be waiting for his report, and more importantly, Betsy would be worried if he was late.

He wrinkled his nose as the scent of creosote filled the air. Must be from the factory, he thought idly. The smell was strong but it did bring a bit of relief, considering that he was hiding behind an old privy with a very distinctive odor of its own. The privy was behind cottage number six. He'd changed hiding places when he'd seen Constable Barnes come charging out of number seven and race up the road. He'd known something odd was happening and had decided the risk of getting close enough to see what was going on was worth taking. If any of the policemen came out this way, he thought he could nip over the back fence without too much trouble.

He peeked out around the corner and took another look at the cottage. From here, he could see down the narrow passage between the two houses, and that gave him a view of who was going in or out of number seven. He'd now seen three additional constables go inside. He made up his mind. Betsy would just have to understand. This was too important, he had to find out what was going on in there.

He pulled his coat tighter as another blast of wind whipped the air around him. Hunkering down, he crept out of his hiding place and moved quietly toward the back window of number seven. He pressed his face against the dirty glass and found he could see inside a bit. The door leading to the sitting room was open at such an angle that he had a partial view. There were policemen bunched in a group around the small fire-place. One of the men shifted position, and Smythe could see that a constable was actually hunkered in the tiny opening, looking straight up into the chimney. Inspector Witherspoon was standing to one side, gesturing with his hands.

'Blast a Spaniard,' he muttered, 'this doesn't make any sense.' He stepped back and shook his head. There must be something up in the chimney, he decided. Cor blimey, if it was some sort of evidence, something that had been tossed down the chimney or burned in the grate, he might be here all day before they got it out.

He pulled out his pocket watch and noted the time again. It was gone three o'clock. If he hurried, he could make it back for the meeting. Smythe ducked down and slipped back to his hiding place, took a quick look about to make sure no one had nipped out to have a snoop and then continued along through the small gardens at the backs of the cottages. He reached the last house, turned and headed for the street just in time to see an ambulance coming from around the corner. What's all this about, then? he thought. He crossed the road and slipped behind a postbox. Peeking out, he saw the ambulance pulling up in front of number seven.

No one had been hurt or wounded in the cottage; Smythe was sure of that. So that meant the presence of the ambulance could only mean one thing. There was another body.

He leaned against the postbox and watched. A few minutes later, he saw three constables come outside. Two of them used their hands as footholds and helped the third one up onto the roof. Then one of them handed him what looked like an old broom. The one with the broom made his way to the chimney, peeked inside and then began poking the handle down it. Smythe shook his head in amazement and stopped worrying about being late to the meeting. The others, including Betsy, would kill him if he didn't stay here till the end and see exactly what was going on.

Betsy cast another glance toward the windows over the kitchen sink. Though it was only four-thirty, the afternoon was darkening with a coming rain. She wished Smythe would get here.

'Stop frettin'.' Luty Belle Crookshank reached over and patted the girl on the arm. 'He'll be here soon.'

Luty Belle was a small, elderly American woman

with white hair, sharp black eyes and a Colt .45 in the deep pocket of her cloak. She was rich, opinionated and loved helping the staff of Upper Edmonton Gardens solve the inspector's murders. Widowed, she and her late husband had made a fortune in the silver mines of Colorado and then come back to her husband's native land and settled in London. She knew everyone in London and had wonderful connections in the legal and financial communities.

'I do hope he has something useful to report,' Hatchet, Luty's butler, said. He was a tall, robust man with a full head of thick, white hair. He'd been in her service for years but didn't let that stop him from arguing with her about anything and everything. 'But I suppose I ought to be grateful for small favors. At least this time we weren't out of the country.'

'Quit cryin' over spilt milk,' Luty replied. She plucked at the white lace on the sleeve of her burgundy day dress. 'That last one wasn't anyone's fault. We were gone when it happened.'

Hatchet sniffed.

'Speaking of which, we really must send Wiggins a telegram tomorrow,' Mrs Jeffries interjected.

'Too bad no one thought to send us a telegram when the last one happened,' Hatchet muttered darkly.

'We were twenty-five-hundred miles away,' Luty shot back. 'Wiggins is only in Colchester. He can get here by tomorrow evenin'. It would have taken us two weeks!'

'What if it turns out to be nothin'?' Mrs Goodge said calmly. 'Even with a dead body, these things aren't always murder. I don't think we ought to be draggin' the lad back until we know for sure one way or another.'

'But we do know for sure,' Betsy pointed out. 'Constable Barnes told the inspector it was murder. I don't think he'd be mistaken about that.' She looked toward the hallway, her attention drawn by the sound of the back door opening.

'That must be Smythe,' Mrs Jeffries said conversationally. 'Betsy, pour him some tea.'

But Betsy was already filling his mug and heaping slices of rich brown bread on his plate.

'Hello, everyone,' Smythe said as he came into the warm kitchen. 'Sorry I'm a bit late, but I've got a lot to tell.' He slipped into the chair next to Betsy and gave her a quick smile. Under the table, he grabbed her hand.

'We thought you'd be back earlier than this,' Betsy said as she clasped his fingers tightly. 'I was starting to worry. It looks like it's going to rain.'

'But we assumed you were detained because something important came up,' the housekeeper added.

'What happened?' Luty asked bluntly. 'Did they find out who the dead man is?'

'Not yet.' Smythe took a quick sip of tea. Having had neither food nor drink since breakfast, he was thirsty and hungry. 'But he's not the only one we've got to worry about. There's another body.'

'What?' Betsy exclaimed.

'You mean there's two murders?' Mrs Goodge asked.

'Good,' Hatchet said. 'That'll make up for us missing one.'

'Nell's bells, two at once, that's got to take the prize,' Luty said eagerly. 'Where do we start?'

'We really must send that telegram,' Mrs Jeffries said softly. 'Smythe, do tell us everything.'

Smythe swallowed the bite of bread and butter he'd just popped into his mouth. 'I don't have much to go on,' he began, 'and I think it would make more sense if I tell it from the start.'

'Go ahead,' she encouraged.

He gave them all the details starting with his arriving at St Paul's on Dock Street. 'I was sure the inspector would hang about askin' questions and managing the house-to-house, but he didn't. The minute they loaded the vicar's body into the ambulance, he and Barnes were off like a shot. I figured they must have found out somethin' important and that maybe it'd be best if I scarpered along and saw where they were goin'.'

'That was good thinking on your part,' Mrs Goodge interjected. 'It's always best to find out as much as possible at the beginning of the investigation. It saves a lot of time and grief later.'

'And where were they going?' Mrs Jeffries pressed. She rather agreed with the cook, but she didn't wish to interrupt the coachman's narrative.

'To a house . . . well, it's not really a house, more like a cottage – it's in Bermondsey. Number seven Dorland Place. It's right across the road from a paint factory and down the end of a lane of abandoned houses. It seemed I had to 'ide for ages before anythin' 'appened, and I'd just about decided to come along home when all of a sudden, Barnes comes out of the house and scurries off up the road. I didn't know whether to follow 'im or not, so I stayed put, and a few minutes later, he was back with a couple of police constables. I got right up to the back window and I could see in a little, but I couldn't really tell too much from where I was standin'. I didn't want to be too bold and risk getting caught.'

'Did you see anything?' Luty asked impatiently.

'Not much,' he admitted with a rueful smile. 'But I noticed that everyone seemed to be doin' something with the fireplace.'

'Doing what?' Mrs Jeffries asked. She'd learned long ago that every detail was important, including the ones that might be unusual.

'Mainly, stickin' their head up it.'

'It sounds like something may have been hidden up there,' Hatchet mused.

'That's what I thought,' Smythe replied. 'But then the ambulance showed up and I knew it wasn't something hidden up there, but someone.'

'You mean there was a body?' Betsy made a face. 'Up in the fireplace?'

'Good God, was they smokin' it like it was a Virginia ham?' Luty tried hard to keep a straight face.

'Really, Madam.' Hatchet sniffed disapprovingly.

'Well, that's how we smoke hams where I come from – stick 'em up over an open fire and let 'em smoke. Why else would someone stick a body in a fireplace?'

'You said the cottages are abandoned,' Mrs Jeffries said to Smythe. 'I'm wondering if the body was placed there to hide it.'

'That's more likely,' Luty agreed. 'No point in smokin' a body. It's not like they's any cannibals around here.'

'It's still disgusting,' Mrs Goodge said. 'Imagine, putting a body in a fireplace.'

'Seems as good a place to hide a body as any,'

Smythe murmured. 'Especially if the place was empty and there weren't any neighbors about to see you do it.'

'Wouldn't it smell?' Betsy asked.

'Probably, but if all the other houses around it are abandoned, and the closest neighbor is a factory, who'd be around to complain?' Smythe leaned back in his chair. 'I think we're dealin' with a very clever killer.'

'Don't you mean two killers?' Mrs Goodge reached for the plate of buttered bread and helped herself to a slice.

'Two killers?' Mrs Jeffries repeated. 'I'm not sure we can make that assumption. We'd best wait until the inspector gets home tonight and I can find out what's what.'

'I didn't tell you the best bit,' Smythe said. 'The police surgeon on the first body is Dr Bosworth. I saw him.'

'That's a bit of luck.' Mrs Jeffries nodded approvingly. Dr Bosworth had helped them on several of their previous cases. He'd been very helpful and, more importantly, very discreet.

'What else did you see?' Hatchet inquired. 'At the first murder. Any idea who the victim might be? Any clues for us to go on?'

'Only that he's a vicar,' the coachman replied. 'Leastways he was dressed like one.'

'You must have gotten quite close to the body to see that,' Betsy smiled at him.

'Not really,' he grinned. 'I just overhead some talkin' from people who did see the corpse.'

'What do you want us to do?' Luty asked the housekeeper.

Mrs Jeffries wasn't certain. 'I suppose you could find out if there's any missing clergymen in the area.'

'Maybe he was Roman Catholic?' Mrs Goodge ventured. 'Priests tend to dress alike, don't they?'

No one knew the answer to that.

'They both wear collars,' Betsy finally said.

'Not to worry,' Hatchet said cheerfully. 'Roman Catholic or C of E, we'll find out soon enough if anyone's gone missing.' He turned to Luty. 'I believe the bishop was a close friend of your late husband's.'

Luty snorted. 'Close friend, my foot. Every time the man came around he had his hand out for some building fund or missionary trust. Considerin' how much I've funneled that way over the years, the man owes me some information.'

'Good,' Mrs Jeffries replied. She looked at the cook. 'What about Wiggins? It's definitely a murder. I think we ought to send for him.'

'I wanted him to have a chance to meet his grandfather,' Mrs Goodge replied. 'But you're right, we did promise him.'

Mrs Jeffries nodded in understanding. 'I'll go along to the telegraph office straightaway and send off the message.' She turned her attention to Luty and Hatchet. 'Can you be back here early tomorrow morning? I'm going to see what I can get out of the inspector when he comes home tonight. We ought to have some decent information for you by then, at least enough details to get us started.'

'We'll be here,' Luty said. She grinned wickedly. 'And tonight, I'll pay that bishop a visit.'

'Madam, one doesn't just drop by to see the bishop,'

Hatchet warned her. 'We must make an appointment.'

'Fiddlesticks.' Luty's bright dress rustled as she rose to her feet. 'As long as I'm dangling my chequebook in my hand, he'll see me. You mark my words.'

Witherspoon was exhausted by the time he climbed the steps to his home. Mrs Jeffries waited for him by the door.

'Good evening, sir.' She reached for his bowler and hung it on the coat tree.

'Good evening, Mrs Jeffries.' He shrugged out of his heavy winter overcoat and handed it to her. 'I do hope dinner isn't on the table. I'd so like a sherry before I eat.'

Mrs Jeffries hung the coat next to the hat. 'Dinner can wait, sir. Let's go into the drawing room. You look like you could use a rest.'

A few minutes later he was settled in his favorite armchair with a glass of Harvey's in his hand. As was their custom, Mrs Jeffries had poured one for herself and sat down on the settee.

'It's been a rather odd day,' he began. 'As you know, the day started off with a murder, and then strangely enough, we stumbled onto another body. Mind you, until the doctor does the postmortem on the second one, we don't know if that's murder or death by misadventure.'

'And you're certain the first victim was deliberately murdered?' She wanted to make sure she got all the facts in this case absolutely correct. They already had two bodies to deal with; it wouldn't do to get muddled this early in the game.

'Absolutely. Poor fellow had a hole straight through the middle of his forehead.' He took a sip of sherry and sighed in pleasure.

'That rules out suicide, then,' she murmured. 'Most people who shoot themselves put the gun in their mouth or at their temple. Where did you find your second body, sir?' She had to ask; they couldn't let on that they already had any information.

Witherspoon leaned forward as though he was sharing a secret. 'In a very unusual place, Mrs Jeffries. It was in a chimney, of all things. We'd not have found it at all if Barnes hadn't pushed against the mantel. He was trying to show me how dilapidated and unsafe the building was. Well, imagine my surprise when a foot dropped out onto the grate.'

'I expect you were quite stunned, sir. It's certainly not what one would expect to happen.' She quickly dropped her gaze to hide her amusement. She knew it really wasn't a topic for levity, but the idea was quite funny.

'And, of course, where there's a foot, there's generally the rest of the body.' He took another sip. 'Sure enough, once we got some more men there, we found the rest of the corpse. It took three police constables to get the poor wretch out as well.'

'Exactly how did they get it out?'

Witherspoon visibly winced. 'Well, we had no choice, really. It was either remove half the chimney, which didn't seem very safe, or poke at the poor thing with a stick. So that's what we did. We sent a PC up to the roof with a broom handle, and he shoved from the top while we pulled from the bottom. That's the only way we could get the thing down.' He shook himself. 'I'm being terrible. It wasn't a thing, it was the body of a woman.'

'You could tell that much about it?'

'Oh yes, it was quite dreadful, really just a skeleton, but Dr Bosworth is sure it was a woman's bones we found.'

'Dr Bosworth.' Mrs Jeffries was surprised. 'He was there?'

'We sent for him after the foot fell out. I'm no expert on corpses, Mrs Jeffries, but I certainly didn't want to destroy any evidence. So I sent along for the doctor. He arrived with the ambulance lads.'

That explained why Smythe hadn't mentioned him, she thought. He'd probably nipped in with the lads and Smythe hadn't noticed him.

'He was very helpful, too, held the lantern and directed the lads on getting the corpse out without too much damage. Mind you, he's got some very advanced ideas on what one can learn from the dead.' Witherspoon paused thoughtfully. 'He was certain it was a woman almost from the moment he saw the foot.'

'How did you come to go to this house, sir?'

'The first victim sent us there,' he said. 'The address was written on a bit of paper. He was holding onto it. We went there hoping to find someone who could identify him for us, but, well, you know what we found.'

'So you have no idea who this poor man might be?' she pressed.

'No, all we know is that he was dressed in clerical

attire and had nothing on him except this bit of paper. The local priest didn't know who he was, and as of late this afternoon, the local bishop didn't know of any missing priests either.'

'Was he Church of England, sir?'

'We think so, but we're checking with the Roman Catholic archdiocese as well. Honestly, Mrs Jeffries, how can priests just end up dead practically on a church doorstep and no one has any idea who they might be?'

'I'm sure you'll find out soon enough, sir. You always do.' She could tell he was having one of his periodic bouts of self-doubt. 'What did the locals have to say about the situation?' She knew his methods well enough to guess that he'd sent police constables on a door-to-door search for information.

He sighed heavily. 'Not very much. No one can recall seeing the poor fellow. But Dr Bosworth thinks he might have been there all night. It's a commercial area, so there wouldn't be many people about once the warehouses and shipping offices closed for the day.'

'The doctor has an estimate of the time of death?'

'Not really, it was only a guess on his part. He'll have more for us by tomorrow. He's doing the post-mortems tonight.'

'On both bodies?' She felt a bit sorry for the poor doctor. He wasn't going to get any rest this night.

'He hoped to complete them both. Mind you, I don't know what he can hope to find out from those bones. But he seemed confident he could learn something.'

'Well, he was able to tell you the victim was a woman,' she said thoughtfully. Mrs Jeffries's mind worked furiously. There were a dozen different ways to approach this investigation, and she wanted to have as much information as possible before they all went off half-cocked. 'Inspector, I'm sure you've already done this, but have you found out who owned the cottage where the body was found?'

Witherspoon tossed back the last of his sherry. 'Indeed I did. Unfortunately, all the cottages in that row belong to the factory across the street. But no one's lived in them for ten years.'

Wiggins was torn between pity and compassion. He wanted to stay really angry at this old man, but it was getting harder and harder to do that as the day wore on. Jonathan Edward Wiggins lay in the center of a huge four-poster bed and stared at him piteously. His eyes were shrunken into his sockets, his face was pale as the sheets and his skin had a waxy sheen to it that didn't look good.

'I'm not sure I know what you're tryin' to tell me,' Wiggins finally said. Through the window next to the bed, he could see the open fields of the farm. The sky was darkening with the fall of evening, and Wiggins wished he were anyplace but here.

'I'm tryin' to explain why I was so harsh,' Jonathan Wiggins whispered. 'It were wrong of me . . .' He broke off as a wracking series of coughs shook his whole body.

'Grandfather, don't strain yourself.' The voice came from the other side of the room, from a lad about Wiggins's age who was his cousin. Albert Wiggins shot Wiggins a malevolent glance. Like his cousin, he had brown hair, round apple cheeks and blue eyes. But there the resemblance to Wiggins ended, for Albert's mouth was a thin, disapproving line, and his chin was almost nonexistent. 'You're upsetting him. Why don't you go back where you came from and leave us in peace.'

'No,' the old man ordered, and even in his disabled state, his voice was authoritative. 'He stays. He's family.'

'I don't want to cause any trouble,' Wiggins replied. Cor blimey, he didn't want to be in the middle of a family quarrel, even if it was his own family.

'Sit down, boy,' Jonathan Wiggins instructed his grandson. 'Sit down and hear me out.'

Wiggins wished he had the meanness or the courage to tell the old man to sod off, but he didn't. He felt sorry for the old fellow. He'd arrived that day and been met at the station by his cousin, the sullen Albert. During the ride from Colchester to the farm, Albert had said very little. When he'd arrived, he'd met his Aunt Alice and Uncle Peter, who were almost as sullen as their son. But they'd shown him his room and then taken him right up to his grandfather's room. The old man had talked to him for a while . . . well, he'd rambled on about how much Wiggins reminded him of his eldest son, Wiggins's father, Douglas. Then he'd fallen asleep and Wiggins had gone to his room.

This was his second meeting today with his grandfather, and he hoped it would be his last. He eased down into the straight-backed chair next to his grandfather's bed. 'All right, I'm sittin'. What do you want to say to me?'

Jonathan Wiggins coughed again. 'I shouldn't have

run your mother off,' he muttered. 'But I was so angry, I blamed her for your father's death.'

'But my father died of pneumonia. How could she have been at fault?' Wiggins replied. He heard his cousin mutter something under his breath, so he turned his head and shot him a fast glare. Albert stepped back and then looked away. Like many others, he'd mistaken Wiggins's good nature for weakness.

'She weren't to blame at all,' Jonathan said softly. 'But I hadn't wanted him to marry her, and he'd defied me and done it anyway. When she come along looking for help after his death, I wanted someone to blame, and she were the one in front of me. I bitterly regret it.' Another series of coughs racked him.

Wiggins got to his feet. 'Don't fret, please. You'll harm yourself. I understand. It's all in the past. It's all over.'

Tears filled the old man's eyes. 'Do you forgive me?'

Wiggins didn't think he could ever really forgive the old man. But right now, he'd say anything to stop the fellow from suffering so much. 'Yes, yes, please, stop cryin', you'll upset yourself.'

'You're not just sayin' it, are you? You truly forgive me?'

He hesitated, not wanting to lie twice in a row. But he was scared his grandfather was going to die on him if he didn't calm down. 'I'm not just sayin' it. Truly, it's over and done with.'

'Will you stay for a while?' Jonathan pressed.

Wiggins paused. He didn't want to make a promise he couldn't keep. 'I might have to go back to London . . .'

'Surely your employer will understand,' Jonathan pleaded. 'I'm an old man, I'm dying. You're my grandson and I need to make my peace with you.'

'Well, I'll stay for as long as I can,' he finally replied. Truth was, he didn't want to miss a murder.

'Promise,' Jonathan asked weakly.

'I promise.'

There was a soft knock on the door, and a moment later, a tall, rawboned middle-aged woman stepped inside the sickroom. It was his Aunt Alice. She handed Wiggins a yellow envelope. 'This come for you.'

'What is it?' Jonathan demanded. He struggled to sit up.

'It's a telegram,' Albert said smugly. 'They probably want him to come back.'

'But you said you'd stay,' Jonathan cried. His eyes filled with tears again. 'You promised. Take pity on an old man. Take pity. You promised you'd stay.'

'It's all right, it's all right,' Wiggins soothed. He knew what was in the telegram. 'If I can, I'll stay.' He tore open the thin flap and read the words. It was short and to the point.

We've got one, come quickly.

Wiggins sighed. He wanted to go back to London more than anything. He didn't want to miss this murder, but then he looked at the old man in the bed and knew he couldn't do it.

'Do you have to leave?' Aunt Alice asked eagerly.

'No, I can stay for a bit.'

They met as soon as the inspector had retired for the evening. Mrs Jeffries told them everything she'd learned, and then she sat back in her chair, her expression thoughtful.

'This is an odd kettle of fish.' Mrs Goodge shook her head. 'It'll be difficult to investigate anything. We don't even have any names.'

'Cor blimey, this isn't goin' to be easy. Where do we even start?' Smythe added.

Mrs Jeffries rather agreed with them, but she didn't wish to sound defeated before they'd even begun. Besides, she'd given the matter some thought, and they did have several avenues that might be worth pursuing. 'This may indeed be a difficult case, but I think we've got enough to start looking about.'

'We do?' Betsy asked.

'Certainly.' She held up her hand and spread her fingers. 'To begin with, the first victim was found at the docks, and no one appears to know who he was. Now, to my knowledge neither the Church of England nor the Roman Catholic Church actually lose their priests. Yet neither of them reported anyone missing or lost. So, that might mean there is a good possibility our clerically garbed victim only arrived in town yesterday, the day he was probably murdered.'

'Which means someone at a shipping company will know who he might be.' Betsy nodded eagerly. 'I see what you're getting at. One of us should check the shipping lines and see what came in yesterday or the day before.'

'That was my thought exactly.' Mrs Jeffries nodded approvingly.

'And one of us should nip around to the neighborhood

where the second body was found and see who lived in that cottage years ago,' Smythe added.

'I thought those cottages were owned by that factory,' Betsy said.

'They are, but someone had to have lived in them at one time or another,' Mrs Jeffries pointed out. 'Someone who knew the place and, more importantly, knew they were going to be abandoned for years. I highly doubt that some stranger came along and shoved a woman's corpse down the chimney.' She frowned. 'Which is odd when you think about it. Why put a body in a chimney in the first place?'

'What do you mean?' Mrs Goodge asked. She was a bit disappointed that they'd no names as yet. It was difficult for her to do her bits and pieces without names. But she didn't want the others to think she was sulking.

'I mean, why a chimney? Why not just bury the body?' She turned to Smythe. 'Were there any places behind the cottage for a burial?'

He thought for a moment. 'Actually, there is. All them cottages have back gardens. They're small, but there's room for someone to bury a body. But I don't see what you're gettin' at.'

She wasn't sure herself. 'It seems to me that putting a body in a chimney involves a great deal of work. Corpses are dead weight. So, whoever put her there had to either stuff her up the chimney, which seems very difficult unless one had enormous strength, or they had to stuff her down the chimney, which means they would have had to have carried the body onto the roof. That couldn't have been easy.'

'It probably wasn't easy, but I expect the killer didn't

44

have any choice. There aren't any fences between the cottages. So if you did try to bury her and someone came outside from one of the other houses, you'd have been seen,' Smythe said.

'And even if they had a place to put her, maybe they couldn't bury her,' Mrs Goodge suggested.

'Seems to me digging a hole is a lot easier than hauling a body up onto the roof,' Betsy said.

'Not if the ground is frozen,' the cook replied. 'And if you'll recall, we had some rather nasty winters a few years back.'

'That's right,' Mrs Jeffries added. 'If the murder was done during bad weather, either the ground being frozen . . .'

'Or soaked,' Mrs Goodge put in. 'If there'd been days of hard rain, you couldn't bury a body.'

'Then that would explain why someone would use a chimney. Especially if they knew the cottages were going to be abandoned.'

'Or they already were abandoned,' Smythe suggested. 'We don't know when the murder was done.'

'Aren't we getting ahead of ourselves?' Betsy said. 'We don't know for certain the second body was murder.'

'Course we do,' Mrs Goodge exclaimed. 'People who die from natural causes don't usually end up in the chimney.'

'I hadn't thought of that.' The maid frowned, annoyed with herself for not seeing the obvious. 'Maybe I ought to nip over there tomorrow and learn what I can about that cottage.'

'That's an excellent idea,' Mrs Jeffries said quickly.

Any information you can get us will be helpful. Smythe, do you think you can go along to the docks and see if you can learn anything concerning our dead clergyman?'

'What if he came in on a ship that docked at Tilbury?' Smythe mused. 'That's where most of the big ships come in at these days.'

'But plenty of ships still come in on the London docks,' Mrs Goodge pointed out. 'And it was close to there where the fellow was murdered.' She was a tad annoyed. In her view, he at least had something to do. The best she could hope for was picking up a few bits and pieces about the murder in general. It was difficult for her to do her investigations without the victim's name. 'Besides, most of the shipping lines still have offices at the London docks.'

'Right, then,' he nodded. 'I'll try the offices first, and if I don't 'ave any luck, I'll 'ave a go at the pubs and seamen's haunts. Not everyone who comes in by ship 'as 'is name on a manifest.'

'What about Luty and Hatchet?' Betsy asked. 'What can they do?'

Mrs Jeffries frowned. 'We did ask Luty to speak to the bishop about whether there are any missing clergy.'

'She'll have done that by tomorrow morning,' Mrs Goodge warned. 'You'd best have something else at the ready for her and Hatchet.'

'Oh, dear, we've so little information to go on,' Mrs Jeffries replied. 'I suppose they could do some general nosing about – especially in the area where the clergyman's body was found. With Wiggins being gone, we

46

need at least one of them asking questions around the neighborhood.'

'It'd better be Hatchet doin' the askin',' Smythe grinned. 'Luty tends to charge in like a bull in china shop.'

'She's direct,' Betsy defended her friend. 'But she can be as bland as butter when it's necessary.'

'You'd better come up with something for her to do,' Mrs Goodge warned, 'or she'll be doggin' everyone's heels and gettin' in the way.' Translated, this meant that Mrs Goodge didn't want Luty hanging around her kitchen – not when she was trying to do her own investigating.

'I'll think of something by tomorrow morning,' Mrs Jeffries sighed.

'Are you going to have a word with Dr Bosworth?' Mrs Goodge asked.

'Yes, as a matter of fact, I think I'll go along to the hospital tonight.'

'All on your own?' Betsy yelped.

'That's not a good idea,' Mrs Goodge said. 'The streets aren't safe for a woman alone at night.'

'Why do you want to go tonight?' Smythe asked.

'Because he's doing the postmortems on both the victims, and if I'm very lucky, I'll be able to speak with him before he goes home. He may have some valuable information for us. But I wasn't planning on going alone. I was hoping Smythe would be good enough to accompany me.'

'Course I will, Mrs Jeffries.' He smiled in relief. 'We couldn't let you go off on your own in the middle of the night. What time do you want to leave?'

She thought for a moment. She had no idea how long it would take to do two postmortems, but knowing how thorough Dr Bosworth was, she suspected he would take his time. 'Why don't we leave here about four. There's no traffic at that time, so we'd get to St Thomas's Hospital by half past. I should think he'd be finished by then.'

'Are you sure he'll be doing the postmortems at St Thomas's?' Betsy asked. 'That's a long way from Bermondsey and Dock Street. Wouldn't he use a closer hospital?'

'I don't think so,' she replied. 'Not all hospitals have the facilities for postmortems.'

'We'll not be able to get a hansom at that hour of the morning,' Smythe said, 'so I'd best nip over to Howards and get the coach.'

'Won't Howards be locked?' Mrs Goodge asked.

Howards was the stable where the inspector's horses and carriage were kept.

'They will, but I've a key.' He grinned again. 'I told 'em I needed one. What with the inspector bein' a policeman, there's no tellin' when I might have to get the coach and horses in the middle of the night.'

'Why, Smythe,' Mrs Jeffries smiled approvingly. 'That was most farsighted of you.'

CHAPTER THREE

Mrs Jeffries felt a bit silly sitting all alone in the coach. But Smythe had refused to let her sit up with him, and of course, if he sat inside with her he wouldn't be able to drive. She stuck her head out and called, 'Are you all right up there?'

'Fine, Mrs J. We'll be there in a few minutes, so stop frettin' about me. I'm enjoyin' myself. It's been ages since I had the rig out at night.'

She popped back down in her seat and then grabbed the handhold as they careened around a corner. 'You might slow down a bit,' she muttered, but she'd not the heart to shout at him; he was obviously having a wonderful time. She bounced up and down on the stiff leather seats as they galloped through the sleeping city. Finally, they pulled up in front of a long, two-story, gray stone building with lights shining out of the basement windows.

Smythe tied up the horses and helped her down onto the cobblestone street. 'There's a light by that door,' he nodded at a door to their left. 'I expect there's a porter on duty who can let us in.'

Moving quickly against the cold night air, they went up the walkway to the door, their footsteps seeming unusually loud in the quiet night. The porter, hearing them coming, opened the door before they knocked.

'Is this an emergency?' he gave them a hard stare. 'You both look healthy enough to me.'

'Are you a doctor?' Mrs Jeffries asked quietly. She took Smythe's arm.

'Well, no,' he sputtered.

'Then I'll thank you to refrain from attempting to diagnose me. Could you please direct me to the morgue?'

'No offense, madam,' the porter replied. 'But you're not supposed to go there. It's for dead people.'

'We're here to make an identification,' Smythe said quickly. 'Dr Bosworth sent for us.'

'No one told me.' He stepped back and waved them inside. 'What are you doing here this time of night? That's always done during the daytime.'

'We're leaving for Australia by ship on the morning tide,' Smythe said smoothly. 'So we're in a hurry. Now be a good fellow and tell us how we find this Bosworth fellow?'

Mrs Jeffries shot him an admiring smile. He was getting quite good at thinking on his feet.

The porter shrugged. 'It's just down these stairs. Go all the way to the bottom and turn left. You'll come right to it, there's a sign on the door so you'll not miss it.'

They followed his directions and a few minutes later they were standing at the door to the morgue.

Mrs Jeffries took a deep breath. She noticed that

50

Smythe did the same. 'Now that we're here, I'm not sure I want to see what's on the other side of that door.'

'Oh, I don't know. I'm sure it'll be all right. There's probably not *too* many bodies in there,' he replied.

'And I'm certain that the dead are decently covered. Right, then.' She stepped forward and grasped the handle. 'Let's have a look.' She shoved open the door, stepped inside and then recoiled as the smell hit her full force. The air reeked; a ghastly mixture of blood, infection, carbolic acid, formaldehyde and the faintest whiff of methane gas. She forced herself to move into the room proper.

'Cor blimey,' Smythe muttered from behind her. 'This is bad enough to make the dead weep.'

The lights were dim but not so low that she couldn't see. Several bodies, decently covered, she was relieved to see, were lying on tables. Along the opposite wall was a row of sinks, and above them, shelves and cupboards filled with medicine bottles, tins of antiseptic, bandages and rolls of toweling.

At the far end of the room, a lone figure was bent over a naked body. 'I'm almost done,' he called chattily. 'Sorry to be so late. I know it's a bother for you, but I'll have a word with the nursing sisters to make sure you're not in trouble. You can't be expected to clean and tidy up when I'm working.'

'Uh . . . Dr Bosworth.' Now that they were here, Mrs Jeffries was a bit embarrassed. The doctor had helped them on several occasions in their investigations, but this was the first time they'd ever hunted him down on the job, so to speak. 'I do hope we're not interrupting . . .'

Bosworth whirled around. 'Good Lord, it's Mrs Jeffries. What on earth are you doing here?' He was a tall, red-haired man with pale skin and generally a nice smile. The smile was conspicuously absent at the moment. He looked rather annoyed. In one hand he held a scalpel dripping with blood and in the other a pair of long slender tongs. His collar was undone, his sleeves rolled up, and there were a multitude of hideous stains on the heavy apron he wore to protect his clothes.

'I'm dreadfully sorry to bother you,' she apologized. 'We were rather hoping you'd have finished by now and we could offer you a lift home. We brought the carriage.'

For a long moment, he stared at them and then he grinned. 'I might have known you'd show up. It's not often you get two corpses on one case. I'll be finished here in a few minutes. Why don't you wait for me out in the hall? This probably isn't very pleasant for either of you.'

'Yes, that'll be splendid,' she replied as she turned and hurried to the door. Smythe was right on her heels. They stepped into the hall and took deep breaths.

'Cor blimey, Mrs Jeffries.' Smythe shook his head. 'I thought for a minute there I was goin' to lose my supper. How does 'e stand it?'

'I expect you get used to the odor,' she murmured. 'But it is rather awful. I do hope the doctor will forgive us the liberty of just dropping in on him.'

Smythe laughed. 'Sure 'e will. The good doctor likes to see justice done just as much as we do.'

'Indeed I do, Smythe,' Bosworth said as he stepped

out and joined them. He rolled down his sleeves. 'And sometimes I'm of the mind that if it weren't for you lot, there'd be many a killer walking the streets of London. There's no need for you to take me home, I've still my reports to write, but if you'll come with me, I know a place where we can have a quiet cup of tea.'

'At this hour?'

He grinned again. 'This is a hospital, Smythe. There's always a kettle on the boil somewhere.' He took Mrs Jeffries's arm and guided her to the staircase. 'I know why you're here, so we can spend a few minutes nattering, then I'll tell you what I've learned about your two victims.'

By the time they got the coach back to Howards and made their way back to Upper Edmonton Gardens, it was full daylight. Mrs Goodge and Betsy were both sitting at the kitchen table, waiting for them.

'We've had quite a time,' Smythe said. 'It's bloomin' cold out there, I don't care if it is spring.'

'Have you had any luck in learning anything?' Mrs Goodge asked.

Mrs Jeffries slipped into her chair at the head of the table. She noticed that Fred, their mongrel dog, had barely wagged his tail when they'd come inside. 'What's wrong with Fred?'

'He misses Wiggins something fierce,' Betsy asked. 'But he'll be fine soon. I expect Wiggins will take the morning train and be here by this afternoon.'

Mrs Goodge snorted. 'He'd better be. We sent the telegram yesterday and he should have gotten it. Should we wait for Luty and Hatchet to get here before you

53

begin? You know how testy Hatchet's been since they missed our last murder.'

'That's a very good idea. That way I'll only have to tell it once.' She glanced at the carriage clock on the pine sideboard. 'It's almost seven. They'll be here right after breakfast.'

They arrived moments after the inspector had left for the day. The household had just finished the clearing up, and the cook had brewed a fresh pot of tea for their meeting.

Mrs Jeffries waved everyone to the table. 'Come along, everyone, we've a lot of ground to cover. I want to tell everyone what we learned from Dr Bosworth.'

'Good,' Luty declared as she plopped down in the seat next to Mrs Goodge. 'I've got somethin' to report too.'

Hatchet gave her a quick glare. 'Naturally you do, madam, considering that we barged into the bishop's residence without so much as a by-your-leave last night. I should hope you'd have something to show for your efforts.'

Luty grinned. She knew he was annoyed that she'd not only made him wait outside, but she hadn't shared what she'd learned with him. Served him right for trying to stop her from bargin' past the feller's secretary.

'Excellent, Luty,' said Mrs Jeffries. She smiled approvingly and then waited a moment before she spoke. 'I won't bore you with the preliminaries of our meeting with Dr Bosworth,' she said. 'I'll get right to the heart of the matter. He was able to determine that the first victim . . .

'That preacher feller,' Luty clarified.

'Yes, or as we call him, the vicar, he'd been dead for

at least twelve hours by the time his body was found yesterday.'

'That would put it at around nine o'clock the previous evening,' Hatchet said.

'Possibly.' Mrs Jeffries frowned slightly. 'But he emphasized the fact that he could be wrong by several hours either way. That was his best estimate, but he couldn't swear to that time in a court of law.'

'So it could have been as early as say, six, or as late as midnight,' Hatchet mused.

'But it would have had to have been after dark, wouldn't it?' Betsy said. 'If it had been before six and still daylight, someone would have seen the body.'

'That's right.' Smythe smiled proudly at his beloved and gave her fingers a squeeze. 'There's enough foot traffic that someone would have spotted him propped up against that wall, even if he was around the side of the building. I think it's safe to say he was killed after dark, which would mean it had gone six by the time the deed was done.'

'But that still leaves a very long time period to cover,' Mrs Goodge complained. 'What about the other one?'

'Now that's quite interesting,' Mrs Jeffries replied. 'There wasn't much Dr Bosworth could tell. Essentially, all he had to work with was a skeleton.'

'Had she been murdered?' Betsy asked.

'He wasn't able to tell, but he did say there were no obvious signs as to cause of death. No bullet holes or anything useful like that,' she replied. 'But he was able to determine she'd been in that chimney for a good number of years. He's having a friend of his take a look at her.'

'You mean another doctor?' Hatchet asked. 'Good gracious, why?' He didn't much like the idea of even more people snooping about in the inspector's cases. It meant there'd be less for him and the rest of them to do.

'I think it's a doctor.' Mrs Jeffries shrugged. 'Apparently, this person is an expert on bones, and he might be able to tell Dr Bosworth something more about the victim. I didn't really understand the details of why he thought it necessary to bring another person in to have a look, but I've faith that Dr Bosworth knows what he's doing. He's going to stop by on his way home this evening if there's any more information.'

'Is that it?' Mrs Goodge asked. She really needed this kitchen empty if she was to get anything done at all on her bits and pieces.

'That's all we know,' Mrs Jeffries replied. She looked at Luty. 'Were you successful at learning anything about our unknown vicar?'

Luty smiled smugly. 'I learned that no one, including the bishop, knows anything about the fellow. As far as he knew, there aren't any missin' priests from any of the London parishes. He's pretty sure the man must be from one of their overseas missions.'

'That doesn't mean there aren't any missing priests from other parishes,' Hatchet point out tartly. 'Just because Bishop Andrews hadn't heard anything doesn't mean there isn't one missing from somewhere. In case you don't know, there are over a hundred bishops in England, and unless you're going to toddle over to the House of Lords and speak to each and every one of them personally, you can't possibly know that this priest isn't from Cheshire or Yorkshire or Nottingham.'

'I don't have to go to the House of Lords,' Luty said. 'I've got a meetin' this morning with the archbishop.'

'Of Canterbury?' Hatchet looked positively horrified. 'You're barging in on the Archbishop of Canterbury?'

'I'm not bargin' in,' Luty retorted. 'Bishop Andrews made the appointment for me. Mind you, I did write out a big check for the Bishop's Building Fund, but I like to think he'd have done it even if I hadn't given him any money. Don't get your nose out of joint, Hatchet, I'll be discreet. I've got a good story all cooked up.'

'You're going to lie to the Archbishop of Canterbury?' If possible, Hatchet was even more horrified. It wasn't that he considered it a grievous sin to lie to the archbishop; he was simply afraid she'd muck it up and they'd be caught snooping in the inspector's case. 'But madam, you can't do that.'

Luty smiled smugly but said nothing.

'Hatchet, I'm sure Luty will be most discreet in her efforts,' Mrs Jeffries said soothingly. Luty was rich enough and wily enough that the housekeeper was fairly certain the worst that could happen was that she'd be considered an eccentric American. In England, there was a long history of tolerance for such people. 'And I'm equally sure she'll do her best to get us more information. Now, unless anyone has anything else to add, I suggest we do our chores as quickly as possible and then get cracking.'

Betsy stared at the row of abandoned cottages and then straightened her spine. There was no point in hanging about staring at the empty houses. They weren't likely to speak to her. The workers at the factory had already gone inside for their shift, so there was no information from that quarter, so she'd best get on up to the commercial areas and start talking to shopkeepers. Surely someone would know something.

She turned on her heel and retraced her steps. It took less than five minutes before she was standing on the busiest street corner in Bermondsey. Betsy leaned against a lamppost and surveyed the area. There was a greengrocer's, a fishmonger, a butcher shop, a dry goods store and a draper's shop. She decided to try the greengrocer's first. She crossed the cobblestone street and went inside. A middle-aged woman was serving a short line of customers. Betsy waited her turn. Luckily, no one had come in behind her, so she was alone with the proprietress.

'What can I get for you, miss?' the woman asked politely as she wiped her hands on her apron.

Betsy smiled shyly. 'I was hoping you could help me.'

The woman frowned slightly and dashed a lock of frizzy, light brown hair off her cheek. 'What do you need, girl?' As Betsy wasn't actually a customer, she'd gone down a peg or two in the woman's estimation.

'I was wondering if you know anything about those abandoned cottages down by the factory.'

'They're empty,' she retorted. She turned away and began straightening a bin of onions.

'I mean, do you know who owns them?' The moment the words were out, she wanted to bite her tongue. Inspector Witherspoon had already found out who owned them.

'The factory people own the whole lot of 'em,' the

proprietress said. She looked over her shoulder and stared at Betsy suspiciously. 'Why are you so interested in 'em?'

'I'm trying to find someone who used to live in one of them.' Betsy already had a story at the ready. 'My aunt and my cousin used to live in number seven. My family emigrated to Canada and we lost contact with them. Me mam died, and I've come back. I've come a long way to find them.'

The woman snorted in disbelief. 'Didn't your people ever hear of writing letters? Sorry, girl, no one's lived in those places for years. The council forced everyone out when the ground began to shift. They're none of 'em safe.'

'So you've no idea where the people who lived there went?' Betsy wisely decided to ignore the comment about letter-writing.

'No.' The woman turned to help a customer who'd entered the shop so quietly Betsy hadn't heard her come in. 'What can I get you, Mrs Pangley?'

Betsy mumbled her thanks to the woman and hurried out. She wasn't certain what to do next. But she wasn't going to give up. Someone around here had to know something about those cottages. She started for the butcher shop. But she had no better luck there. Nor did she find out anything at the fishmonger's, the dry goods shop or the draper's.

She stared at the busy street. She supposed she could try the shops on the next road, but that was even farther away from where the houses were located. She'd learned nothing except that the houses had been abandoned for years.

'Excuse me, miss,' came a woman's voice from behind her.

Betsy whirled around. It was the lady from the greengrocer's, the one who'd come in so quietly.

'I'm Ada Pangley,' she continued. 'I couldn't help but overhear your conversation at the greengrocer's.' She was a tall woman with graying brown hair, blue eyes and thin lips. She was dressed in a sensible brown coat, plain brown bonnet and sturdy shoes.

'You know something that might help me?' Betsy couldn't believe her luck.

Ada Pangley shrugged. 'I'm not sure. But I did know someone who used to live in those cottages. I used to do some sewing for the people who lived in number five. Where did your people live?'

Betsy was ready for this question. 'I'm not sure. You see, I was just a little girl. It might have been number seven or number six. It was one of the ones at the end.'

'It must have been number six, then,' Ada nodded wisely. 'The woman in number seven didn't have any children.'

Betsy wasn't going to let this lady get away. Not if she knew something about the woman who'd lived in number seven. 'Is there a tea shop nearby? I'd love to buy you a cup of tea and ask you a few more questions.'

'There's nothing like that around here,' Ada replied. 'But I live just around the corner. Come along, I could do with a cuppa myself.'

'Oh, I don't want to put you to any trouble.'

'It's no trouble at all.' Ada smiled again and started

for the corner. 'Since my Stan died, I'm a bit lonely. Come along, it'll be nice to have some company.'

Betsy trailed after her. 'If you're sure it's no trouble.' She knew that if Smythe found out she was going off with some stranger, he'd have a fit. But this lady looked harmless enough, and it was worth the risk if she was going to find out anything useful.

Hatchet was determined to find out something important today. He stared at the spot where the dead vicar had been found and saw absolutely nothing but an empty wall. Well, what had he expected? A clue the police had overlooked. Not likely. His mind worked furiously. There was no point in questioning anyone at the church proper because the police would have taken care of that task. He turned and headed for the end of the street, coming out on a busy road with a host of shops, offices and businesses lining each side. He wasn't sure where to start, so he walked into the first one, which was a secondhand furniture shop.

The shop was poorly lighted and crowded with all manner of old furniture, most of it in fairly bad condition. Tallboys with missing handles, uneven tables, and oversized chairs with half their stuffing missing were piled haphazardly around the room. Broken footstools, chairs and even some small tables were suspended on hooks along the walls.

A long narrow counter ran the width of the room, behind which stood a tall, thin woman wearing a beige dress and a stained brown apron. She stared at him. 'May I help you?'

Hatchet gave her his most charming smile. It

appeared to have no effect whatsoever. 'Thank you, madam. I'm just having a good look around, if you don't mind.'

'Looking for anything in particular?' she pressed.

'Actually, I came into your charming establishment because of the plethora of quality goods I saw from the window,' Hatchet replied. She'd been a handsome woman in her youth, he thought. Her eyes were a nice color of blue, and she had a lovely bone structure.

She smiled faintly. 'That's funny, them windows is so dirty you can barely see inside.'

Hatchet wanted to tell her that her manner wasn't the best approach to ensure a sale, but he thought better of it. But before he could say a word, she spoke.

'Look, let's not shilly-shally about. You're no more interested in my goods than the man in the moon. People like you don't buy this kind of old furniture.' She gestured around the shop. 'So let's talk about what you are interested in.'

'And what would that be, madam?' he asked curiously. He should have worn one of his old suits and his scuffed shoes before venturing out to this neighborhood. The polished top hat and his gold-handled walking stick didn't help his cause either. In the future, he'd leave them at home.

'You're one of them reporters from the newspaper, aren't you? And you're interested in that there dead vicar they found propped up by the church wall.'

Hatchet stared at her in surprise.

'If you want any of my information,' she said bluntly, 'you'll have to pay for it. It's not like we're made of money around here, you know.'

'How much?'

'A couple of quid.'

Hatchet hesitated. He wasn't sure whether reporters actually paid for information or not, but then again, he wasn't a reporter. But a real journalist would negotiate. 'How do I know what you've got to tell me is worth that much?'

'That's just a risk you'll have to take,' she shot back. 'If I didn't say nuthin' to the police, I'm not likely to say much to you unless you cross my palm with silver.'

He reached in his pocket and drew out his purse. Opening it, he took out two half-sovereigns and held them up. 'Let's start with these,' he said to her, 'and if what you've got to say is worth it, I'll give you two more.'

Her eyes narrowed but she grabbed the coins. 'It'll be worth it, just you wait. Come along to the back. We might as well give my feet a rest while we're talking.'

Hatchet followed her through a dingy gray curtain that separated the shop from a back room that was even darker than the shop. She struck a match and lighted a tiny gas lamp that stood on a table. She motioned for him to take a chair, and then sat down herself.

Hatchet lowered himself into the flimsy seat very carefully, and they sat facing one another. The woman said, 'My name's Jane Bilkington.' She stared at him, her expression expectant. It suddenly occurred to him that she was waiting for him to introduce himself.

He was suddenly a bit ashamed. This woman was poor and quite willing to sell information, but she was still deserving of common courtesy. 'My name is Hector Clemente,' he said, using the name of a deceased friend of his who didn't need it anymore.

'What paper d'you work for?' she asked conversationally.

Again, he hesitated. Did real reporters reveal who they wrote for? He didn't know. 'I'd prefer to keep that confidential.' He gave her a sly smile. 'If you don't mind.'

She shrugged. 'As long as you're payin', I don't care who you work for. I was just bein' sociable-like. Anyways, let's get on with this, I've got work to do.'

'Thank you, Miss Bilkington,' he replied.

'Mrs Bilkington,' she corrected. 'I'm a widow.'

'Sorry, Mrs Bilkingon. If you'd tell me what you know about the dead vicar, I'd be most appreciative.'

'I can tell you he weren't alone, that's for certain,' she sniffed delicately. 'He was runnin' helter-skelter when he come past here last night. Mind you, it was hard to see anything, what with the heavy fog and all, but he weren't alone. I know that much.'

'Why don't you tell me exactly what you saw?' he suggested. 'Start at the beginning.'

'I'd gone out front to bring in a new entry table we'd just bought, nice thing it was too, just had a few scratches and nicks on the top. We'd sold it already, you see. Course I knew it would sell fast, that's why I bought it. Entry tables do well for us. A lot of our customers live in small places, and a decent-sized entry table can be used to eat on . . .'

'Yes, I'm sure that's true,' he interrupted. 'But what did you see?'

'Just give me a minute,' she scolded. 'As you're payin' for this, I want to make sure I get it right. Anyways, like I was sayin', I was bringing in that table when all of a sudden, I hears footsteps comin' down the road. They was comin' fast and hard, too, so I stopped what I was doing and stepped out a bit into the street. It was dark, and with the fog and all, you couldn't see more than a foot or so in front of your own face.'

'Do you know what time it was, exactly?' Hatchet asked.

'It was almost six, I know that. We close at six and I was due at my sister's at half past. She lives up on Rayners Lane, which is a good twenty-minute walk. So I timed it to bring in the table, lock the shop and then go. Well, as I said, I heard footsteps coming hard down the road. They kept comin' closer and closer, but with the fog I couldn't see anything even if it were right in front of my eyes. All of a sudden, when the vicar couldn't have been more than ten feet from me, there was one of them partings that you get. You know, one of them spots where the fog shifts and you can see. Lo and behold, I saw the man runnin' like the hounds of hell was on his heels.'

'Did he see you?' Hatchet had no idea why that was important, but for some reason, it was.

'No, he were too busy lookin' over his shoulder, but he was lookin' the opposite direction. Then, before I could do so much as a by-your-leave-sir, the fog closed in again and I couldn't see anything. Just heard his footsteps. A few seconds later, I heard a second set. They was runnin' hard too.'

Hatchet drew a sharp breath. 'Did you see this second person?'

She shook her head. 'The fog was too thick. Mind

you, I thought it odd, but then again, it never pays to stick your nose into things that don't concern you.'

'You mean you didn't summon a policeman.'

'How was I to know the vicar was in danger? I thought the man was runnin' to get to church on time. It was almost time for the service.'

He stared at her in disbelief. 'Let me make sure I understand. You saw a gentleman wearing a clerical collar come running past your establishment and a few seconds later you heard another set of footstep, apparently chasing the poor man, but you didn't think it wise to summon a policeman?'

'And tell him what? That I saw a vicar runnin' toward St Paul's?' She glared at him, shoved back from the table and got to her feet. 'You've got no call to be passing judgment on me. Like I said, the evensong bells was ringing. I thought they was late for church. It was only later that I realized what I'd really heard. Now get out of here.'

'I'm sorry, Mrs Bilkington. You're right, I've no right to pass judgment on you.' He got up as well. 'Please accept my apologies.' He reached in his pocket for his purse, but she held up her hand.

'I don't want any more of your money, just get out of my shop.'

Hatchet realized he'd deeply offended the woman and that there was no going back. She might have wanted money for the information she had, but she'd genuinely not known the vicar was in danger. He walked out of the room and into the shop. She followed him. At the door, he stopped and turned. 'Again, I'm sorry to have offended you.'

She said nothing.

Hatchet stepped out into the sunny spring day.

Witherspoon buttoned his coat as he and Barnes stepped out of the offices of the Far East and India Shipping Company. The traffic on the Commercial Road was heavy, but Barnes spotted a hansom and gave a toot on his police whistle. A few moments later, they were climbing into a cab. Barnes gave the driver an address in St John's Wood.

'It was very clever of you to think of this.' Witherspoon gestured at the offices they'd just left as the cab pulled back into the traffic.

'It wasn't me that thought of it, sir. It was Mrs Barnes. I was telling her over breakfast how frustrating it was not to be able to identify the victim, when she suggested the vicar might be from overseas.' Once Barnes had suggested the idea to the inspector, it had then been decided that as they had no other clues to follow, it wouldn't hurt to check with the shipping companies to see if any priests had come in recently on one of their vessels. Armed with copies of the *Times* detailing arrivals from foreign ports, they'd started making the rounds of the shipping companies. The Far East and India line had been the fourth one they'd tried. Their vessel, the *Eastern Sun*, had arrived on Monday morning, the day before the priest's body had been discovered.

'Then thanks to your good wife for being so clever. At least now we might have a name.'

'The Reverend Jasper Claypool.' Barnes repeated the name they'd gotten off the passenger manifest at the shipping offices. 'Now why does that sound so familiar? Let's keep our fingers crossed it's him. We've had a bit of luck on this one, sir, and that's a fact.'

They'd not only found out a priest had come in on the ship, but they'd gotten his local address from the manifest and learned that the man had relatives here in the city.

'Hopefully one of his relatives ought to be able to identify the poor fellow,' Witherspoon said. 'That'll give us a place to start. It's very difficult to investigate a murder properly when one doesn't even know the name of the victim.'

Barnes grabbed the handhold above his head as the hansom hit a particularly deep pothole. 'We ought to know fairly soon, sir.'

The traffic didn't get any better, and it was almost two o'clock by the time the hansom pulled up in front of number four Heather Street in St John's Wood. The house was a three-story red–brick Georgian with a white painted door on the left-hand side of the building. There was a huge fanlight over the top of the door and freshly painted white trim around the windows.

Witherspoon and Barnes went up the short walkway, and the constable reached for the knocker. But before his fingers touched the brass, the door was flung open and a butler stuck his head out and inquired, 'May I help you?'

'We'd like to see . . .' Witherspoon hesitated. He didn't actually have a name of a person.

'The master of the house,' Barnes put in smoothly.

The butler raised his eyebrows. 'Do you mean Mr Christopher?'

'Is Mr Christopher a relation of the Reverend Jasper Claypool?' the inspector asked.

The butler's eyebrows climbed even higher. 'No, but Mrs Christopher has an uncle by that name.'

'May we speak to Mrs Christopher, then?' Barnes asked. He was getting impatient.

The butler looked uncertain. 'If you'll come in, I'll see if she's at home.' He held open the door, and they stepped into a wide foyer with a beautiful Persian rug on the floor. Through an archway just ahead of them was a wide staircase carpeted in deep red. A huge fern in an ornate brass urn stood next to the staircase. Its twin stood on the second-floor landing which they could clearly see from where they stood.

'This isn't a social call,' Barnes said to the butler. 'It's a police matter. Kindly tell your mistress it's urgent that we speak with her.'

The butler look faintly alarmed, but he nodded and hurried off past the staircase to a room farther down the hall. They could hear the low murmuring of voices, and a moment later, the butler reappeared. 'Please follow me.'

He led them into an opulently furnished drawing room. The walls were painted a pale green, green velvet drapes with gold fringe framed the tall windows, there was a parquet floor with another beautiful Persian carpet and several glorious paintings of the English countryside were on the walls. Twin cream-colored chairs were on each side of the marble fireplace, and there were also several cabinets, two occasional tables covered with Dresden figurines and a three-seater cream-colored sofa, as well as a padded satin emerald-colored settee.

A beautiful woman with red hair was sitting on the settee. She stared at them curiously out of eyes the same color as the walls. 'Good day, gentlemen. My name is Hilda Christopher.'

'Good day, madam,' Witherspoon replied. 'We're sorry to barge in on you so unexpectedly, but I'm afraid I might have some very distressing news for you.'

'Distressing news? For me?' She rose to her feet, her expression confused. 'I'm afraid I don't understand.'

Suddenly they heard footsteps pounding down the hall, and a second later, a tall, dark-haired man burst into the room. 'Hilda, what's going on? Blevins said the police were here.'

'They are.' She gestured toward the two men.

'I'm Carl Christopher. Why are you here? Has something happened?' He crossed the room and stood next to his wife.

'I'm Inspector Witherspoon and this is Constable Barnes. I'm afraid we might have some rather unpleasant news for your wife.' He directed his attention to Mrs Christopher. 'Do you have an uncle named Jasper Claypool, and is that person a clergyman?'

Hilda Christopher looked even more confused. 'Yes, but my uncle's in India.'

'I'm afraid not, madam,' the inspector replied. 'Your uncle arrived in England two days ago. We'd like you to come with us.'

'Come with you?' Carl Christopher protested. 'What's this all about? Why should we come with you?'

Witherspoon hated this part of his job. 'We'd like you to come with us to the morgue at St Thomas's Hospital. We need someone to identify a gentleman who was found dead yesterday. He was wearing clerical garb and we have reason to believe he might be Jasper Claypool.'

'Dead? Do you mean he's had a stroke or a seizure of some kind?' Hilda Christopher said.

Witherspoon winced inwardly. But knew he must do his duty. It was better she be told the truth in advance than see it at the morgue. 'No ma'am, I'm afraid he's been murdered.'

CHAPTER FOUR

Mrs Goodge held the telegram in her hand and read it for the third time.

'Grandfather very ill. Can't come home yet.'

Considering that she'd been the one to insist the lad go visit his grandfather in the first place, she wasn't sure if she should be pleased or annoyed. But it wasn't like the boy to miss a murder. On the other hand, he was a kindhearted sort, so if he'd arrived and the old man had whined at him to stay, he'd do just that.

She sighed and looked over at Fred, who was staring at her with a forlorn expression, as though he understood what was written on the slip of paper in her hand. 'Sorry, boy, he's not comin' home just yet.'

'Who's not coming home?' Mrs Jeffries asked briskly as she stepped into the kitchen. She noticed the telegram. 'Ah, I see. It's our Wiggins. So they've prevailed upon him to stay?'

'Afraid so.' She pursed her lips. 'Maybe I oughtn't have encouraged him to go. He didn't want to and now he's going to miss the murder.'

'Of course you should have encouraged him.' Mrs

Jeffries stepped over to the table and began setting out the plates that were stacked on the end. 'He needs to make peace with his family, not for their sakes, but for his. Now don't you fret over it, Mrs Goodge. You did the right thing.'

The cook put the telegram in her apron pocket. 'I like to think so. There may come a day when the lad will be glad he's got a family to give him aid and comfort. We'll not be here forever. I'd best get that kettle on the boil; the others will be here soon.'

'I'm going to set an extra plate,' Mrs Jeffries announced as she went to the pine sideboard and opened the cupboard, 'just in case Dr Bosworth arrives in time for tea.'

In the next ten minutes, the others drifted into the warm kitchen and took their usual spots at the table. Mrs Jeffries waited till everyone had a cup of steaming tea and a thick slice of freshly baked bread before she made her announcement. 'Before we begin, I want to tell you that we've heard from Wiggins. Apparently his grandfather is quite ill and he won't be coming back just yet.'

'Poor Wiggins,' Betsy said. 'He's going to miss the murder.'

'More like poor Fred.' Smythe reached down and patted the animal on the head. 'He's so lonely he's even doggin' *my* 'eels.'

'Fred will be fine as soon as the inspector gets home,' the housekeeper replied. 'He'll take him right upstairs with him and then they'll go for an extra long walk.'

'And probably let him sleep on his rug too,' Mrs Goodge said. 'But enough of this. If no one minds, I'd like to go first. Frankly, without names, I'm workin' in the dark, so to speak. But I did find out a bit about those abandoned cottages. Oh, bother, I didn't really find out anything about the wretched things except that the gossip is they're used for nefarious purposes.'

'Nefarious purposes,' Hatchet repeated. 'You mean by criminals?'

'No, no,' Mrs Goodge wave her hand impatiently. 'The other sort of nefarious dealings. Unmarried men and women doing things they wouldn't confess to the vicar.'

'I think we all understand,' Mrs Jeffries said quickly. 'Did you learn anything specific?'

Mrs Goodge shook her head in disgust. 'Not yet. But as soon as I have some names, I'll track down all sorts of good gossip.'

'I found out something interesting,' Betsy said slowly. She wasn't sure if her information was useful or not. 'One of the people in the shops told me that some of those cottages weren't let at all. The one on the end, the one they found the body in, never had any real tenants. But everyone who lived along the row knew that someone occasionally stayed there. But they never knew who it was. Only that it was a woman, because no matter how careful she was, someone would spot her going in or out.'

'What did she look like?' Mrs Goodge asked eagerly. 'Did your source know?'

'No, she always wore a heavy veil when she arrived.'

'How often was she there?' Mrs Jeffries asked.

'My source wasn't sure,' Betsy replied. 'She said the neighbors sometimes spoke of her like she was a tenant, which would imply she was there quite often, and sometimes they talked about her like she just occasionally came for a visit. She always came in at night and locked the shutters tight so no one could see inside.'

'You mean someone was just using the place without permission?' Mrs Goodge looked confused.

'That's the funny part,' she replied. 'This Mrs Pangley that I was talking to said the neighbors had gone to the factory supervisor and reported what they'd seen. They were told it was none of their affair and to leave it alone.'

'Did you get the name of the foreman?' Mrs Jeffries asked. This was very intriguing.

'No, Mrs Pangley didn't have that many details. She didn't actually live there, she was just repeating the talk she'd heard.'

'How long ago was this?' Smythe asked. 'I mean, how long ago was it that there was gossip about someone usin' number seven?'

'Well, she did know that everyone had to leave the cottages about ten years ago, but I didn't think to ask her how long before that the neighbors had been talking.' Betsy sighed. 'That was silly of me. That might be important.'

'Don't fret, love,' he said softly. 'I wouldn't have thought to ask it either, and if it's important, we'll find it out another way.'

'That's excellent, Betsy.' Mrs Jeffries nodded approvingly. Considering how little information they'd started with, they were doing quite well. 'Who would like to go next?'

'If it's all the same to everyone,' Hatchet said, 'I do

believe I've found out something interesting.' He told them about his visit to the used furniture shop and his talk with Jane Bilkington. 'So it sounds as if our victim knew he was being pursued,' he finished. 'According to Mrs Bilkington, he was running like the devil was on his heels.'

'That doesn't sound like he was just worried about bein' late to church, either,' Luty added. 'Poor feller. Must have been awful, an old man like him bein' chased down like that and killed.'

'So he was killed around six o'clock,' Mrs Jeffries murmured. She was trying to think of how she could get this information to the inspector. 'Too bad this Mrs Bilkington didn't share this with the police.'

'We'll find a way of seein' that he gets it,' Luty replied. 'Anyways, if that's all Hatchet's got, can I go next?'

'All that I've got?' Hatchet glared at her. 'I'll have you know, madam, that learning the time of death is no small accomplishment.'

'Course it ain't,' Luty grinned. 'But if that's all you got, I'd like the floor now. You ain't the only one who found out something useful.'

Mrs Jeffries decided to intervene. 'Go ahead, Luty. Tell us what you found out.'

'The archbishop says our dead vicar is from overseas. So we was right to send Smythe off down to the docks to have a snoop around the shipping offices. The murder is causin' quite a stir, what with the victim bein' a clergyman and all. So I guess the archbishop already had his minions lookin' into how they could help identify the feller. Anyways, when I got into his

76

office, he had a list of clergymen that were supposedly comin' to England from their overseas churches.'

'I don't suppose he shared the names with you?' Mrs Jeffries asked.

'Course he didn't, but I didn't let that stop me. The list was sittin' right there on his desk – we got lucky, his secretary had just brung it to him a few minutes before I arrived. Anyways, when we was alone, I pretended to faint so that when he went to get me a glass of water, I memorized the three names on the list.'

Hatchet laughed, Betsy giggled, Mrs Jeffries smiled, Smythe chuckled and even Mrs Goodge snickered.

'Sometimes my bein' an old woman works to our advantage.' Luty grinned broadly. 'Anyways, when he jumped up to get me that water, I got a good look at them names. First one was John Smithson, the second was Edgar Woodley and the third was Jasper Claypool.'

'Very good, Luty. You are a clever one.' Mrs Jeffries was very pleased. 'Now we've really got something to go on.'

'It's too bad them names didn't have any dates with 'em.' Luty shrugged.

'I don't expect that matters much,' Mrs Goodge put in. 'Seems to me the archbishop probably only asked for the names of people who'd only just arrived in the country. Anyone who'd been here awhile would have been reported missing if they didn't turn up at their home or their hotel. According to the inspector, no one's reported any priests missing.'

Mrs Jeffries nodded in agreement. 'That sounds logical.' She turned to Smythe. 'I don't suppose you came across any of those names during your inquiries today?'

'Only one of them: Jasper Claypool. He came in on the *Eastern Sun* early Monday morning. She came in from Calcutta. No one mentioned any of the other priests.'

'They might have come into Southampton or Liverpool,' Mrs Goodge suggested.

'Was Claypool's luggage picked up?' Mrs Jeffries asked.

Smythe winced. 'I forgot to check. Cor blimey, I must be losin' my mind. That's important! If we've time after our meetin', I'll nip back and see if I can find out.'

'Why is it so important?' Betsy frowned thoughtfully. 'I don't see what difference it makes . . . oh, of course. Now I see what you're getting at. He didn't have any luggage with him when he was running through the streets, otherwise that Mrs Bilkington would have seen it.'

'Right, which means that he either had it sent somewhere else, in which case why hasn't the hotel or the boarding house where it went made inquiries as to his whereabouts. Or, he didn't take it with him when he left the ship.'

'Why wouldn't he take it with him?' Mrs Goodge asked.

'Sometimes you leave it at the shipping company,' Smythe replied. 'When I made my trips to Australia, I used to leave my bags down at the dock until I could find a nice lodging house. He probably wasn't sure where he was goin' to stay and didn't fancy carryin' his bags with 'im. Whatever it was, I'll make it my business to find out tomorrow.'

Fred suddenly leapt up, paused for a split second and then charged toward the back door, barking as he ran.

'What's got into him?' Smythe charged after the animal.

They heard the excited sound of the dog's paws bouncing against the floor, the door opening and then a familiar voice saying, 'This is a fine greeting. Hello, old fellow, I haven't seen you in ages. Looks like you're being fed very well.'

'I hope that's Fred that Doctor Bosworth is talking to,' Betsy giggled. 'Otherwise, Smythe's nose will be out of joint.'

When the two men and the animal came back into the kitchen, it was obviously the dog who'd been the focus of the good doctor's attentions. Fred was bouncing at the doctor's heels and his tail was wagging furiously.

'Good evening, Doctor,' Mrs Jeffries got to her feet. 'We're so glad you decided to drop in. Do have a seat.' She pointed to the empty spot they'd saved for him. Betsy was already pouring him tea, and the cook was loading his plate with bread, butter and buns.

Bosworth gave Fred one final pat on the head and sat down. 'I can't stay long. I've been up for hours and I've got to get some rest. But I did want to give you a quick report on my findings. Ah, this looks wonderful.' He nodded his thanks to Betsy as she handed him the tea and took a quick sip. 'I won't bore you with too much detail, but it appears that our victim that was found in the chimney was a young woman.'

'Any idea how old she might have been?' Mrs Jeffries asked.

'She could be anywhere from fifteen to thirty,' he replied, 'At least that's what I thought when I examined her, but Dr McCallister – he's that friend of mine I mentioned to you,' he said, nodding at Mrs Jeffries. 'His opinion is that she was probably in her early twenties when death occurred.'

'Does he know what he's about?' Betsy asked softly. She couldn't think how someone could become a 'bone expert', but she didn't want to insult Dr Bosworth or his colleagues. Besides, she knew she was ignorant of such matters.

Bosworth grinned. 'He knows what he's about. He's been studying bones for years now and knows more about them than anyone.'

'Did he have any idea of how long the bones had been up there?' Smythe asked.

'His best guess was ten years. The bones were beginning to weather from the elements. That means they've been up there a fair bit of time. Considering that the cottages were inhabited up until ten years ago, I think it's fair to assume that if someone had been living in the house, they'd have noticed a corpse in the chimney.'

'But that's just it, no one was living in that particular cottage,' Mrs Jeffries said. She gave him the information Betsy had gotten from Mrs Pangley.

His expression grew thoughtful as he listened and then shrugged. 'Even if the cottage was uninhabited, if this woman was occasionally coming in and using the place, she'd have noticed the smell. I know there's a paint factory across the road and it smells awful, but you couldn't miss the scent of decomposing flesh if you were inside the cottage proper. And if you tried to light the fireplace, well,' he shrugged and made a face. 'Let's just say it wouldn't be very nice.'

'Could the body have been up there less than ten years?' Mrs Jeffries wanted to clarify this point as much as possible. The entire investigation could go badly if they operated under a false assumption as to when the body had been placed in the chimney.

'That's doubtful.' Bosworth gulped more tea. 'As I said, the bones had begun to weather, and that does take time.' He yawned widely. 'Forgive me but I'm dreadfully tired. I've been on duty for over twenty-four hours straight.' He rose to his feet and Fred jumped up as well. 'I really must be going. Oh, there is one other thing I noticed about the corpse. She'd broken her right arm in childhood and it hadn't been set very well. It was a very old break and done well before the murder.'

'Do you have any idea what killed her?' Mrs Jeffries asked. Gracious, that was one of the most important points, and she'd almost forgotten to ask.

'There were no obvious signs of trauma on the bones.' He yawned again. 'But she could easily have been asphyxiated or even stabbed to death. There are a number of ways to commit murder without disturbing the bones. Poison, stabbing through soft tissue, a garrot.' He stifled another yawn. 'I must admit, I'm very curious as to how these two murders can possibly be connected. Do keep me informed.'

Mrs Jeffries knew she had to let the poor man go home. He was dead on his feet. 'We'll do that, Doctor.'

She got up and followed him out of the kitchen. 'Let me walk you to the door.'

Inspector Witherspoon was always uncomfortable around bodies, but even more so when he was escorting some poor unfortunate to identify a loved one. He glanced over at Mr and Mrs Christoper and was relieved to see that they were quite calm.

Barnes pushed through the door that led to St Thomas's mortuary and held it open for the others.

Inside, a porter stood respectfully at attention, waiting for them. 'Inspector Witherspoon? We got your message, sir. Everything is all set up in the viewing room.' He turned to his left and beckoned for them to follow, leading them to a small room off a short corridor.

Witherspoon blinked as he entered. The room was unnaturally bright. Even though it was daylight, all the gas lamps had been lighted and there was a good half-dozen lit lanterns hanging from hooks along the wall. He looked at the oblong table in the center of the room. A sheet-draped body lay on top of it. 'I'm afraid this isn't going to be pleasant,' he said to the Christophers. They'd come just inside the door and then stopped. The inspector didn't much blame them. He didn't fancy looking at that dead body either.

'Must my wife do this?' Carl Christopher put his arm around her protectively. 'Can't I identify him?'

'Did you know your wife's uncle very well?' Witherspoon asked.

'Well enough to know if it's him,' Christopher replied.

'It's all right, Carl.' Mrs Christopher smiled bravely.

'Let me do it. It's been years since you've seen Uncle Jasper.'

'And it's been the same amount of time since you've seen him,' her husband replied softly.

'Yes, I know, but he virtually raised me. So no matter how long it's been, I'll recognize him.' She looked at Witherspoon and Barnes. 'Is he horribly disfigured? I mean . . .'

'He was shot in the head,' Barnes put in quickly. 'There's a hole, but it's a small one. He's been cleaned up as much as possible. But it'll not be very nice.'

'I understand.' She moved away from her husband's protective embrace and stepped to the table.

Barnes went over, picked up the sheet and held it back so that she could get a good look at the deceased. 'Is this your uncle?'

She gasped, bit hard on her lip and closed her eyes. Then she nodded her head affirmatively. 'That's him. That's my Uncle Jasper. But who on earth would want to kill him? Who would want to harm him?'

'Are you certain, ma'am?' Barnes pressed. 'It's been a long time since you've seen your uncle.'

'It's him.' She drew a long, jagged breath and covered her face with her hands. 'Oh God, why would anyone hurt Uncle Jasper? He was such a good man.'

Carl Christopher rushed over to his wife and drew her away from the table. 'Oh darling, this must be dreadful for you.'

'Let's go outside,' Witherspoon said quickly. 'Now that we know he's your uncle, unfortunately, we've a number of questions we must ask you.'

Mrs Christopher kept her hands over her face as her

husband led her out of the room. Once outside, Carl Christopher said, 'My wife's had a terrible shock. Must you pester her with questions just now? Can't you ask them later?'

The inspector hesitated. The woman didn't look very well, but on the other hand, they really couldn't waste any more time. 'I'm sure your wife is most dreadfully upset,' he replied. 'But we really must have some answers to move forward on this investigation. Perhaps we could go back to your house and you could answer some of our questions. If Mrs Christopher isn't feeling up to it, we could come back tomorrow to speak with her.'

'I'm fine, Carl,' she said. 'It's been a shock, but I'm capable of coherent thought.' She looked at the two policemen. 'I don't know what you think we can tell you. We didn't even know Uncle Jasper was in England.'

'Nevertheless, we must speak with you,' Witherspoon insisted.

Barnes secured two hansoms and they went back to St John's Wood. The Christophers arrived first, so that by the time the two policemen entered the drawing room, a maid was pouring tea.

'Please sit down,' Carl Christopher said, nodding toward one of the settees, 'and let's get this over with.'

They each took a seat and accepted a cup of tea from the maid. The cups were delicate bone china that looked like it would crack if you so much as breathed hard. Taking great care, Barnes set his tea down on an end table covered with a fringed shawl, then he whipped out his little brown notebook.

Witherspoon balanced his cup and saucer on his knee and hoped he wouldn't disgrace himself by dropping the wretched thing. 'When was the last time you communicated with your uncle?'

'We had a letter from him three months ago,' Mrs Christopher replied. 'He said nothing about returning to England. It was one of his usual missives, he told us all about his church doings and his congregation. That was all.'

'Do you have any idea why he would have come home?' Barnes asked.

She shook her head. 'None at all. He was quite happy living in India.'

Witherspoon took a quick sip. 'Had he been there long?'

She smiled sadly. 'Almost ten years. He retired from St Matthew's in Finsbury Park and was at loose ends. For some odd reason, he took it into his head to go out to India and take up a church there. I gather it's quite difficult for the church to find priests who are willing to work overseas.'

'How old was your uncle?' Barnes asked.

She thought for a moment. 'He's seventy-five.'

'Perhaps he came home because he wanted to retire here.'

'No. He loved India. He planned on staying there for the rest of his life. He owns property and has a wide circle of friends. Oh, dear, I expect I'll have to write to them now, let them know he's not coming back.'

'And you've no idea why he came home unexpectedly,' Barnes pressed.

'She's already said she hasn't,' Carl Christopher

snapped. 'Now look, we've told you all we know. Uncle Jasper was probably killed by a robber or something.'

'We doubt that, sir,' the constable replied. 'Most robbers don't murder their victim. Especially a victim of your uncle's advanced years. It would have been much easier simply to knock him down and take his purse instead of putting a bullet through his forehead.'

Witherspoon asked, 'Do either of you know anything about a cottage at number seven Dorland Place in Bermondsey?'

For a moment, neither of them spoke. Then Carl Christopher said, 'That's a very odd question, Inspector. I presume you have reason for asking.'

'When your uncle's body was discovered, he was holding a slip of paper in his hand that had that address on it. Do you have any idea why?'

It was Mrs Christopher who replied. 'Actually, we do know that address. Oh dear lord, what am I thinking? He doesn't know about Jasper. He and Eugenia will be so upset. Nothing like this has ever happened to our family before.' She covered her face with her hands and began to weep softly.

Witherspoon winced, but Barnes looked unperturbed.

'There, there, dear.' Carl Christopher put his arm around his wife and drew her close. 'It's all right. I'll tell Horace and Eugenia straightaway.' He looked at the policemen. 'Horace Riley is my wife's cousin. He's also Jasper's nephew. His father was Uncle Jasper's halfbrother. He's one of the owners of the factory across the road from those cottages you mentioned. We all are. As a matter of fact, the cottages belong to the factory as well.'

'That's why the name sounded so familiar,' Barnes murmured. 'Claypool Manufacturing. It was written on the sign in front.'

Christopher nodded. 'We all own part of that factory. Including Uncle Jasper. Actually, he owns the lion's share.'

Witherspoon didn't wish to upset Mrs Christopher any further, so he wasn't sure it was wise to mention the body in the chimney.

'Could you give us Mr Horace Riley's address, sir?' Barnes asked. 'We've found a body in the chimney of one of those cottages, and we're hoping that he, or perhaps even one of you, could shed a bit of light on it.'

Smythe glanced at the clock on the sideboard. 'It's not gone five yet. If I 'urry, I can make it to that shippin' office before it closes and see if Claypool's luggage is still there.'

Mrs Jeffries got up as well. 'While you're there, see if you can find out from one of the clerks if there is a London address for the man. That would at least give us a start tomorrow morning.'

He nodded and turned to Betsy. 'Walk me to the door, love.'

'All right,' she replied cheerfully. 'Then I've got to finish dusting upstairs. I want to have plenty of time tomorrow to get out and about.'

'Smythe's errand will give the rest of us time to get things caught up around here,' Mrs Jeffries said. They were a very efficient lot, but when they had a murder, they were always a bit pressed to get their household chores done properly.

Smythe and Betsy walked down the dim back hall, and as they reached the door, Smythe drew her close for a quick kiss.

'They know what we're doing,' she whispered. 'But I don't care.'

'Neither do they,' he said as he touched her cheek. 'I won't be too late, so save me some supper.'

'We'll not eat until you get back,' she promised.

Mrs Jeffries met the inspector at the front door that evening. 'Good evening, sir,' she said brightly.

'Good evening, Mrs Jeffries,' he said, handing her his bowler. 'Is there any word from our Wiggins?'

'His grandfather isn't doing very well, sir.' She took his coat from him and placed it on the coat tree just under his hat. 'Would you like a glass of sherry before dinner, sir?'

'That would be lovely,' he sighed. 'It's been a very full day.' They went down the hall to the drawing room, and within moments, he was sitting in his favorite chair. Mrs Jeffries poured him a Harvey's and then, as was their custom, poured one for herself. 'How is your investigation proceeding, sir?'

'Actually, it's going quite well,' he replied. He smiled proudly. 'We know the name of our first victim. He's the Reverend Jasper Claypool, and apparently he's just arrived from India. We were able to track down his relations, and they identified the body.'

'I must say, that was good work on your part, sir. Do tell me how you did it?'

'Thank you, Mrs Jeffries. We were rather proud of ourselves.' He told her every little detail of how he and Barnes had solved their identity problem. Then he went on to tell her of his meeting with the Christophers. She listened carefully, occasionally asking a question or making a comment.

'I must say, Mrs Christopher was quite calm until Barnes mentioned the body in the chimney. Then she got most upset.'

'Did she know who it was?'

'Oh, no no,' he replied. 'Nothing like that. As I said, we'd just come from identifying her uncle's body and I think that when Constable Barnes mentioned the cottages and the body, it all became a bit overwhelming for the poor woman. She'd held up rather well until that moment. But it was a rather gruesome conversation, and I'm afraid Constable Barnes did rather blurt it out in a, well, rather frightening sort of manner.' He took a quick sip from his glass. 'Anyway, as I was saying, it turns out that by mentioning the cottages, we did find out who owns them.' He gave her the remainder of the details of his visit with the Christophers. 'By the time we'd finished with the Christophers, I'd found out that Dr Bosworth's reports on both the . . . uh . . . victims had been sent to the station. I wanted to have a look at them before I proceeded any further.'

'Was there anything interesting in the reports?'

He told her essentially the same thing they'd already learned from the doctor. As usual, she listened carefully and discreetly asked question after question. By the time he was ready for his meal, she had more than enough information for them to tackle the next day.

Witherspoon ate his dinner and then took Fred for an especially long walk. Both man and dog were tired when they returned. Fred stayed close to the inspector's heels and trotted up the stairs with him. Before the inspector retired for the night he gave them instructions to wake him a bit earlier than usual. He had a very full day planned.

So did the household of Upper Edmonton Gardens, but they didn't share that information with their dear employer.

Wiggins wasn't in the least bit hungry, but he knew if he didn't eat every bite of the shepherd's pie his Aunt Alice had given him, she'd be offended. She was easily offended. So was the rest of the family, except for his grandfather. No matter what he did, no matter what he said, the whole lot of 'em wouldn't give him so much as a smile. They were a silent, sullen bunch of people, and he bitterly regretted that he'd agreed to stay.

'What's the matter, the stew not good enough for you?' Albert asked nastily.

'The stew's fine,' he replied quickly. He picked up his spoon and shoveled it into the bowl.

'You'll not get your fancy London food here, boy,' his uncle warned. 'You'll get plain, good country cooking. Won't he, Alice?'

'Yes, sir.' Wiggins wouldn't have minded plain, good country cooking, but his Aunt Alice's food was either half-raw or burnt beyond recognition. Tonight's offering was a combination of both. The carrots in the stew were almost raw while the meat had the consistency of an old shoe. 'It seems that Grandfather's feelin' a bit better today.'

'You a doctor now?' Albert sneered.

'No, but his color seemed a bit better, and he was able to sit up without coughin' his lungs out.'

'Eat your supper,' Alice snapped. 'I'm wanting to get this kitchen cleared.'

'Yes, ma'am.' Wiggins looked down at his bowl and doggedly took another bite. When he looked up, his cousin smiled at him maliciously. Wiggins wished he were anywhere but here.

The next morning, Luty and Hatchet arrived less than ten minutes after the inspector had gone. Mrs Goodge and Betsy had already cleared off the table, so everyone took their usual place.

'We've got a lot to go over this morning,' Mrs Jeffries said briskly. 'We have confirmation that the first victim was Jasper Claypool. He's been in India for the past ten years, and according to his relatives, he'd no plans for coming home.'

'That's an interestin' bit,' Luty muttered.

'Agreed,' the housekeeper nodded. 'But what's more interesting was the connection between Jasper Claypool and the cottage where the second corpse was found.' She told them everything she'd gotten from the inspector, taking care not to leave out any detail, no matter how insignificant it might seem. More than one of their cases had been solved on seemingly insignificant details.

When she'd finished, no one said anything. But by

the expressions on their faces, it was obvious they were all considering their next step.

Finally, Luty said, 'It seems to me I ought to find out everything I can about the finances of the Christophers and the Rileys. If they're his relations, they might be the ones who'd benefit from his death.'

'Don't you think you ought to find out if he had any money to leave them?' Hatchet said softly. 'I believe most churchmen take a vow of poverty . . .'

'That's Roman Catholics,' Luty interrupted. 'You can be rich as sin and be a priest in the Church of England.'

'Are you sure about that, madam?' he asked skeptically.

'Archbishop of Canterbury didn't look like he was hurtin' none,' she shot back. 'Fellow lives in a palace. Besides, it seems to me if this here Claypool's got the cash to buy a ticket all the way from India, he probably ain't hurtin' none either. Matter of fact, I think I'll make it my business to see what I can find out about how much money he had and, more importantly, who he left it to.'

'That's a wonderful idea,' Mrs Jeffries said quickly. 'Finding out who directly benefits from someone's death is always a good idea.'

'But if no one knew he was coming home,' Betsy mused, 'how could any of them have had him killed?'

'Because I, for one, am not sure that the family is as much in the dark as they profess to be.' Mrs Jeffries tapped her fingers on the tabletop. 'The trip from India to England is quite a long one. Most vessels make several stops on the way. Surely, unless the gentleman was estranged from his family, he'd have let someone know he was coming home. And if he didn't, why not? I certainly think we ought to find out.'

'What about the servants?' Betsy asked. 'I mean, if Jasper Claypool did let someone know he was coming home, wouldn't a servant know?'

'That's an idea worth pursuing,' she replied. 'He'd have had to have sent a cable, and someone in one of the houses must have seen it arrive, if, indeed, he contacted anyone.'

'I'll work on the Christophers,' Hatchet said. 'Miss Betsy, why don't you see what you can find out about the Rileys?'

Betsy nodded.

'And I'll track down where that luggage was taken,' Smythe put in.

'You mean Claypool's luggage?' Mrs Goodge looked confused.

'Oh, dear,' Mrs Jeffries smiled apologetically. 'I forgot, Smythe found out quite a bit at the shipping office last evening.'

He'd told Mrs Jeffries and Betsy, of course, but not the others. 'I 'ad a bit of luck when I got there,' he grinned. 'One of the clerks had gone home sick, so there was only one person in the office when I went inside. I've found that people talk more easily when there's no one else about, especially if it's late in the day like that and they're wantin' to go home.' What he didn't tell them was that when he'd seen the clerk on his own, he'd whipped a couple of sovereigns out of his pocket and dangled them under the fellow's nose as he'd asked his questions. He'd found it was much easier that way. But he didn't want the others to know how often he paid for information. 'It seems Claypool's luggage was picked up. But it was picked up by a freight company on Monday afternoon.'

'Freight company?' Luty frowned. 'That's odd. Why would Claypool have done that? Why not send a hansom for the luggage, or a street Arab? That's what most folks would do.'

'I don't know, but I'm goin' to find out,' he replied. 'It's just one more piece of the puzzle. We'll suss it out eventually.'

Betsy frowned. 'This isn't goin' to be easy, especially as we don't have Wiggins. We're spread a bit thin on this one. Who's going to keep on about the woman in the chimney? We can't forget her. We don't even know who she is.'

'Don't worry, Betsy,' Smythe soothed. 'We'll not be forgettin' her.'

He knew she was very sensitive to people who were overlooked or neglected. She'd seen members of her own family die because no one cared enough to provide even the kindness of a crust of bread or a bowl of soup. That was one of the reasons he loved her so much. She genuinely cared about those less fortunate than herself. 'We'll find out who killed her and make sure she gets a decent burial.'

Even if he had to pay for it himself.

CHAPTER FIVE

'This is the house, sir,' Constable Barnes said to Witherspoon as their hansom pulled up in front of a four-story red-brick detached house. 'Number sixty-eight Canfield Lane, Hampstead. Looks fairly posh but not quite as fancy as the Christopher home.' He paid off the driver and stepped down. 'Let's hope Horace Riley's not gone off to work already, sir.'

'It's still quite early,' the inspector replied, 'and if he's not here, we'll go to his office at the paint factory. At the very least, we'll be able to have a word with his wife.'

They went up a short, paved walkway to the white painted front door. Barnes lifted the heavy, brass door-knocker and let it fall. A moment later, the door opened and a middle-aged woman wearing the dark dress of a housekeeper stared out at them. She raised her eyebrows at the sight of Constable Barnes. 'Yes?'

'May we please speak with Mr Horace Riley?' Witherspoon asked politely.

The housekeeper hesitated for a moment and then held the door wider. 'Please come inside. I'll tell Mr Riley you're here.'

They stepped into a large foyer that was wallpapered in deep red brocade. The floor was covered with a crimson and gray patterned rug, and directly ahead of them was a mahogany staircase that wound around to the upper floors. On the wall across from the staircase there was a lamp table with a marble top, and above that, a painting of a huge bowl of colorful fruit in a gold-painted baroque frame. Two brass urns, each of them with ostrich feathers sticking out the top, flanked the sides of the table.

'This place is bright enough to make you blink,' Barnes whispered. 'The house looked nice enough from the outside, but I wasn't expecting this.'

'Obviously, Mr Horace Riley is doing quite well,' the inspector replied. A hallway running the length of the house ran off the far side of the staircase, and Witherspoon watched the housekeeper as she disappeared. 'At least we know he's home.'

'Yes, let's just hope he's able to shed some light on this case, sir,' Barnes replied. 'If you don't mind my saying so, sir, it's a real baffler. It's not often that we get two bodies on the same case.'

'If it *is* the same case,' Witherspoon murmured.

'It must be, sir,' Barnes said. 'It would be too much of a coincidence that a dead man would be holding an address in his hand for a house with a body stuck in the chimney. Coincidences do happen, sir, but not like that.'

'I rather agree.' The inspector sighed silently. He wasn't at all sure he was going to solve this one. If that second body hadn't been stuck in that ruddy chimney, the first murder could have been classified as a simple robbery gone wrong. It happened that way sometimes; the victim shouted or tried to run off or even fought back, which would cause the robber to panic and fire his weapon. It happened that way sometimes – not often, but sometimes. Then Witherspoon caught himself. He mustn't think like this. These victims deserved justice. It didn't matter how hard the cases were going to be, he must do his best to bring their killers to trial. 'Coincidences like that simply don't happen.'

The housekeeper returned and motioned for them to follow her. 'This way, please. Mr Riley will see you in his study.'

She led them down the hall and into a room with heavy rust-colored drapes on the windows, dark paneling along the walls and an amazing number of tables, tallboys, bookcases and cabinets, all of which seemed to have an equally amazing number of figurines, knick-knacks, vases, candleholders and china bowls on top or inside of them.

A man of younger middle age with stringy brown hair sat behind a huge desk next to the fireplace. He stared at them over the top of his spectacles. He didn't get up. 'I'm Horace Riley. My housekeeper says you want to speak to me. Why?'

'I'm Inspector Gerald Witherspoon and this is Constable Barnes. We'd like to ask you a few questions about your uncle, Jasper Claypool.' From the corner of his eye, he saw Barnes take out his little brown notebook.

Riley drew back in surprise. 'My uncle. What on earth has my uncle to do with the police?'

'Mr Riley, I take it you haven't been in

communication with your cousin, Mrs Christopher.' Witherspoon found it odd that Carl Christopher hadn't sent him a message. He'd said he would inform the family. But then again, perhaps he hadn't really wanted to take care of such a grim business.

'I haven't seen Hilda since Christmas. Now what's all this about?' He gestured toward two straight-backed chairs in front of his desk. 'Please sit.'

They did as he requested. Witherspoon decided to be as tactful as possible, but he had the impression that Horace Riley wasn't going to become unduly emotional about the death of his relation. 'I'm afraid your uncle is dead. He was murdered two days ago. Your cousin and her husband identified the body.'

Horace's jaw dropped. 'Uncle Jasper dead? But he's in India. How could someone kill him if he's in India? I don't understand this. I don't understand this at all.'

'Do you know if your uncle had any enemies?' Barnes asked quickly. He watched Riley carefully.

'Enemies? Why would he have enemies? He was a priest. He never harmed anyone. Good Lord, he spent his life in service to his church. Where did it happen?'

Witherspoon gave him the barest facts about the case. He didn't want to give too much away. One never knew with family – they could act dreadfully upset about the departed while at the very same time hiding the fact that they'd helped dispatch the poor victim into the next world! 'Did you know your uncle was coming to England?'

Riley shook his head. 'No. I had a letter from Uncle Jasper last month. He never mentioned coming home.'

'May we see the letter?' Witherspoon asked. He'd no idea why he thought this important, but he did.

'Why?' Riley looked perplexed. 'It was simply his monthly duty letter. He said nothing of importance in it.'

'He wrote to you every month?' Barnes asked. He made a note to remind the inspector that the Christophers apparently didn't hear from their uncle as regularly as Horace Riley. They hadn't heard from Claypool in three months, or so they claimed.

'Like clockwork,' he replied. 'I receive them the first week of every month.'

'You say you got one last month,' Witherspoon said. 'It's now the fifth of April. Did you get this month's letter?'

Riley's mouth opened in surprise. 'Gracious, that's right. I haven't received one to date. I should have noticed . . .' He opened the drawer on the side of his desk, reached inside and pulled out an envelope. 'Here's his letter from March. You can read it if you like. But it won't help you. He simply natters on and on about his congregation and the weather and some very dull old family matters.'

The door to the study opened and a woman wearing a beautifully fitted sapphire-blue jacket, and matching veiled hat and gloves stepped inside. Though not a great beauty, she was nonetheless quite pretty and a good fifteen years younger than Horace Riley.

She stared at the two policemen and then at Riley. 'Horace? What on earth is going on? I was just on my way out to go shopping when Mrs Staggers told me the police were here.'

Horace got to his feet. 'My dear. I'm afraid we've some bad news. Uncle Jasper's dead.' He turned to the policemen. 'This is my wife, Mrs Riley.'

Witherspoon and Barnes had both risen when she'd entered the room. They nodded politely at the introduction.

'I'm sorry for your loss, madam,' the inspector said.

'Thank you,' she murmured. She looked at her husband, her expression confused. 'I still don't understand why the police are here. Uncle Jasper's in India. He's in some little village outside of Calcutta. Is that why they've come, because something happened to Uncle Jasper in India? Did the bishop send them?'

'No ma'am, the bishop has nothing to do with our being here,' Barnes said quickly. 'Your uncle was murdered, and it didn't happen in India. It happened at St Paul's Church over on Dock Street.'

Smythe wasn't having any luck at all. He'd tried every freight company within two miles of the West India docks and hadn't come up with anything. He sighed as he stepped outside the offices of Winklers Freight Forwarding and stared glumly at the heavy traffic. What was he to do next? It was past noon, and he had the feeling that whoever had picked up that luggage hadn't been a local company. Which meant there were dozens of firms from all over the greater London area that could have done it. He wasn't sure why Claypool's baggage was important, but he knew it was. A vendor pushing a fruit cart trundled past and almost collided with a boardman advertising a pantomine. 'Watch it, mate,' the vendor shouted.

'You watch it,' the boardman shouted back. 'You don't own the ruddy streets.'

Smythe deftly moved around the skirmish and headed across the road. He wasn't going to waste more time. He was going to see an expert on information. He hailed a hansom. 'The Dirty Duck. It's a pub down by the river—'

'I know where it is, mate,' the driver called back.

It took less than ten minutes before the cab pulled up in front of The Dirty Duck pub. Smythe paid off the driver and then pulled out his pocket watch. He was in luck; there was still a good half hour before closing.

He stepped inside and paused for a moment to let his eyes adjust to the dim light. The air was a pungent combination of beer, gin, unwashed bodies and smoke from the fire. The pub catered to dock workers, day laborers, food vendors and all manner of working people from the great commercial area of the docks. It was also the unofficial office of one Blimpey Groggins, ex-thief and purveyor of information to most anyone who'd cross his palm with silver.

'Over here, Smythe.' Blimpey's voice rose above the din of the crowded pub.

Smythe spotted him at a table by the fireplace. Blimpey's companion, an elderly man dressed in an old-fashioned top hat, got up and went to the bar as Smythe made his way to Blimpey's table.

'Nice to see ya, Smythe.' Blimpey was a short, round, middle-aged man with ginger-colored hair and a ruddy complexion. He was dressed in his usual brown-and-white checked coat, a white shirt that had seen better days and a brown porkpie hat. Around his neck he wore a long, red scarf. He nodded at the seat across from him. 'Have a sit down and rest your feet.'

'Thanks.' Smythe sat. ''Ow are ya?'

'In good order, my fine fellow, in good order. The plans for the nuptials are proceeding nicely.' Blimpey grinned broadly. Smythe had given Blimpey some advice that had helped him work up the courage to ask his Nell, a woman who was a few years younger than himself, for her hand in marriage. She'd agreed, and they had a June wedding planned. 'How are the plans for your own wedding coming along?'

Smythe shrugged. 'We're in no 'urry. But we're thinkin' of a June wedding as well.' He wasn't going to admit to Blimpey that it was going to be June of the following year. 'Anyways, I need some information from you.'

He laughed. 'You always do, mate. What is it this time?' Blimpey had started his career as a small-time housebreaker and thief. But when he'd realized that his phenomenal memory, coupled with a vast network of information sources, could provide him with a rather large income without the attendant risks one ran as a thief, he'd changed his course and not looked back. As a purveyor of information to all sorts of people, including, it was whispered, the Foreign Secretary, Blimpey was honorable, honest and very reliable. He was also careful in who he worked for, and wouldn't pass on information to anyone planning grievous bodily harm to another human being – unless, of course, he was of the opinion that said human being deserved grievous bodily harm.

Smythe thought for a moment. Now that he was here, he might as well get Blimpey to find out as much as possible. He could well afford the man's services. 'There's a couple of things I'd like you to look into. Let me get us some drinks.' He waved at the barmaid and held up two fingers. 'Two pints, please,' he called. Then he turned his attention back to his companion. 'You might 'ave a bit of a problem trackin' this down, but I want to know the name of the freight company that picked up some luggage from the Far East and India line. It came in on the *Eastern Sun* this past Monday. More importantly, I want to know where they took the luggage.'

Blimpey raised his eyebrows but said nothing as the barmaid brought their drinks. He waited till she'd moved out of earshot before he said, 'That's goin' to cost you a bob or two, *and* I'll need a few more details.'

Smythe told him as much as he felt Blimpey needed to know, mentioning only the victim's name and not the fact that he'd been murdered.

'Jasper Claypool?' Blimpey repeated the dead man's name. 'He's that one who were murdered the other day and propped up outside St Paul's over on Dock Street.'

'How'd you find out about it?' Smythe asked. 'His body was only identified yesterday afternoon.'

'It's my business to know about things like that,' Blimpey replied modestly. 'I've got sources all over town, includin' the hospital morgues and the police stations. It pays to know who's died or been nicked.'

'Cor blimey, no wonder you know everything that's goin' on in this town.'

'And I'll tell you somethin' for free, 'cause I owe you

a favor,' Blimpey said earnestly. 'Claypool wasn't killed so he could be robbed. It weren't none of our local villains that did him.'

'You know that for a fact?' Smythe took a sip of beer.

'Wouldn't say it if I didn't know it,' he replied. 'I put my people on it as soon as I heard a priest had been killed. Don't hold with murderin' children, women or parsons.'

Smythe was grateful. 'Thanks, I appreciate you tellin' me.'

'So what else do you want me to find out about the Reverend Claypool?' Blimpey asked.

'Anything you can,' Smythe replied. 'He arrived in England from India at six a.m. on the morning he was murdered. But he wasn't killed till six that night. So what did he do for that twelve hours?'

'Something that got him killed, apparently.'

'And I want you to get me some names of the other passengers who were on the vessel with him. Preferably, people who he spent some time with.'

Blimpey nodded and finished off his beer. 'This is goin' to cost you an awful lot.'

Smythe shrugged. 'I can afford your rates providin' you give me something worth havin'.'

'Don't be daft. I always give you your money's worth,' Blimpey grinned. 'Anything else you want?'

Smythe considered it for a minute. He was tempted to tell Blimpey about the body in the chimney, but the truth was, the fellow probably already knew. Besides, if he came up with too much information about both cases, the others would really get their collective noses out of joint. 'This'll be all for now. But there might be something later.' He got to his feet, pulled a half-sovereign out of his pocket and tossed it to Blimpey. 'Make sure the barmaid gets some of this.'

'Right, mate,' Blimpey caught it easily. 'One thing I like about you, Smythe. You're always generous with your coin. Give us a day or two and then nip back here in the afternoon. I ought to have something for you by then.'

Betsy stood in front of the tobacconist's window and pretended to read a sign advertising a lecture on the fascinating subject of mesmerism, but she was really keeping an eye on the middle-aged woman who'd just gone into the shop. She was hoping her quarry was the Riley housekeeper.

She'd spent half the morning keeping an eye on the Riley house in Canfield Lane, hoping a servant or even a tradesman would come out so she'd have some chance at finding something out. But the only activity she'd seen was Inspector Witherspoon and Constable Barnes going inside. Then, just when she was about to give up, this woman had come out carrying a shopping basket.

She'd been following her now for a good hour. They'd traversed the length of the High Street, and Betsy had watched her go to the grocer's, the fishmonger's and the baker's. But she was of two minds about approaching the housekeeper. Betsy had noticed the woman didn't smile very often, not at the shopkeepers and certainly not at any other pedestrians on the busy street.

Betsy wished she'd been able to find a footman or a

maid. She'd found that the lower the servant was in the household pecking order, the looser their tongues. But the hours were passing quickly, her feet were hurting and she'd not found out a blooming thing. The door of the tobacconist's opened and her prey stepped outside. The woman moved directly ahead, crossing the road and nimbly dodging hansoms, wagons and omnibuses before making it safely to the other side.

Betsy was right after her. The housekeeper turned onto a side street and was now moving very fast. Betsy quickened her pace, keeping sight of the woman as she weaved in and out amongst the heavy foot traffic. Finally, after a good five minutes, Betsy saw her quarry stop and then enter a building. When Betsy came abreast of the place, she saw it was a pub.

She went in after her. The light was dim, the air reeked of stale beer and the place was crowded with people.

Betsy stood on tiptoe and looked around. She spotted the woman standing at the far end of the bar, a glass of gin in her hand. As it was nearly closing time, Betsy knew that if she wanted to make contact, she'd best be quick about it. She pushed her way through the crowded room and squeezed in next to the woman. 'Crowded in 'ere, isn't it?' she said conversationally.

'It's a pub and the drink's cheap. Of course it's crowded,' the woman replied. She didn't look at Betsy.

'Can I buy you another one?' Betsy asked. She signaled to the barman, who promptly ignored her.

The woman slowly turned and stared at Betsy, her expression suspicious. 'Why would you want to buy me a drink?'

Betsy's mind worked furiously. She'd come up with and discarded several different stories since walking into the pub, but all of them sounded silly. 'I want some information,' she said bluntly, 'and I'm willing to pay for it by buying you as much gin as you can drink.'

Because of Smythe, she had more than enough coins in her pocket to buy a few drinks. He was adamant that she was not to leave the house without plenty of money for a hansom home or any other kind of trouble that might come her way.

'Information about what?' The woman's eyes were still suspicious, but she also looked curious.

'Your employer,' Betsy replied. She waved at the barman again, and this time, he ambled toward her. 'So will you talk to me, or do I have to go elsewhere?'

'I'll have another gin,' she smiled slyly.

'Two gins, please,' Betsy told the barman. She wasn't much of a drinker herself – the truth was, she couldn't stand the stuff. It brought back too many bad memories from when she was a child and living in the East End. But she'd choke a few sips down if it would get this woman talking. 'I'm Betsy,' she said to her companion.

'I'm Lilly Staggers. So what do you want to know about my employer?'

'You do work for Horace Riley?' Betsy nodded her thanks to the barman as he put their drinks down on the counter.

'And Mrs Riley.' Lilly grinned and took a long, slow sip of her gin.

'Aren't you curious as to why I'm asking?'

'Not in the least,' Lilly shrugged. 'I don't care. If talking about them will do them harm in any way, that's fine by me. She's probably going to sack me as soon as she finds another housekeeper. Goes through staff at a fairly good clip, she does. Anyway, what do you want to know?'

Betsy wasn't shocked. Many domestic servants loathed their employers. But generally, they didn't share their opinions with strangers. Obviously, Lilly Staggers didn't care, though. Yet now that she was here, she wasn't quite sure what to ask. 'Uh, were both the Rileys at home around six in the evening this past Monday night?'

'Monday night?' She frowned thoughtfully. 'As a matter of fact, they weren't. Mr Riley didn't come in until seven forty-five, and Mrs Riley came home a few minutes later.'

'Was that the time they both generally arrive home?' Betsy asked.

'Oh, no. Mr Riley is usually home for his dinner by six every evening, and Mrs Riley is almost always there, if you get my meaning. The only time we ever have a moment's peace from the woman is when she's out shopping. But ever since her husband's put his foot down about her spending, she's always at home, always hanging over your shoulder, always looking to catch us out doing something wrong . . . honestly, she's a terror, she is.' She paused long enough to take another quick drink of her gin. 'That's why I remember them being out so late that night. It was nice and peaceful for a few hours that day.'

'Do you know where they were?'

'She'd not tell the likes of us her business,' Lilly replied.

'So you've no idea where she went?' Betsy pressed.

'No.'

'What time did she leave the house that afternoon?'

'Around one o'clock. I remember that because she stuck her head in the drawing room as I was measuring for the new curtains and told me she was going out.' Lilly laughed. 'At the time, I thought perhaps she'd sweet-talked that old fool she's married to into reopening some of her accounts.'

Betsy took a sip of her gin and tried not to make a face. 'Had anything unusual happened that day?'

'Unusual? Nah . . . don't think so . . . wait a minute.' Her words slurred slightly as she spoke. 'I tell a lie, something did happen. We got a telegram. That's right. It came at eleven o'clock and I remember Mrs Riley was in the study with the door closed so I couldn't give it to her right away. We're not allowed to disturb her when she's got the door closed. So she didn't see it till she came out for lunch.'

'Did she read it right away?'

'She read it all right,' Lilly snickered. 'Turned dead white, she did. Didn't even bother to eat the lunch that cook had made. Just went upstairs, changed her clothes and then went off. Didn't come home till that evening,'

Betsy wasn't sure what to make of this. 'Do you know what she did with the telegram?'

Lilly finished her drink and shrugged. 'Don't know. Probably tossed it away.' She was staring at Betsy's unfinished drink. 'You don't really like that, do you?'

Betsy pushed the glass toward her. 'Help yourself. But, uh, don't you have to go back to work?'

'Should be back there now.' Lilly snatched up Betsy's

glass and drained the contents in a single gulp. 'But I'll come up with some story to keep the old bitch at bay. Truth is, she can't afford to sack me until she's got someone else. Mr Riley said he wasn't paying the agency's rates anymore, so she's got to find someone on her own, and that'll take her ages.'

Betsy suddenly thought of something. 'Was Mr Riley surprised when he got home Monday evening and she was still out?'

'Time, people. Drink up,' the barman announced.

She thought about it for a moment. 'Not really. Come to think of it, when he came in that evening, he didn't ask about her at all.' She burped softly and stepped back. 'Well, dear, it's been lovely, but I've got to run. The silly cow isn't the smartest pig at the trough, but even she can read a clock.' She headed for the door, moving easily through the thinning crowd.

Betsy dashed after her. 'Won't she notice the . . . gin . . . I mean . . . the smell?' She couldn't think of a polite way to ask the question. But she didn't want the woman to lose her position. Now that she'd asked her questions, she felt a bit guilty about plying the woman with alcohol.

Lilly reached the door and pulled it open. 'Don't worry about me, love. She's got no nose. She could be standing in a privy and if she had a blindfold on, she wouldn't know where she was.' She stepped out into the street. 'Oh, there's one other thing about that day. When she did get home, she and Mr Riley went into the study and had a right old dustup. They was tryin' hard to keep their voices down, but I could hear them going at it like two cats tossed in a barley sack.' She started up the road.

Betsy hurried after her. 'Do you have any idea what they were fighting over?'

'Like I said, they was keepin' their voices down. But I did hear Mrs Riley say that if he had botched it up, she'd take care of it herself.' She increased her pace.

'Thanks for talking to me,' Betsy said. 'Getting information hasn't ever been this easy for me.'

'Glad to be of help.' She gave Betsy a sly, sideways glance. 'Truth to tell, girl, I figured you for one of Eric's girls. Blighter's been trying to get control of the factory for two years now, and I reckoned he sent you along to find out the lay of the land. Mind you, I don't care. He's always been decent to me, better than that one I work for.'

'Eric who?' Betsy dodged around a couple of ladies walking arm and arm. Keeping up with Lilly was proving harder than expected.

'Eric Riley, Horace Riley's half-brother.' She started moving even faster. Betsy was almost running to keep up.

Lilly halted briefly at the corner and then started across the road, neatly dodging the traffic. Betsy charged after her. She cleared the wheels of a hansom by inches but managed to stay on Lilly's heels. 'How could Eric get control of the factory?'

'His uncle's back from India,' Lilly called over her shoulder. 'Eric's been trying to get the old fellow to turn control of his share of the firm over to him. Oh bother, I really can't talk anymore. I've got to get back. I don't want to make her too angry. If she has one of her tantrums, she just might sack me on the spot.' With that, she took off at a run down the street.

'Well, blast a Spaniard,' Betsy muttered as she watched the woman disappear. 'Trust me to spend my time asking all the wrong questions.'

Mrs Goodge set a plate of treacle tarts on the table and then picked up the teapot. 'Don't be shy now, Letty. You help yourself,' she told her guest as she poured out the tea.

Letty Sommerville was a woman well into her middle years. She had a round face, brown eyes and a generous mouth. She was dressed in a brown bombazine dress that was only fitting as she was a housekeeper and she wore her graying brown hair tucked neatly up in a tidy bun. 'Thank you, Mrs Goodge,' she replied as she reached for a tart. 'These look wonderful. But then again, you always were a good baker.'

Mrs Goodge laughed and took the chair across from her. 'I've always enjoyed baking much more than cooking.' She stared at her old colleague. The two women had once worked together in the same house. Only then Letty Sommerville had been a downstairs maid. 'I was a bit surprised to see you when I opened the door this morning.'

'I hope you didn't mind my coming by,' Letty replied. 'But I happened to run into Maisie Daniels, and she mentioned you were working for a policeman. Of course after I'd chatted with her, I had to come along and talk to you myself. Especially as I happen to work just around the corner from Heather Street. That's where the Christophers live, and they've had them a murder in their very household! Can you imagine it?' She snorted delicately. 'Back in our day it wouldn't have done at all. People didn't work for houses where murder was done, did they?'

'Well, I expect it happened a bit more often than we'd like to think,' Mrs Goodge replied. She was racking her brain, frantically trying to remember the conversations she'd had with Maisie. She remembered inviting Maisie for tea on one of their earlier cases, but for the life of her she couldn't recall what case it was or what she had actually said to her old friend. How much had she given away about their activities? Gracious, did the whole town know they helped their inspector on his cases?

Letty grinned. 'Of course it did. I always wondered about old Mrs Claxton's fall down those back stairs when we worked at Claxton Hall. But back in our younger days, no one had the nerve to suggest that the young master's gambling debts gave him a good reason for helping his grandmother to go meet her maker.'

'Do you really think he pushed her?' Mrs Goodge had already left Claxton Hall when the 'accident' had occurred, but she'd heard the gossip.

'Everett Claxton was no good.' She shrugged. 'He was quite capable of pushing that poor old woman down them awful stairs. But if he did, he was careful and he didn't do it in front of anyone. But I didn't come here to talk about old news, I come to tell you what I know about Carl and Hilda Christopher. Mind you, I don't think they had anything to do with Jasper Claypool's death. Jasper Claypool helped raise Hilda and her sister. I don't think she or her sister will inherit very much. Not that it'll make any difference to Hilda Christopher – the only thing she's ever spoken about wanting was his collection of rare books.'

'Are they valuable?'

'Probably. But not valuable enough for her to have wanted her uncle dead.'

'Maybe the other sister wanted him dead?' Mrs Goodge said the first thing that popped into her head.

'Edith's not even in London. She's off on the continent doing who knows what and having a high old time, she is. She was the scandal of that family before she left. I think she's one of the reasons the Reverend Claypool went off to India, probably hoped to set an example for the girl. Not that it did much good – Edith left town within a day or two of her uncle's sailing. I daresay the rest of the family was relieved. No, it seems to me your inspector shouldn't be wasting his time looking at the Christophers. I can't imagine that they had anything to do with Reverend Claypool's murder.'

'How do you know all this?' Mrs Goodge interrupted. She couldn't believe her ears. They were in deep, deep trouble. The entire town apparently knew what they were up to.

Letty blinked in surprise. 'How do I know?' she repeated. 'Oh, that's easy. I've told you, I work just around the corner from the Christophers. I have tea every week with their housekeeper, Mrs Nimitz. She doesn't care all that much for her employers, but she's well paid and they keep enough staff that her work isn't too difficult. Mind you, she's always complaining that they work her to death, but if you ask me, she's a bit of a whiner. Anyway, as I was sayin', you ought to have

114

your inspector take a look at Horace Riley or his half-brother, Eric. They are the ones that'll get a good bit of what the Reverend Claypool had in this old world, and from what I hear, they both need it.'

'And I take it the good reverend had quite a lot?' Mrs Goodge interjected. Oh Lord, what on earth were they going to do? She simply couldn't think of a way out of this mess. She could hardly tell Letty to shut up, that she wasn't interested. But the more she spoke, the more obvious it was that she was fishing for information.

'He had plenty.' Letty took a quick sip of her tea. 'Mind you, I think he was going to leave it all to Edith and Hilda. He was very close to them both. They're so identical he was one of the few people who could tell them apart. But then there was pressure put on him by others in the family not to leave his nephews out of his will. Horace is the general manager of the factory, and it's common knowledge he wants his uncle's share of it for himself. Eric works for Horace, but the two of them don't get on, even though they're half-brothers. Why, Horace Riley only hired Eric because the reverend forced him to do it before he went off to India.'

'Really.' Mrs Goodge could barely take in what the woman was saying, she was still so upset by the realization that all her efforts to be subtle about her investigations over the years had been for naught. Everyone could see right through her.

'Of course.' Letty reached for another tart. 'Both the Rileys have very big plans, at least that's what I've heard. They want to sell off all the adjacent property to the factory and put the capital back into the business.'

Mrs Goodge got a hold of herself. Worrying that everyone knew about their activities wasn't going to stop her from doing her duty, but there were a few things she did want to make clear. 'Uh, Letty, I'm not sure what Maisie said to you, but I don't really have that much interest in the inspector's investigations.'

Letty stared at her blankly. 'The inspector's investigations? What on earth are you on about? I only mentioned your inspector to be polite.'

'But . . .'

'The only thing Maisie said about you was that you loved a good gossip.'

Mrs Goodge's jaw dropped. 'She said I was a gossip!'

'Oh yes,' Letty grinned widely. 'And that was just fine with me. I like a good natter myself. Now, where was I?'

'It's most unfortunate that Mrs Riley got so upset,' Inspector Witherspoon said. 'I'd have liked to have asked her a few more questions.'

'We can always go back, sir,' Barnes assured him. 'I'd like to have a word with their staff . . . you know, confirm that both of them were home on Monday evening.'

'Do you think they're lying?' Witherspoon kept a lookout for a passing hansom.

'I'm not sure, sir,' Barnes replied. 'But their answers sounded almost as if they'd rehearsed them in advance. I think there's a cab stand around the corner.'

'Good.' The inspector started for the intersection. 'I can never tell if someone's lying. But if they are, we'll find out. We really should get over to the factory and try to have a word with Mr Eric Riley before it gets too late today.'

'We can have another look at those cottages while we're there,' Barnes agreed. As they rounded the corner a hansom was discharging a fare, and the constable waved it over.

Witherspoon frowned as he climbed aboard. 'I do wish we had more information on the chimney corpse. What if those two deaths don't have anything to do with one another?'

'The Claypool factory on Dorland Place in Bermondsey,' Barnes told the driver as he swung in next to the inspector. 'Not to worry, sir. We'll get it solved one way or another. I'm sure they are connected. As you pointed out, corpses don't stuff themselves in a chimney. Someone went to a lot of trouble to hide that body up there, and I'm sure it's the same someone that put a bullet through that poor vicar's head.'

'Yes, er . . . well, that's the assumption we're working under, so to speak.' He couldn't recall pointing anything out, but that happened to him quite frequently. He no longer worried about all the intelligent things he said that he couldn't remember. 'What did you think of Horace Riley?'

'I think he's worried,' Barnes said bluntly. 'As I said, sir, I want to have a word with his staff. I think he's hiding something about his movements on the day his uncle was killed. When we asked him what time he'd come home from the factory on the day Claypool died, he was a bit too ready with the answer.'

'I agree. If he really was home by half past four, as he

claims, someone in the household other than his wife should be able to vouch for it.'

'Maybe Mr Eric Riley will be able to give us some additional information.' Barnes grinned. 'Matter of fact, I have a feeling we'll get an earful from him.'

'Why is that?' Witherspoon asked curiously.

'Because, sir, I was watching Horace Riley very carefully when he mentioned his brother, and if I'm not mistaken, I don't think he likes him very much. Every time he said Eric's name, his hand clenched into a fist.'

CHAPTER SIX

Luty glared at the three men sitting on the other side of the long mahogany table. 'All I'm asking for is an itty, bitty favor,' she said. It's not like I'm wantin' you to bust into Westminster Cathedral and steal the gold plate.' She thumped her parasol on the carpeted floor for emphasis.

None of them so much as blinked. They were used to her tantrums. Herndon Rutherford, Thomas Finch and Josiah Williams had been her solicitors for over thirty years. Rutherford, a tall man with a long face, gray hair and a perpetually disapproving expression, spoke first. 'Madam, it's not that we don't wish to accommodate you, it's that what you're asking us to do is quite difficult.'

'I don't see why. This feller's already dead,' Luty exclaimed. 'Before too long, his will is gonna be a matter of public record. Nellie's whiskers, they publish that kind of information in *The Times*.' Blasted lawyers. Why wouldn't they just do what she told them to do and stop giving her so much trouble? Generally, she got her information through other, less rigid, sources.

But she'd been in a hurry to find out who was going to benefit the most from Jasper Claypool's death.

'That's correct, madam,' Thomas Finch agreed, 'but only after the estate's been through probate and all the other necessary legal steps.' He was a short, rotund, balding man with brown eyes and a perpetually worried expression.

'Oh, forget I asked,' she snorted. 'I'll find out what I need to know myself.' She started to get up.

'Now, now, madam,' Josiah Williams, the youngest of the three, waved her back into her chair. 'Let's not be hasty, here. I'm quite sure we can get this information for you, it's simply going to take us a day or two.'

'A day or two,' Herndon snapped. He glared at his associate. 'I don't think we'll be able to get it at all. We have no business snooping about in this deceased person's business.'

'But I already told ya, Claypool's dead. He ain't goin' to give a tinker's damn about whether or not we find out who his heirs might be.'

'Reverend Claypool's attitude isn't relevant.' Herndon's frown deepened. 'Our firm has a reputation for discretion, and I intend to see that we keep it.'

'Can you tell us, madam, why you want this information?' Josiah asked softly. Despite the fact that she was an American, he'd always liked her more than their other clients.

Luty shrugged. 'I need it for a friend.' She was sure that she'd made a mistake. She should have known better than to come here for her snooping. 'I don't have any more time to waste with you all. Since ya can't help me, I'll be on my way.' She got up, shot them one last frown and started for the door. 'I ought to fire the bunch of you,' she muttered.

'But then you'd just end up hiring us back,' Herndon replied. 'We're the best, and whether you'll admit it or not, you're actually quite fond of us.'

Luty snorted and thumped her parasol on the floor again. What he said was true. She did like them, even if they were a bunch of nervous nellies.

'Let me walk you to the door, madam.' Josiah Williams hurried after her.

As she went into the outer office, she waved at the grinning clerks. They waved back. Luty was a favorite amongst the staff.

'Let me get that for you, madam,' Josiah reached past her for the handle to the front door. 'If you'll give me a day or so,' he said softly, 'I'll get that information for you.'

Luty stared at him. 'You think you can?'

'I'm fairly certain I can find out something,' he replied. He shot a quick look over his shoulder to make sure neither of his partners had followed him out. 'As you pointed out, the man is dead, so it's just a question of time until the contents of the will are a matter of public record. I'll stop around to see you as soon as I know one way or the other.'

She grinned broadly. 'Thanks, Josiah, you're the only one of the bunch with a sense of adventure.'

'I'm not sure that's a good attribute for a solicitor,' he replied, but he was smiling as he said it.

Witherspoon wrinkled his nose as the clerk led him and Barnes down a long corridor toward the offices.

The air had an acrid, chemical smell that wasn't very pleasant. As a matter of fact, it made his eyes water. He wondered how the people who worked here could stand it, and then assumed they must be used to it.

'It's just in here, sir.' The clerk opened a door and ushered them into a large office with two young men sitting opposite one another at desks. Both of them had open ledgers in front of them. At the far end of the room was a door leading to an office, and opposite that, on the other wall, was another office. The clerk turned to his left and popped his head into the nearest office. 'The police are here to see you, Mr Riley.' He turned to the two policemen. 'Go on inside.'

A tall, thin man who looked to be in his mid-thirties rose to his feet. He had dark brown hair, deep-set brown eyes and a fine-featured face. 'Hello, I'm Eric Riley. I've been expecting you. Please make yourselves comfortable.' He gestured at the empty chairs in front of the desk.

'Thank you. I'm Inspector Gerald Witherspoon and this is Constable Barnes.' They each took a chair, and Riley sat back down behind his cluttered desk.

'We've come to ask you a few questions about your uncle, Jasper Claypool,' Witherspoon said.

Eric sighed sadly. 'Horace told me what happened. I can't fathom it. No one even knew Uncle Jasper was coming home. Who would want to kill him?'

'That's what we're going to find out,' Witherspoon replied. 'When was the last time you had any communication with your uncle?'

'Let me see,' he stroked his chin. 'I'm not really certain. We didn't correspond regularly. But I did send him the occasional letter, and he always replied. I received a letter from him at Christmas.'

'Did he mention that he was thinking of coming back to England?' Barnes asked.

'No, he wrote about his congregation and how he wished they'd more money as the church roof needed repair and the hymnals needed replacing. That sort of thing.' Eric leaned back in his seat. 'He mentioned a few mundane family matters.'

'What kind of family matters?' the constable pressed.

Eric's dark eyebrows shot up. 'I don't really think it's of any consequence. It was just the musings of an elderly man. He wished my brother and I were closer, he wished we'd all spent more time together when we had the chance; he wished that my cousins, Hilda and Edith, were closer. He was getting on in years, Constable, and frankly, I think he was getting a bit maudlin. But he never said a word about coming to England.'

'Where were you on Monday evening?' Witherspoon asked.

Eric looked surprised. 'Where was I? I was here, Inspector. I worked late that evening. I was going over some invoices.'

'Can anyone verify your whereabouts?'

He shook his head. 'I'm afraid not. My clerks leave at half past five, and the night watchman doesn't come on duty until eight. I saw no one, Inspector. But I assure you, I often work late here on my own.'

'Was your uncle one of the owners of this concern?' Witherspoon waved his hand about, indicating the factory. He already knew the answer, but he wanted to hear what Riley had to say and, more importantly, how he said it.

'He owns half an interest,' Eric replied. 'But he controls more than that, and of course, it isn't just the factory. There's a good bit of adjacent property.'

'What do you mean, he controls more than his share?' Witherspoon asked.

'He owns half an interest. The other half is divided up into four shares. Horace and I each inherited a share when our father died, and each of the twins inherited their shares when their mother died.'

Barnes looked up from his notebook. 'What's the other sister's name?'

'Edith Durant. Their mother was Uncle Jasper's sister, Elizabeth Claypool Durant. For what it's worth, Horace and I have control of our shares, but Uncle Jasper controls the twins' shares. So even though he only owns half, for all intents and purposes, he's a majority shareholder in the concern. But he wasn't interested in running a business. He was a clergyman, a servant of his church.'

'So he had no interest in the factory at all?' Barnes pressed.

'None whatsoever,' Eric replied. 'He never interfered. He left the day-to-day running of the business to Horace and myself.'

'Then can you explain, sir, why in his letter to Mr Horace Riley, he asked for a full report on the company's profits and losses?'

Eric frowned and shook his head. 'A full report? But he's not due for a report until the end of the year.'

'Nevertheless, he asked Horace Riley for a report in

his last letter. Mr Riley showed us the letter,' Wither-spoon replied.

'I've no idea why he'd want to know such a thing, Inspector,' Eric replied slowly. 'It certainly isn't like him. He's shown no interest in the factory what-soever for the past ten years. We only send him an annual report out of courtesy. I'm sure he never reads it.'

'Well, he apparently was developing an interest,' the inspector said softly.

'Did you ever visit the cottages across the road'?' Barnes asked.

'Of course, they're part of the property. Horace and I both have had occasion to examine them. But I've no idea who that corpse you found up the chimney could possibly be. Those houses haven't been inhabited for years.'

'Do you have the names of the last tenants?' Barnes asked. 'We'd like to interview them.'

Witherspoon had no idea what he ought to ask next. He was profoundly grateful the constable was taking such an active part in the inquiry. It gave him a chance to think. But no matter how hard he thought about the matter, between the dead vicar and the corpse in the chimney, he was completely confused. What he needed was a nice long chat with Mrs Jeffries. She was so very helpful in helping him to sort all the bits and pieces out correctly.

'I've already had my clerk make up a list,' Eric replied. 'Good luck finding these people. It's been ten years. Most of them have probably moved on.'

The inspector suddenly thought of a good question.

'Why weren't the cottages torn down when they were deemed unsafe?'

'We wanted to do just that,' Eric replied, 'but my uncle wouldn't let us . . .' His voice faltered as he spoke. 'Oh my God, I've only just realized. It was Uncle Jasper who wouldn't let us tear the wretched things down. He wouldn't hear of it. He kept putting it off, saying that we couldn't stand the expense.'

Barnes looked at the inspector. He could tell by his expression that both of them were thinking along the same lines. 'So it was your Uncle Jasper who refused to let them be torn down? Are you certain of that?' the constable asked.

'Absolutely,' Eric replied. 'I remember it very well. We met with Jasper only hours before he boarded the ship because he kept putting off making a decision. But he was in a foul mood that day, which was very unusual for him. He'd just had a terrific row with Edith, and that had upset him. She was always his favorite. Horace told Uncle Jasper he was going to get an estimate for a tear-down price from a local firm, and Jasper had a fit. He told us to board the cottages up and leave them alone. He was adamant about it. We were both rather stunned.'

'For a man who didn't take any interest in the running of the business, Reverend Claypool certainly seemed to have strong opinions about the cottages,' Witherspoon pointed out softly.

'He was occasionally a bit eccentric,' Eric replied. His voice had a defensive edge to it. 'After all, he took it into his head to go out to India at the age of sixty-five.'

'From the way the ground has shifted, it doesn't look

like those cottages will ever be safe,' Barnes said. 'Do you have any idea why your uncle wanted them left alone?'

'He didn't say.'

'Did anyone ever ask him?' Witherspoon asked. It seemed to him a perfectly reasonable question.

'Horace wrote to him a number of times about the issue,' he replied. 'But Horace never saw fit to confide our uncle's reasons to me. At that time, I'd just started here and was a lowly office clerk.' He smiled bitterly. 'Unlike my dear brother, I actually had to work my way up in the family business.'

Witherspoon was as confused as ever, but that didn't stop him from forging ahead. 'But you owned equal shares in the company.'

'Yes, but Uncle Jasper had appointed Horace the general manager. You've got to understand my position, Inspector. I was very much the odd man out. My mother didn't come from money. Her people were in trade. She was our father's second wife and not overly popular with the rest of the Claypool-Riley clan. Horace was very put out when I was born.' He gave a short bark of a laugh. 'Our family isn't in land, sir. No primogeniture. When my parents died, our father's fortune was split between Horace and I. But there wasn't a lot of cash, just his share of the factory and some shares of stock.'

'I don't suppose you know who's going to inherit your Uncle Jasper's estate?' Witherspoon asked.

Eric laughed. 'All of us, I expect. Uncle Jasper was always very fair in his dealings with the nieces and nephews. Not that cousin Hilda needs anything from this place. Their father was very rich. When he died, she inherited his estate outright.'

'What about the other girl?' Witherspoon asked.

'Edith was the second born of the twins.' Eric shrugged. 'She inherited some of the money, but the bulk of it went to Hilda as the eldest. Their father was very old-fashioned, he didn't believe in splitting up the family money. Besides, Edith had already shown herself to be a good deal more independent than their father thought proper. I expect he thought that Hilda, who was always the sensible one, would take care of her sister.'

'And has she?' the constable queried.

Again, Eric laughed. 'Edith is the last person to need taking care of, Constable. She's . . . how can I say this without being indelicate? . . . I suppose the kindest thing one can say is that she is an adventuress, or perhaps a better word would be courtesan. She never lacks for male companionship. The family never speaks of it, but I do believe that she's been seen cavorting about Brighton with the heir apparent.'

It took a moment before Witherspoon understood. 'Oh, dear,' he murmured. 'Then I expect she doesn't know her uncle has been murdered.'

'I don't expect she'd much care,' Eric replied with a sad smile. 'As I told you, the last time she and Uncle Jasper had any contact was just before he left for India. They had a fierce row over how she was living her life. She was involved with a married man at the time. Horace later told me that Uncle Jasper told Edith he never wanted to see her again. It must have broken his heart, too.' He sighed and looked away briefly. 'Poor

Uncle Jasper. I hope he was happy in India. Frankly, we were all amazed at how long he lasted out there. We fully expected the place to kill him.'

'Apparently it was coming home that killed him, sir,' Barnes said.

'I've got you a sherry already poured, sir,' Mrs Jeffries said as she took the inspector's bowler from him. 'Dinner will be a bit tardy, sir. The butcher's delivery didn't get here until quite late this afternoon.' The truth was, she wanted to hear what he'd learned that day. She'd already decided that a case this complex was going to require all of her mental agility and listening skills.

Witherspoon slipped off his coat. 'That's quite all right, Mrs Jeffries. I could do with a drink. It has been a very difficult day.'

They went into the sitting room and took their usual places. Mrs Jeffries picked up her sherry from the table. 'I take it the investigation isn't going very well?'

He sighed and took a sip. 'That's just it. I don't really know. I feel we've learned an awful lot, but I'm not terribly certain that everything I've learned has anything to do with the case. For instance, we went along and had a chat with Horace Riley – he's Jasper Claypool's nephew.' He told her everything about his visit to the Riley household. 'And of course, I felt a bit odd reading his private letter from his uncle, but then again, he did offer to let me see it, and this is a murder investigation.'

'What did the letter say?' she asked.

'Not much, really. Just the usual sort of thing one would expect an elderly vicar to be concerned about.

His church in India needed new hymnals and pews, and there was never enough money to do anything properly. He was distressed by the lack of converts but he found the local people wonderfully kind. You know, that sort of thing, grousing about the lack of support from the church here in England.'

She nodded. 'I see. So the letter was all about his life in India?'

'Not completely,' Witherspoon frowned. 'At the very end he did mention that he wished the family was closer to one another.'

'Did he mean closer physically or emotionally?'

'It wasn't really clear.' The inspector pushed his glasses up his nose. 'It could have been either.'

'So perhaps he was hinting that he might be thinking about coming home,' Mrs Jeffries suggested. 'Which would mean that perhaps Horace Riley wasn't completely surprised by the news that his uncle had come to England.' She had no idea what the letter might or might not have meant. She was merely throwing suggestions out to see if any of them might be useful. It never hurt to stir the waters a bit and then have look after the silt had settled.

'I hadn't thought of it like that,' he replied. 'But I suppose it's possible.' He took another sip from his glass and then told her about the rest of his day. 'I must say the smell around that factory is rather appalling. I can't think how the workers stand it.'

'I expect they're used to it,' she replied. 'And of course, a smelly factory would be quite handy if one wanted to stuff a body down a chimney. It would hide the scent of decomposition.'

'Is that how you think they did it?'

'I should think it would be much easier to put the body in the chimney from the top rather than trying to stuff it up from the inside of the fireplace. That would have taken enormous strength.'

'But putting a body down a chimney would require you going outside and carrying the corpse up to the roof. That's very risky for the murderer. He might have been seen.'

'True, but perhaps he did it late at night.'

'Yes, I suppose that's possible. It certainly sounds like a logical way of going about such an activity.'

'I don't suppose you're any closer to identifying who the victim was?' she asked softly.

'Not really. Only that it was a young woman.' He sighed. 'We've got a list of former tenants, and we'll be interviewing anyone who lived there that we can find. Perhaps that'll shed some light on this mystery. I've also got some lads going over old missing-persons reports for young women. But frankly, that's not going to be worthwhile. There are a lot of young women that go missing, and we've no real idea how long that body was up in the fireplace. Dr Bosworth's expert could only give us a guess. Mind you, he was fairly sure she'd been up there close to ten years. Something about the bones being weathered . . .'

'You spoke to Dr Bosworth today?' she interrupted.

'We stopped by to see him after we'd seen Eric Riley,' Witherspoon replied.

Her mind worked furiously. She had dozens of ideas and questions racing around her head, yet she knew she

131

needed more facts before any of them could coalesce into a useful pattern.

They discussed the case for another fifteen minutes, and then Betsy popped her head into the drawing room and announced that dinner was served. Mrs Jeffries accompanied him to the dining room, got him settled and then went down to the kitchen for her own dinner.

The kitchen was empty except for Fred. Dutifully, he wagged his tail, but Mrs Jeffries could see his heart wasn't in it. 'I'm sorry, boy, but he's still not back.' She leaned down and patted his head. 'I'm sure Wiggins misses you as much as you miss him. I'll tell you what, let's give it a few minutes, give the inspector time to eat his meal and then I'll take you upstairs. He'll take you for a nice, long walk.'

'You chatting with Fred now?' Mrs Goodge inquired as she came into the kitchen. She was carrying a sack of flour.

'Just trying to cheer the poor thing up a bit,' she replied with a laugh. 'Where is everyone?'

'Smythe's gone to Howards to give the horses a bit of a run, and Betsy's upstairs putting the linens away so she won't have to bother with it tomorrow. It's going to be a busy day for all of us.'

'That's true. Do you think we ought to send Wiggins another telegram?' She still felt very guilty about the lad not being there.

'He knows we've a murder,' the cook replied. 'So his not being here is more or less his own doing. He's not bein' held against his will.'

'That's true.' She smiled suddenly. 'I guess he needs

to take care of his relations with his family. They've obviously become important to him.'

'Get out of my way.' Albert shoved Wiggins to one side and hurried over to the kitchen table. He gave him one last glare and then sat down and picked up his fork. 'Well, what are you waitin' for?'

'Hurry up, Wiggins, it's time for supper,' Aunt Alice snapped. 'I don't want to spend all evening cleanin' up this kitchen because you can't get to the table when it's ready.'

'I was reading the newspaper to Grandfather,' Wiggins replied. He sat down at the table. But he had no appetite. His relatives were a sorry lot. They obviously hated him. He wished he'd not given the old man his promise to stay. But what was done was done, and now he was stuck here with this miserable bunch. Cor blimey, but having a conscience could sometimes cost a body a lot. He'd give anything to be back in London with the others.

'Don't know why he needs to have the paper read to him,' Uncle Peter muttered. 'Seems to me he ought to be resting, not getting all upset over the troubles of the world.'

'He asked me to read it to 'im,' Wiggins said defensively. 'And I didn't want to leave 'im till he'd fallen asleep. I was only tryin' to be nice.'

'We know what you're trying to do,' Albert sneered.

'What does that mean?' Wiggins was more mystified than angry.

'You two stop it now, and eat your dinner,' Aunt

133

Alice warned. 'These walls are thin, and sound carries right up them stairs. You don't want to be waking Grandfather now that he's finally asleep.'

But Albert apparently wasn't in the least concerned with waking his grandfather. 'You show up here and all of a sudden the rest of us is no more to the old man than a tick in a feather bed,' he snapped at Wiggins. 'Let me tell you something, no matter how much you lick his boots, you'll not be getting your hands on this farm. It'll belong to us when he goes. You understand. Us. Not you.'

'I don't want the ruddy farm,' Wiggins cried.

'Hush, Albert,' his father warned. He shot Wiggins a quick glance. 'He didn't mean that. He's just a bit jealous is all.'

'I'm not jealous of him,' Albert snapped as he glared at Wiggins. He shoved his chair back and got to his feet. 'I don't know why everyone's fallin' all over themselves to be nice to him. He's nothing more than the blow-by of a whore who wasn't even properly married to his father.'

Wiggins jumped to his feet with such force his chair went flying. 'You take that back,' he shouted, his hand balled into a fist. 'My mother was no . . .' He couldn't bring himself to repeat the word.

'Whore,' Albert laughed maliciously. 'That's the word you're looking for, boy. She was a whore. A common, street-walking whore who got her hooks into poor Uncle Douglas . . .'

Wiggins swung at his cousin, wincing as his fist connected solidly with Albert's jaw.

★ ★ ★

Luty and Hatchet arrived only moments after the inspector had left for the day. 'I've got a lot to do today,' Luty announced as she plopped down at the table, 'so let's get this meetin' started.'

'Really, madam.' Hatchet took the seat next to his employer. 'I do believe we can take the time to be properly civil to one another.'

'I wasn't sayin' we ought to be rude.' Luty put her muff on the table and pulled off her green kid gloves. 'I was sayin' we ought to be fast. We're a man short on this investigation, and in case you've forgotten, we've got us two murders.'

'We're well aware of that, madam,' Hatchet replied. He smiled at the others. 'But I, for one, am of the opinion that the two killings are connected.'

'So am I,' Mrs Jeffries added. 'We just have to keep moving right along. Luty is correct, though. We do have a lot to cover this morning. If you don't mind, I'll start.' She told them everything she'd learned from the inspector, taking care not to leave out even the smallest detail.

'I heard about Eric Riley,' Betsy said as soon as the housekeeper had finished. She told them about her meeting with Horace Riley's housekeeper. She left out the bit about the pub. 'She was ever so chatty. I think she hates Mrs Riley.'

'And she was sure about the time that Mrs Riley left the house?' Mrs Jeffries pressed. This might be very important information.

'She was, and equally sure of the fact that both the Rileys were late getting home that night,' Betsy said. 'I only wish I could get my hands on that telegram.'

'Maybe we can,' Smythe said softly. 'If she tossed it in the dustbin, it might still be on the property.' He looked at Mrs Jeffries. 'How important do you think that telegram is?'

'Very,' she replied. 'The contents of it sent Mrs Riley out of the house without her lunch. It might have been from Jasper Claypool.'

'Should I try my hand at getting hold of it?' Smythe grinned. 'I've a feelin' I can lay my hands on it.'

'It might not still be there,' Betsy warned. 'She could have tossed it in the cooking fire.'

'But she might not 'ave,' he countered. 'At least let me give it a try.'

'Mind you don't take any risks, Smythe,' Betsy said lightly. 'It'd be ever so awkward if you got arrested for trespassing.' She tried to keep her tone casual, but he could tell she was concerned.

'Don't worry, I'll be careful.' He patted her arm under the table. 'I'll nip over and suss out the lay of the land this afternoon.'

Betsy opened her mouth to speak, to tell them the best part about her meeting with Lilly Staggers, but before she could get the words out, Mrs Jeffries started asking questions.

'Were you able to find out where Claypool's luggage had been taken?' she asked the coachman.

He shook his head. 'I'm still working on that one. But I did find out that Claypool's murder wasn't a robbery. At least that's the word down at the docks. I got that from a good source, too, so we can rule out a common by-your-leave bit of pilferin' gone bad.'

'That's useful to know,' Mrs Jeffries said thoughtfully.

'And I'm workin' on getting names of the other passengers from the ship,' Smythe added. 'But that might take some doin'.'

'Perhaps I might be of some assistance there,' Hatchet offered. 'I could stop by the Far East and India offices and see what I can learn. Frankly, it would be a relief. I'm not having a lot of luck finding out any information about the Christophers.'

Smythe could hardly admit he'd already hired Blimpey to find out that information. 'Thanks, that would be good. Save me a bit of trouble.'

'It'll be my pleasure,' Hatchet replied.

'I take it that means you've not had much success,' Mrs Jeffries queried. She knew how easy it was to get downhearted when one hadn't found out anything useful.

Hatchet sighed. 'Not really. The best I managed was a bit of old gossip about Mrs Christopher's sister. Apparently, Edith Durant was a complete hoyden, and the only person who had any influence on her whatsoever was her Uncle Jasper.'

'So you weren't able to find out if either of the Christophers had an alibi for the time of the murder?' Mrs Jeffries pressed. They already knew about Edith. What they needed now was to know where everyone was at the time of the killing.

He shook his head in disgust. 'The only person from the household that I managed to speak to was the tweeny, and she didn't know much of anything.' He didn't reveal that he'd paid the girl for the pathetic scraps of information he'd brought to their table. 'Unfortunately, the day of the murder there were painters at the Christopher house, so most of the staff had gone out. She knew nothing.'

'But she knew gossip about Mrs Christopher's sister,' Betsy said. 'Someone she hadn't even met.'

'Oh, but she had,' Hatchet replied quickly. 'Apparently, Edith Durant visits her sister every once in a while. She never stays more than a few hours, but the girl had glimpsed her going in and out.'

'We do need more information about the Christophers,' Mrs Jeffries said. She looked at Betsy. 'Do you think you could have a chat with the local shopkeepers tomorrow?'

'Of course, but before I nip along there, you might want me to go back over to the Riley neighborhood. I wasn't finished with my telling. I found out something else today, something that I think is important. Apparently, Eric Riley knew his Uncle Jasper was back in London.'

'How'd you find that out?' Luty exclaimed.

'From Lilly Staggers, she sort of yelled that at me as she was leaving today and I didn't have a chance to ask her any more questions. I've got to talk to her again.'

'Of course you must,' Mrs Jeffries replied. She was annoyed with herself for not realizing that they'd all interrupted the girl. 'And from now on, if you're not finished with your report, do let us know.'

'That's right, we don't want to be interruptin' you,' Mrs Goodge added.

'It's all right,' she smiled sheepishly. 'I should have said something.'

'How are you going to speak to her again?' Mrs Goodge asked. 'Won't she get suspicious?'

Betsy shrugged. She'd planned on watching the pub tomorrow about the same time she'd been there today. To her way of thinking, the Riley housekeeper probably visited that pub quite often. 'Not really. She's got quite a loose tongue on her.'

'It seems to me that if the housekeeper to the Horace Rileys told Betsy that Eric Riley knew Claypool was coming home, then it stands to reason that there's a good chance the Horace Rileys knew he was comin' home too,' Luty said.

She was a bit put out. Suddenly, learning the contents of Jasper Claypool's will didn't seem so very important. But then again, you never knew what was going to be useful or not till you got to the very end.

'I don't see the connection, madam,' Hatchet said.

'I do,' Mrs Goodge put in. 'Unless she had reason to be talking to Eric Riley directly, Lilly Staggers probably overheard Horace Riley telling Mrs Riley he'd heard from Eric that Claypool was coming home.'

'I think she did have reason to talk to him herself,' Betsy said quickly. 'She seemed to know quite a bit about Eric Riley and his doings. Did I mention that she said he'd been trying to get control of the factory for the past two years?'

'You didn't mention that time period,' Mrs Jeffries said softly.

'I'm sorry, I'm getting sloppy.' Annoyed with herself, she shook her head. 'Now that I think of it, her whole manner was odd.'

'Odd how?' Smythe pressed.

'Odd in the sense that she seemed almost like she was used to reporting on her employer.' Betsy smiled sheepishly. 'I'm sorry. I'm being silly, it's just now when I look back on the whole thing, that's the impression I get.'

'Your impressions are usually very reliable,' Mrs Jeffries said. 'Do you think it's possible that Lilly Staggers is working for Eric Riley? Reporting to him about the Horace Rileys?'

'I think it's worth finding out,' Betsy replied. She wondered how much gin it was going to take to get Lilly to tell her the whole truth. 'And I think I know how I can do it.'

'You be careful now, lass,' Smythe warned. 'This woman may not take kindly to bein' accused of spyin' on her employers.'

'I'll be very subtle.' Betsy gave him a reassuring smile. 'I'll be talking to her in broad daylight in front of dozens of people. I don't think she'll try and box my ears if I offend her.'

'Can I have my turn now?' Mrs Goodge asked. At the housekeeper's nod, she told them about her visit from her old colleague, Letty Sommerville. 'So you see, according to Letty, both the Riley men have big plans for that factory and all the property.'

'And apparently, Hilda Christopher gets nothing but a set of old books.' Luty shook her head in disgust.

'Not necessarily,' Mrs Goodge replied. 'Letty only gets gossip thirdhand, it might not be worth much. Besides, from what Mrs Jeffries told us, it looks like Hilda's the only one who doesn't need an inheritance from her uncle.'

'It would be interesting to find out about Edith Durant's financial situation,' Hatchet mused.

'It would be nice if we just knew her address,' Mrs Jeffries added. 'But apparently, not even the police have been able to find out where the woman lives.'

'I expect once the word that he's dead gets spread, she'll come out into the open,' Luty said. 'Especially if she's one of his heirs. Money always brings relatives sniffing around, even ones that don't need it.'

'But he'd told her he never wanted to see her again,' Betsy reminded her. 'So maybe she doesn't care if he's dead.'

'He told her that ten years ago,' Smythe said. 'They might 'ave made it up by now.' He looked at Mrs Jeffries. 'Do you want me to try and find out where she lives?'

'Do you think you can?'

'I'll give it a try,' he replied. He'd get Blimpey on it right away. If anyone could find the woman, he could.

'From everything we've learned about Jasper Claypool,' Mrs Goodge muttered, 'it seems he liked his nieces a good deal more than his nephews. Who knows what he actually left them in his will?'

Luty stifled a grin. By this time tomorrow, she certainly hoped she'd know who got what from the good reverend.

CHAPTER SEVEN

Mrs Jeffries yawned as she went down the stairs the next morning. She hadn't slept well. There were far too many bits and pieces swirling about in her head for a restful night's sleep. She hurried into the kitchen and came to an abrupt halt.

Wiggins and Mrs Goodge were sitting at the table. There was a plate of buttered bread, a dish of orange marmalade and a pot of tea in front of them. Fred was sitting next to the footman's chair with his head resting against the lad.

'Gracious, Wiggins, this is a bit of a surprise. Welcome back.'

'I took the early train back this mornin'. I'm glad to be 'ome, Mrs Jeffries,' he replied. 'It feels like I've been gone for ages instead of a few days.'

'How is your grandfather?' She got a cup down from the sideboard.

'Well, uh, he's about the same,' Wiggins said softly. He reached down and patted Fred. 'I come 'ome because I 'ad a bit of a dustup with my cousin.'

'He punched him in the nose,' Mrs Goodge added.

'But from what Wiggins told me, the boy had it coming. He kept insulting Wiggins's mother.'

'I see,' Mrs Jeffries poured herself a cup of tea. 'If that's the case, then it's just as well you came back.'

Wiggins looked up and met her eyes. 'I tried to get along with my relations, Mrs Jeffries, I really did. But the only one who wanted me there was my grandfather. My aunt and uncle weren't very nice either, and my cousin hated me from the second he picked me up at the station. But I didn't mind all that, I tried to keep out of everyone's way. But when Albert started callin' my mam them horrible names . . .'

'You don't have to explain to us.' She held up her hand. 'We know you, Wiggins. You're a good and gentle soul. If you resorted to fisticuffs, I'm sure it was for a good reason.' She couldn't believe she'd just said those words. She'd always believed violence never really solved anything, but then again, perhaps she'd been wrong. Perhaps there were moments when a good smack in the nose was just what the situation needed. 'So, now that you're back with us, let's get you out there working on our case. We've been stretched a bit thin on this one.'

'Course you 'ave,' he nodded eagerly, relieved not to have to keep talking about his dreadful relatives. 'What with there being two corpses and all.'

'I've told him everything we've learned so far,' Mrs Goodge said as she got up and walked over to the counter. She lifted the cloth off her bread bowl and frowned at the dough. 'I don't think I've left anything out. Oh blast, this is takin' its sweet time to raise. Perhaps it's just as well I've got those hot cross buns in the larder. I've got my sources coming along this morning.'

Wiggins looked at Mrs Jeffries. 'What do you want me to be doin'?'

She thought for a moment. 'I think we need someone working on the Bermondsey murder. We haven't really covered that neighborhood very well. Betsy had a bit of luck a couple of days ago, but since then, we've found out very little. I think it would be a good idea if you went around there and had a go at it.'

He took a quick sip from his cup. 'Exactly what should I be askin'? From what Mrs Goodge told me, no one has any idea who that poor woman was.'

'Just find out what you can about either the woman or the cottage,' she replied, 'and follow your nose. You've always been quite good at that sort of thing.'

The housekeeper was referring to their last case, when Wiggins had taken the initiative and ended up stealing a piece of evidence.

'Just see that you don't get in trouble,' Mrs Goodge warned. 'And be back here by teatime for our meeting.'

'I'll be 'ere,' he said. 'Where's the others? Out and about already?'

'Everyone had an early start,' the cook replied. She sat back down. 'But they'll all be here this afternoon.'

'What about you, Mrs Jeffries? Are you goin' out lookin' for clues today?'

'Certainly, just as soon as I get the inspector fed his breakfast and out the front door.' She pushed back from the table and got up. 'I thought I'd see what I could learn about Jasper Claypool before he went to India. Claypool was at St Matthew's Church in Finsbury

144

Park. The family is from that area. Perhaps I'll find out something useful about either our suspects or our victim.'

'I'd best get crackin', then.' Wiggins finished off the last of his food and got up. 'Come on, Fred, let's go see what's what.'

They waited till they heard the back door slam before either of them spoke. Then Mrs Goodge said, 'He was in a terrible state when he arrived this morning. His knuckles are red from where he hit his cousin, but it's his conscience that's really hurting him. He told me he'd broken his promise to his grandfather by leaving. Apparently, the old man had got him to give his word that he'd stay until the grandfather either died or got well.'

'But the old man didn't see to it that his family kept a civil tongue in their heads,' Mrs Jeffries mused. 'And from the sound of it, they made our Wiggins miserable.'

'They're afraid the grandfather is dying and that he's going to leave part of the family farm to Wiggins. Albert, the cousin that Wiggins smacked, accused Wiggins of licking the old man's boots to get a share of the estate.'

'I don't think I like Wiggins's family much,' Mrs Jeffries said. 'Perhaps it's just as well he came home.'

'I hate seein' him so upset,' the cook muttered.

'You think he wants to go back?'

'He wants to be right here,' she replied. 'But he doesn't like breaking his promise.'

'Then let's hope he can find a way to make peace with his decision,' Mrs Jeffries said softly.

★ ★ ★

Constable Barnes waved a passing cab over to the side of Holland Park Road. 'Where to first, sir? The Mayberrys are in Islington, and that's the closest.'

'Let's give them a try,' Witherspoon said as he climbed into the hansom. They had the list of the former tenants of Dorland Place they'd gotten from Eric Riley. 'Let's keep our fingers crossed that someone will give us a clue to who that poor woman was.'

Barnes gave the driver the address and then settled back next to the inspector. He whipped out his notebook. 'If we don't learn anything useful from the Mayberrys, we got the address of a Mrs Colfax who used to live at number three on that road. She lives in Chingford now and is quite elderly.'

'Were those the only two names we were able to track down?' Witherspoon asked. As the days passed, this case was becoming more and more difficult. They had no real suspects, no motive, and one of the corpses hadn't even been identified. He was beginning to think he wasn't ever going to solve this one.

'I'm afraid so, sir,' Barnes admitted morosely, 'Ten years is a long time. We only got these two addresses because they'd kept in touch with the local vicar.'

'I suppose it's a start. Has there been any sign of Claypool's luggage?' Witherspoon asked.

'None, sir,' Barnes replied. 'No one can remember what freight company picked it up, only that they had the proper documents and took it away.'

'But they did confirm that it was picked up on the Monday?'

'Right, sir.' Barnes scratched his chin. 'Which is odd, when you think of it. If he was killed Monday evening and the luggage was picked up Monday afternoon, was he the one that sent for it, and if so, where did he have it taken?'

'I take it the bishop was no help on this problem?' Witherspoon had no idea what this missing luggage meant, but he knew it meant something.

'No, sir, he checked with Claypool's old parish and with some of his former associates and the bags weren't taken anywhere he could find.'

'And they weren't taken to either of the Rileys or the Christopher home or the factory.' Witherspoon shrugged. 'Then where on earth did they go?'

'Maybe they were picked up by Miss Durant, sir,' Barnes suggested. 'She's the only one in this case we haven't spoken with.'

'Do we have an address yet?'

'Not yet, sir. I was only mentioning her as a possibility. Also, sir, I've got the final reports from the lads that did the door-to-door. We've got a report from a woman who actually saw the poor man running down the street.'

'Egads! You mean she saw him being chased by his killer?'

'She didn't exactly see his killer, but she did see Claypool running towards the church,' Barnes said. 'It was a real peasouper that night, and all she caught was glimpses of him running through the fog. She didn't think anything of it because she thought the man was simply late to church. But she was able to pinpoint the time for us, sir. It was six o'clock.'

'And she didn't see the murderer?' Witherspoon asked, his expression hopeful.

'No, sir, but she did hear another set of footsteps. But again, she took no notice. She thought it was someone late for church. That's about it, sir. No one else saw or heard anything.'

For the duration of the journey, they discussed the few facts they had about the case. Barnes, who'd had a brief word with Mrs Jeffries when he'd gotten to Upper Edmonton Gardens that morning, dropped some pertinent bits of information and a goodly number of helpful hints in the inspector's path. But he didn't think they were having the desired effect on his superior, for by the time the hansom pulled up in front of a tiny house in Islington, Barnes could tell by the inspector's glum expression that he was still having grave doubts about the case.

'Constable, I fear this case is going to be one of those that get away from us.' Witherspoon closed his eyes briefly. 'We're dealing with a very clever killer.'

'Not to worry, sir. We'll get the blighter.' He pulled some coins out of his pocket and paid the driver. 'Like you always say, sir, they always make a mistake.'

'I certainly hope so,' Witherspoon said fervently. 'But honestly, I do admit this one has me baffled. Frankly, Constable, I'm not even certain whether we're looking for one or two murderers.' He peered at the small row houses. 'What's the address?'

'It's number eight.' Barnes pointed to the middle of the row. The two-story brick house had dilapidated drainpipes and needed a decent paint job about the window sills. 'Let's hope there's someone home.'

The door opened almost as soon as the constable had finished knocking. An elderly woman wearing spectacles and a clean white apron over her brown housedress peered out at them. 'Yes? What is it?'

'Are you Mrs Mayberry?' Witherspoon asked politely.

'I am, and who might you be?'

He introduced himself and Barnes. 'We'd like to come in and speak to you, if we might.'

She opened the door. 'Come into the parlor, then.' She gestured to a room that opened off the tiny entranceway.

They entered a small sitting room containing an aged three-piece suite of an indeterminate dark color and two side tables with brown matching lamps. Antimacassars were laid neatly on the backs of the settee and chairs.

'Please sit down.' Mrs Mayberry indicated the settee. She took a seat in the chair. 'Now what's this all about?'

'We'd like to talk to you about when you lived in Bermondsey,' Witherspoon began.

'You mean on Dorland Place? That was ten years ago.' She looked at him, her expression mystified.

'Actually, we'd like to know if you ever saw any activity at number seven. That's the one at the very end of the row.'

'I know which one it is,' she said. She smiled slyly. 'No one lived in that one, you know.'

'We understand that,' Barnes said. 'But just because no one lives in a place doesn't mean it doesn't get any use.'

She laughed. 'You can say that again. Mind you, they always tried to be crafty about it when they was using the place. But all of us knew what was goin' on.'

'Uh, exactly what was going on?' Witherspoon wanted to make sure he understood her correctly.

Mrs Mayberry shrugged. 'What do you think? They was usin' it for immoral purposes, that's what.'

'Immoral purposes,' he repeated. 'You mean for illicit assignations?'

She nodded eagerly. 'Supposedly the people that owned the factory across the road, they were our land-lords, you understand, they was supposed to be keeping number seven empty for their own use, but the only time it ever got used was when he was meetin' her.'

'When who was meeting who?' the inspector pressed. It would be most helpful if she knew their names.

Mrs Mayberry shrugged again. 'I don't know their names. Actually, they were pretty crafty about stayin' away from pryin' eyes. But I know they used the place because sometimes you could see smoke comin' out of the chimney, and even though they'd pull the blinds, you could see light comin' from out the bottom crack.'

'Did these people break into the cottage?' Barnes asked.

'They had a key,' she replied. 'There was never any windows broken, and the one time one of the neigh-bors went over to the factory to speak to them about it, they were told to mind their own business.'

'So you never saw the people who were using the place?' Barnes pressed.

'Only once, I saw a woman come out late in the afternoon. She stood at the door and tried to wait until she thought it was safe before she showed her face, but I was back behind the tree across the road and she didn't see me. I saw her all right. She was a tallish woman, well dressed and posh looking if you know what I mean.'

'What did she look like?' the constable asked. 'Could you describe her?'

'No, she had on a veil. But she was dressed fancy and carried herself like a queen, I remember that much. I never got a look at the man, but I know there was one because my Billy was creeping around the back of the cottage when they was in there and he heard them talking.'

'How often did they uh . . . use the cottage?' Witherspoon asked. Gracious, this was a very peculiar conversation.

She pushed her spectacles up her nose. 'Let me see, they only really started usin' the place the last year we lived there. I don't remember how often they was actually there, but it was more than a few times. Too bad you can't speak to Mrs Hornby, she was right next door to the place. But she died last year, had the scarlet fever, she did, and it took her in less than three days.'

'Are you sure it was the same people all the time?' Barnes asked. 'Or did different people use the premises?'

'It was the same ones all the time,' she said.

'But how can you know for certain?' he pressed.

'Because they come in the same way each time,' she insisted. 'They come by hansom cab and the woman always wore a heavy veil over her face and the man had his collar pulled up high. He looked pretty silly when it was summertime. But it was always the same – they went to a great deal of trouble not to be recognized.

Seems to me that casual people using the place wouldn't have taken such care, would they.'

'Yes, I see your point.' The inspector nodded. He wasn't sure what any of this meant, but it had to mean something. 'Do you recall the last time you saw anyone at the cottage?'

'Not really,' she smiled. 'It was ten years ago, Inspector. I only remember about the man and woman because it was so interesting.'

They asked her more questions, but it was soon obvious that she'd told them everything she could remember.

'Is there anyone else here who was in your household when you lived at Dorland Place?' Barnes asked.

She smiled sadly. 'My Billy is gone for two years now, and we never had any children.'

Witherspoon felt very sorry for the poor lady. She sounded very lonely. He got to his feet. 'Thank you for your time, Mrs Mayberry. You've been most helpful.'

She started to get up but he waved her back to her chair. 'It's all right, ma'am, we'll see ourselves out. Good day.'

Mrs Jeffries stepped out of the train station at Finsbury Park and stopped to survey her surroundings. She needed someone local to point her toward St Matthew's Church. Across the road, she spotted a newsagent's. She slipped around a hansom cab and darted through the heavy traffic to the other side. She waited till the shop was empty before stepping inside. 'Hello,' she smiled at the woman behind the counter. 'I'm hoping you can help me. I'm trying to find St Matthew's Church.'

'It's up the road a piece.' She gestured toward the window and to her left. 'It's a good fifteen minutes' walk from here.'

A few moments later Mrs Jeffries, aimed with precise directions, started up the busy road. As she walked, she thought about the case. They had two bodies, two victims, but the murders might be as much as ten years apart. Then again, what if the two killings weren't even related to one another? No, she shook her head as she turned the corner, she simply didn't believe that. It would be far too much of a coincidence for the first victim to be holding an address that had a second victim up its chimney.

But then again, coincidences did happen.

She slowed her steps as the idea took root in her mind. Life was full of coincidence. What if this was one too? Then what? They'd have wasted a huge amount of time and effort trying to tie the two killings together instead of investigating them separately.

She pulled her jacket closer against the sudden cold from a gust of wind. The neighborhood had changed as she walked, going from small row houses with tiny gardens to larger homes the farther one walked from the station. A row of tall oaks lined each side of the road, and the homes were set well back from the street. Most of them had gardens with deep green lawns and beautifully tended flowerbeds.

She came to the intersection and stopped. St Matthew's was on the corner. It was made of gray stone and set back in a churchyard that was surrounded by a low stone fence with a wrought iron gate leading to the church door. She walked up to the gate and stared at the building. It was only half past ten, so there might not be anyone in the church. Well, then, she'd wait about until someone showed up. She pushed through the gate and stepped into the yard. She was almost to the door when a voice said, 'You'll not be able to get inside. They don't unlock the doors till noon.'

She whirled about and saw an elderly man standing on the path. He was holding a wheelbarrow. 'Are you wantin' to see the vicar?'

'Actually, I'm not certain.' She smiled hesitantly. 'I'm trying to locate a Reverend Jasper Claypool.' Though Claypool's murder had been in the papers, she was pretending ignorance, hoping the mention of his name might get someone to talk to her. In her experience, people were always willing to pass along a bit of bad news.

He sat the wheelbarrow down and gazed at her sympathetically. 'You're not a relative are you?'

'No, we were on the same ship coming back from India. I got off in Cherbourg. I arrived back in England late yesterday. Unfortunately, I've lost the address where I was supposed to meet him, but I do recall him saying he was coming up here to visit his family. I've got some contributions for his church building fund in India, and I wanted to give them to him personally.'

'You must have misunderstood him, ma'am,' the gardener shifted uneasily. 'Reverend Claypool's got no family around here. They all left the area years ago. But that's not the worst of it, ma'am. I'm sorry to have to tell you this, but the Reverend Claypool is dead. He was murdered a few days ago near the London docks. It was in yesterday's papers.'

She gasped in pretend surprise and clasped her hands together. 'Oh no, who would want to kill such a nice man?'

'They don't know, ma'am. The police haven't caught anyone.' He reached into his pocket and pulled out a key. 'You look a bit pale, ma'am. I've a key here, so if you'd like to go inside and have a sit down, I'll unlock the doors for you.'

'Thank you, I would be very grateful,' She felt just a bit guilty. But she shoved the feeling aside and carried on with her plan. She wanted this man talking. He'd apparently been here for quite a while and was a good source of information. 'I do feel a bit faint.' She stumbled ever so slightly.

Alarmed, the gardener leapt to her side and took her arm. 'Let me help you, ma'am. This 'as been a real shock to you, I can tell.'

She let him lead her through the narthex and into the sanctuary. He helped her into a pew on the last row.

'Thank you,' she said softly. 'I simply can't believe he's gone. He was so looking forward to coming here. He was so looking forward to seeing his family. He'd missed them all so much, especially his nieces and nephews.'

'I'm sure he did miss 'em, ma'am. He helped raise the twins after their parents died,' the gardener said. 'And it weren't no easy task, either.'

'It's never easy for a single man to raise children,' she murmured. She hoped she was saying the right thing to keep him talking.

'Oh, even if he'd had a wife, raising the girls all

those years would have turned him gray. I'm Arthur Benning,' he said. 'I've been the groundsman here for twenty years.'

'I'm Penelope Mortiboys,' Mrs Jeffries said. She hoped that God would forgive her for lying in his house. After all, she was trying to catch a killer, and surely that took precedence over a petty white-lie sin. 'I hadn't realized that poor Reverend Claypool had spent so many years rearing his nieces.'

'Oh, yes,' Benning smiled broadly. 'He was ever so kind to those girls. Mind you, Miss Hilda was always as good as gold and Miss Edith wasn't a bad girl, just a bit high-spirited. He was a good man, the reverend. He didn't have to be their guardian. His half-brother and his wife was quite willing to take the girls in and give 'em a proper home.'

'You mean their aunt and uncle?' She wanted to make certain she got the details correct.

'Right,' he frowned slightly. 'Mr and Mrs Riley would've been quite chuffed to give the girls a home, but Reverend Claypool said it were his responsibility. He was the one named guardian in their father's will. Course, the gossip was that the only reason the Rileys offered was to get their hands on Miss Hilda's money. But I don't put much credence in that sort of talk. John Riley was a decent sort, and both of his wives was real nice women. The girls spent a lot of time at their house as they were growing up. And the Rileys didn't even make too much of a fuss when Miss Edith played that awful prank.' He laughed. 'I expect they was used to it. Miss Edith was always doin' something naughty, she was.'

'All children play pranks,' she said conversationally.

'Not like this,' he said. 'She leapt out the bushes waving a cloth when young Mr Horace had all the children in the pony cart. It spooked the horse so badly he reared up like a stallion and the cart overturned, The children were tossed out onto the embankment and poor Mr Horace ended up with a broken ankle and missed a whole school term because of it. Mr Eric was just a toddler, and he landed on a clump of grass with just a few bruises, and Miss Hilda broke a bone or two, and, of course, Miss Edith walked away without so much as a scratch.' He laughed again. 'But that was generally the way of it. Miss Edith always seemed to get out of most things with no mishaps.'

Mrs Jeffries sighed sadly. 'I know the reverend was hoping to reconcile with his niece. He mentioned they were estranged.'

'Miss Edith's been estranged from the whole family,' Arthur Benning said bluntly. 'They'd left here by the time it happened, but everyone around here knew about it. Well, you couldn't expect the reverend to forgive something like that, could you?'

Mrs Jeffries knew she had to be careful. She couldn't let on that she had no idea what he was talking about. 'No, of course he couldn't. But all the same, it's a shame the way it all turned out.'

'Oh, I don't know, last I heard, Miss Hilda was happily married to her Mr Christopher and Miss Edith is off running about the continent, doin' what she wants and answerin' to no one. Mind you, I expect the way she's livin' her life probably upset the good reverend, him bein' a vicar and all.'

At that moment, a man dressed in clerical garb stepped into the front of the church and peered at them from behind the baptismal font. 'Arthur, is something wrong?' He advanced down the aisle toward them.

'This lady felt a bit faint, sir,' he replied, gesturing at Mrs Jeffries. 'I brought her inside to have a sit down. She was lookin' for Reverend Claypool and didn't know that he'd died.'

'Oh my dear lady, how very unfortunate,' the vicar said kindly.

'It was a bit of a shock.' She smiled and got to her feet. 'But your Mr Benning has explained everything and been most considerate. Obviously, I misunderstood Reverend Claypool. From what Mr Benning has told me, both he and his family left this area some time ago.'

'That's correct. I never met the man, but he was quite well loved in the parish.' He pulled out a pocket watch and checked the time. 'Arthur, you'd best get that trimming done on the Harcourt graves. They'll be here fairly soon to pay their respects.'

'Yes, sir.' Arthur smiled a goodbye and nodded his head at Mrs Jeffries.

'Thank you for your kindness,' she said. Then she turned to the vicar. 'It's such a shame about the poor man. Do they have any idea who killed him?'

'I'm afraid I don't know,' he said. He took her elbow and began edging them down the aisle toward the door. 'It's most unfortunate, but the police are quite good at catching murderers. I'm sure they'll find out who did it.' He hustled her down the aisle and out the front door before she could gather her wits about her to ask more questions. 'Do have a good day,' he said as he hurried back inside. She stared at the closed door for a moment and then glanced around the churchyard. Arthur was nowhere in sight, and besides, she didn't want to get him in trouble by taking him away from his work anymore.

She went up the path to the pavement, turned and stared at the church. On the property next to the church, there was a house made of the same kind of stone as the church. She guessed that was the vicarage. She decided there was no harm in spending a bit more time in the neighborhood. No telling what she might be able to find out.

'I'd like to have a word with the staff,' Barnes said to the inspector. 'Now that we know when Claypool was killed, it'll be interesting to know if Mr and Mrs Christopher was at home.' They were seated in the Christophers' drawing room waiting for either the master or the mistress.

Witherspoon frowned slightly. 'Do you suspect something?'

Barnes shrugged, 'We're not learning much, sir. I keep thinking that Claypool arrived back in London early that morning, yet he didn't die till six o'clock in the evening. Where was he all that time?'

Mrs Christopher swept into the room. She was dressed in a fur-trimmed fawn jacket and carried a pair of gloves in her hands. 'My housekeeper said you wanted to speak to me,' she said softly.

'Actually, either you or your husband would do.' Witherspoon rose to his feet. The constable got up as well.

'My husband is out,' she replied. 'So you'll have to speak with me.'

'I was wondering, ma'am, if you've any idea where your uncle might have gone on the day he arrived here?'

Her eyes widened in surprise. 'I'm not sure what you mean.'

'I mean, he arrived in London early that morning and he didn't die until that evening. He must have been somewhere for all those hours. Mr Horace Riley insists he wasn't at the factory or at his home, and Mr Eric Riley says the same thing. You and your husband both say he wasn't here, so we're hoping you can give us some idea of where he might have gone.'

She said nothing for a moment. 'I've no idea. Perhaps he went to visit old friends.'

'I doubt that, ma'am,' Barnes said dryly. 'There's been plenty of newspaper coverage about his death. We've asked for anyone who'd seen him to come forward and make a statement. No one has. Also, ma'am, would you mind if we had a word with your staff?'

'My staff? If you mean the servants, there'd be no point. Most of them never even met my uncle. They could tell you nothing.' She pulled on one of the gloves.

'So you've no objection to our speaking to them,' Barnes persisted.

'None whatsoever.' She pulled on the second glove. 'Now, if there's nothing else, I must be off. I've several appointments this morning.'

'Actually, ma'am, there is something else. I believe you have a sister. Does she live here in London?' He knew she didn't, and from everything he'd been told,

Edith Durant was a fairly delicate subject. He wanted to be as discreet as possible, but he had to ask. They couldn't find hide nor hair of the woman anywhere.

'My sister lives abroad,' Hilda Christopher said coolly. 'In Paris. The Metropole Hotel.'

'Does she ever come to visit you?' Barnes asked.

'Not often. But she does come occasionally. We saw her last year as a matter of fact, on Boxing Day.' She sighed. 'Look, Inspector, Constable, my husband doesn't really welcome Edith into our home, so I generally meet her somewhere else.'

'Is it possible your uncle was meeting her on the day he died?' Barnes asked softly.

Her shapely brows drew together. 'I suppose it's possible. But if that's the case, then why hasn't Edith contacted you about it?'

The two policemen looked at one another.

Mrs Christopher followed their glance, and then a puzzled expression crossed her lovely face, quickly followed by one of outrage. 'Now see here, Inspector. What are you implying?'

'Absolutely nothing, Mrs Christopher. We're merely asking very routine questions,' Witherspoon said quickly.

'My sister may be a bit unconventional, sir, but I assure you, she isn't a murderess.' Hilda straightened her spine. 'The very idea is unthinkable.'

'Does your sister own a gun?' Barnes asked softly.

'A gun.' Hilda Christopher repeated the word as if she'd never heard it before. 'Why on earth are you asking me that?'

'Do you own a gun, ma'am?' the inspector

interjected. 'As I said, our questions are merely routine. We're asking everybody.' He was annoyed with himself. He'd not thought to ask Horace or Eric Riley if they owned a weapon. He made a mental note to rectify that error as soon as possible.

'I don't understand this. My uncle, who I didn't even know was in England, gets murdered, and all of a sudden, my family and I are subjected to these humiliating questions.' Her voice had risen perceptibly, and her beautiful eyes filled with tears. 'You have no right to come in here and make these disgusting implications.'

'As I said before, ma'am,' the inspector said, wishing she'd calm down, 'our intention was never to imply anything untoward, we're merely trying to find your uncle's killer. You want us to find out who did it, don't you?'

'Of course I do,' she cried. She clasped hands together in distress. 'Of course I want you to find his killer. I loved Uncle Jasper, he was like a father to me.'

The drawing room door opened and Carl Christopher charged inside. 'Hilda, what on earth is wrong?' He crossed to her and drew her close, his expression concerned. 'I could hear you from outside.'

'I'm sorry, darling.' She gestured at the two policemen. 'I'm afraid I've let myself get upset. They were asking some questions about Edith. About whether or not Uncle Jasper might have met with her on the day he died. About whether or not Edith has a gun. It was most distressing, and I'm afraid I allowed myself to get terribly overwrought.'

'We didn't mean to upset Mrs Christopher,'

Witherspoon said quickly. 'As I pointed out to her, our questions are merely routine.'

'They asked me if I had a gun,' Mrs Christopher added. 'And if I had any idea where Uncle Jasper might have been those hours before he died.'

'We know your uncle arrived quite early that morning,' Barnes said. 'And we asked Mrs Christopher if she had any idea where he might have gone.'

'They also want to speak to the servants,' she said.

'Of course they can speak with the staff,' he said smoothly. He turned to Witherspoon. 'We're not trying to be uncooperative, Inspector. We'll answer any questions you like.'

'Do you own a weapon, sir?' Witherspoon asked.

'No, neither I nor my wife own a weapon of any sort.'

'Does your sister-in-law own a gun?' Barnes asked.

He hesitated for a fraction of a second and then looked at his wife. 'We have to tell the truth, dear.'

She made a sound of distress.

'Hush, darling.' He put his fingers over her lips. 'We'll not do Edith any good by lying for her.' Turning back to the inspector, he said, 'Edith owns a small revolver. She carries it for protection, as she travels so much.'

CHAPTER EIGHT

'So what do you think of this turn of events, sir?' Barnes whispered to the inspector. They were downstairs in a small, dimly lighted sitting room, waiting for the housekeeper.

'I'm not sure,' Witherspoon replied. He glanced at the partly closed door, not wanting to be overheard. 'It's a bit difficult to question someone who doesn't appear to have an address. Miss Edith Durant sounds very much like an adventuress. We've no idea if she's even in England.'

'But at least we know she had a gun,' Barnes pointed out. He turned toward the door as they heard the sound of footsteps coming down the hall. A moment later, the door opened and a tall, austere middle-aged woman wearing a gray dress stepped into the room.

She nodded respectfully at the policemen. 'Good day, I'm Irma Nimitz. Mrs Christopher said you'd like to speak with me.'

Witherspoon smiled warmly. 'I'm Inspector Witherspoon and this is Constable Barnes.'

'Do you mind if I sit down?' She moved toward an

old, overstuffed chair on the far side of the settee. 'I like to rest my feet whenever I've a chance.'

'We wouldn't mind in the least,' he assured her. 'I believe I'll have a sit down too.' He took a seat at the end of the settee closest to her. 'We won't take up much of your time.'

She smiled wanly. 'Take as long as you like, I could use the rest. This is a big house, and frankly, there simply isn't enough staff to run it properly. But that's neither here nor there. You're not interested in our domestic arrangements.'

'Er . . . uh could you tell us if anything unusual happened on this past Monday?'

'The day the old vicar was murdered,' she said. 'I can't think of anything.'

'You didn't have any unexpected visitors or unusual messages,' Barnes asked.

'Not that I know about,' Mrs Nimitz replied with a shrug. 'But then again, I was out for most of the day. The painters were here doing the downstairs, and the smell was awful. We couldn't do our work so Mr Christopher let most of us have the day out.'

'The whole day?' Witherspoon asked. 'That was very generous of him.'

'Not really,' she shrugged again. 'We took the day in lieu of our normal time off for the week. It was a bit annoying, if you know what I mean. We knew the painters were scheduled to come that day, but the master hadn't told us we'd have to take our day out then. It was a trifle inconvenient. My usual day out is Wednesday, and I'd already made plans to go to see my niece in Hackney on Wednesday afternoon.'

'So getting the day off was a surprise to the staff?' Witherspoon asked. He wanted to make sure he understood her correctly. That was the sort of fact that ended up being most important. Sometimes.

'Yes.'

'What time did you leave the house?' Barnes leaned against the table.

'Are you going to repeat what we say back to them?' she jerked her chin upward, toward the drawing room.

'We do not tell employers what their staff say about them in the course of an investigation,' Witherspoon said firmly. 'Your statements are completely private unless used as evidence in a court of law.'

Her expression was still skeptical.

'We don't run tellin' tales,' Barnes added softly. 'If we did, no one would tell us a blooming thing.'

She still didn't look completely convinced, but her expression relaxed a little. 'Right, then. It was a bit of an odd day. We all left fairly early. Blevins, he's the butler, had come downstairs at seven to tell me to get everyone out of the house as soon as breakfast was over. The painters arrived just after eight. As soon as the breakfast things were washed and put away, I let the kitchen girls go on. Then I went upstairs and checked that the beds were made. By the time I came downstairs, Mrs Christopher had shooed everyone out and was pushing me to go as well.'

'Mrs Christopher was still here?' Barnes looked up from his notebook.

'Yes, both she and Mr Christopher were still in the house. They planned to stay the day, too, despite the smell.'

'They told you that?' the inspector asked.

'No, they gave the impression they were going to be going out as well. Supposedly, that was the reason she was rushing us out the door. She kept muttering they had a train to catch. That they were going to spend the day in Brighton. But I know that was a lie. I had to run back upstairs to get my coat, you see.' She smiled impishly. 'They thought I'd already gone. I'd left, but before I got to the corner, I'd realized it was too cold for just my shawl so I came back to get my coat. The front door was unlocked, so I slipped inside. That's when I overheard them talking. Mrs Christopher was telling Mr Christopher that no matter what, they were to stay here until it was finished. I just assumed she was talking about the painters.'

'Why would they insist the staff leave because of the smell and then inflict it upon themselves?'

'Rich people do plenty of things that don't make sense,' Mrs Nimitz replied. 'I've been in service all my life and I've seen things in other houses that would drive a saint to drink. Frankly, I was so glad for a chance to have a few hours off my feet, all I could think of was getting out of here before they changed their minds and decided they needed someone to stay here and fetch and carry for them. Knowing Mrs Christopher as I do, she probably insisted they stay to make sure the painters did the job right. She's real particular and,' she tossed a quick glance at the door, 'not very trusting, if you know what I mean.'

'I'm not sure I do,' Witherspoon said. 'Do you mean she keeps a close eye on her staff?'

The housekeeper grinned. 'Not just her staff,

Inspector. She keeps a pretty good eye on her husband too, especially if that sister of hers comes to town.'

'Does she come very often?' Barnes asked.

'Not anymore. She used to come around a lot right after the old vicar went off to India. I know because every time she'd been here, Mr and Mrs Christopher would have a blazing row.'

'What about?' Witherspoon asked.

'About Miss Edith bein' in the house,' Mrs Nimitz replied. 'Mr Christopher kept insisting that her reputation was so awful he didn't want the neighbors seeing her come here to visit Mrs Christopher. Finally, Mrs Christopher must have had enough of his carping because the last few years she's always met her sister at a hotel.'

'Which hotel?' Barnes looked up from his notebook. 'The St John's on Teesdale Lane,' she replied. 'It's a small but very posh place. Miss Durant stays there when she's in town.'

Witherspoon was confused. 'I don't understand. You said Mrs Christopher kept a close eye on her husband when her sister was in town, yet you also said he doesn't want Miss Durant in the house? Could you explain that remark?'

Mrs Nimitz glanced at the door. 'Like a lot of men, he's a hypocrite. He's terrified the neighbors will get wind of Miss Edith and her wild ways, but at the same time, he's a yen for her himself if you know what I mean.' She leaned closer and lowered her voice. 'I heard that before he married Miss Hilda, Mr Christopher was madly in love with Miss Edith. It's not just gossip, either, because I've seen Mr Christopher at the

St John's with Edith Durant twice in the last year. Plus, a couple of times when Mrs Christopher was out of town visiting her mother's people, he'd bring Miss Durant here late at night.'

'How do you know he was with Miss Durant?' the inspector asked. 'I understand the women are identical in appearance.'

'They may be identical twins,' Mrs Nimitz replied. 'But you can tell them apart by the way they act and the way they dress. Believe me, I can tell Miss Durant from the mistress, that's for sure.'

'Quick, come inside.' Luty grabbed Josiah Williams's arm and dragged him through her front door. 'I don't want him to see us together.' She pushed him toward the drawing room and through the double oak doors. She shoved him quite hard. 'He's way too nosy and he'll want to know what you're doin' here.'

Josiah stumbled on an exquisite Persian carpet, righted himself and then staggered toward a cream-colored overstuffed chair. For a tiny elderly lady, she was very strong. 'Who don't you want to see us?'

'Hatchet,' Luty said grimly. She glanced up and down the hall and then drew the doors shut. 'I've got Jon on guard duty, but Hatchet's crafty, he could easily get past the boy.'

Faintly alarmed, Josiah leapt to his feet. 'Excuse me, madam, but are you frightened of your butler? Has he been threatening you?'

'Threatening me?' Luty repeated incredulously. She threw back her head and laughed. 'Of course not, he just asks a lot of questions. Now sit down and tell me what you found out. I hope you didn't go to much trouble.'

'It was actually quite easy. Uh, excuse me for asking ma'am, but you never mentioned why you needed this information.' He looked at her expectantly.

Luty had a story ready. 'Oh, let's just say that a long time ago, I knew the feller. He's a good man and he always dreamed of giving a big chunk of his fortune to those less fortunate than himself. Unfortunately, he's got a whole pack of relatives bending his ear about what's right and proper. I guess you could say that I want to know if he was able to leave any of his money to a particular charity that I know he supported. If he couldn't, then in his honor, I'll make the contribution for him.' She watched his face as she spoke, hoping to tell by his expression if he believed her. She knew he wouldn't actually challenge her on the matter. After all, she was an important client and paid a good part of his salary. But it would be nice to know that she could be convincing.

But Josiah Williams was too good a legal man to give anything away by so much as a twitch of his nose. 'I see. That's most generous of you, madam. But the fact is, Jasper Claypool's will hasn't changed in ten years. The only bequest he makes to charity is to a benevolence fund for retired clergymen. Was that by any chance the charity you thought he supported?'

'Nah,' she shook her head, 'I was thinkin' he'd leave a few pounds to the foundling home in Watford. But I guess he didn't. Well, Nellie's whiskers, the old fellow swore to me that he'd leave some money to them poor children.' She narrowed her eyes at Josiah. 'Are you sure about this?'

'Of course I'm sure,' he replied stiffly. 'The division of his estate hasn't changed in ten years, not since he left for India.'

'But that's about the time he swore he'd leave them young'uns some money,' Luty insisted. 'Right before he left, he told me he'd leave the bulk to his nieces and nephews but that he'd give a good ten percent to the Watford Foundling Home.'

'Apparently he wasn't entirely truthful to you,' Josiah retorted, 'because he left his estate to his nephews, not his nieces. One of them was specifically disinherited and the other was only left his collection of rare books.'

'And you're sure the will hasn't changed?' Luty pressed.

'Very sure,' Josiah said. 'I spoke to the clerk myself. No one at Claypool's law firm has seen or heard from him for ages. So if he was coming back to England to change his will, he didn't let his solicitors know and he'd not made any appointments to see them.'

The door opened and Hatchet stuck his head inside. He pretended to look surprised. 'Excuse me, madam, I didn't realize you were with your solicitor. May I remind you, madam, we are expected in Holland Park in half an hour. We really mustn't be late. I've taken the liberty of having the carriage brought around. I trust you'll be through with Mr Williams shortly.'

'Keep your collar on, Hatchet. I'll be ready to go by the time the carriage is here.'

'Thank you, madam.' Hatchet smiled politely and withdrew.

171

Luty snorted faintly and then turned back to her companion. Hatchet was already picking at her. That meant he might not have had much luck today either. 'I'm real grateful to you for getting me this information.'

'It was my pleasure, madam.' He rose to his feet. 'Would you like me to contact the Watford Foundling Home on your behalf?'

As Luty wasn't even sure such a place existed, she shook her head. 'That's all right, I'll take care of it myself.'

'It wouldn't be any trouble,' he persisted. 'I'd be happy to do it for you.'

'That's kind of you, but I'd prefer to handle it myself,' Luty couldn't swear to it, but it seemed his face twitched a bit, like he was trying not to laugh. 'But I'm much obliged for the offer.' She'd been going to ask him which niece had been disinherited, but she thought better of it. Besides, she was fairly sure she knew which one it was.

'Do let me know if I can be of further service.' He smiled broadly. 'Your inquiries are always so much more interesting than my usual work at the firm.'

Luty stared at him suspiciously. All her lawyers knew about her close association with the Witherspoon household. Her 'inquiries' had nothing to do with charity and everything to do with snooping for clues in the inspector's murder cases. She made a mental note never to ask her lawyers for help again. The old stodgy ones wouldn't give it and this one was too clever by half. 'Uh, thank you, I think. Uh, you won't get in trouble with the others for helping me, will you?'

'Not at all, ma'am. You're our best client and the truth is, they're all very fond of you. Now, if you'll excuse me, I'll be on my way.' He turned toward the door, and she started to get up. 'Don't bother to show me out,' he called over his shoulder. 'I know the way. Do have a nice time at the illustrious Inspector Witherspoon's household.'

Mrs Jeffries was the last one to arrive for their afternoon meeting. She dashed into the kitchen, taking off her hat as she walked. 'I'm terribly sorry to be late, but the train was held up just outside the station.'

'We only just got here ourselves,' Luty said.

'Wiggins has been tellin' us all about his visit to his relations,' Betsy added.

'And we're glad to 'ave 'im back,' Smythe interjected smoothly.

Mrs Jeffries gave them a grateful smile, approving of the way they were making Wiggins's return to the fold less awkward. 'Indeed, we told the lad we've been stretched thin on this case.' She took her seat at the head of the table and reached for the teapot.

'If no one has any objection,' Mrs Goodge said. 'I'd like to go first.' She paused a moment and then plunged ahead. 'I don't have much to report, but I did hear a bit of gossip this morning. I'm not even sure it has anything to do with our case, but it might. It seems that Horace Riley isn't overly fond of his half-brother, Eric. Supposedly, before Claypool went to India, Horace was trying to talk him into making sure that he had complete control of the factory. Seems he went out of his way to imply that young Eric was incompetent.

Apparently, the lad was quite wild in his youth and had a bit of a gambling problem.'

'You mean Horace Riley wanted his brother's share?' Wiggins asked. He looked disgusted.

'No, he couldn't get Eric's actual share of the property, it was left to him by their father. But as Claypool controlled both of the twins' share and owned half of the factory himself, he could easily have kept Eric Riley from having a position at the factory. That's really what Horace Riley wanted,' Mrs Goodge explained. 'The reverend didn't go along with it. He had very strict views on what was fair and what wasn't. He insisted that Eric be given a position in the family firm and allowed to work his way up. Another thing I heard was that Eric has proved to be far better at business than his half-brother.'

Mrs Jeffries thought for a moment. 'So Horace Riley approached his uncle before he went to India?'

'That's right,' the cook nodded eagerly. 'My source said they had words over it. Mind you, supposedly Horace was already upset with his uncle over the old man's refusal to let them sell off the cottages.'

'But wouldn't those houses be worthless?' Betsy asked. 'The ground is shifting. They're not safe to live in.'

'You can fix that,' Smythe said. 'There's no great caverns or anything like that under London, so it probably wouldn't be that big an engineering effort to find out what's causing the cottages to shift. Believe me, that's a big piece of property sitting there doin' nothin'. Considerin' the cost of land in London, there's plenty of developers that would go to the trouble and expense of making that patch of ground safe for something or other.'

'Why was Claypool so determined to hang on to them old houses?' Luty muttered.

'Maybe when we know the answer to that, we'll know who killed the poor old fella,' Wiggins replied sadly.

Mrs Jeffries glanced at the footman. He was staring morosely at the floor. Poor lad, she thought. He wasn't very happy. Well, he'd have to make peace with his decision one way or another. That wasn't a battle she or any of the others could help him with. 'Would you like to go next, Wiggins? That is, if Mrs Goodge is finished.'

'I'm done,' the cook assured them.

Wiggins took a deep breath. 'Well, uh, actually, I didn't find out much of anything. None of the shopkeepers could remember anything about any of the former tenants of Dorland Place, and the only other person I talked to was an elderly woman who couldn't remember what day it was, let alone anything that happened years ago.' He sighed. 'I'm sorry. I'm not bein' very helpful, am I.'

'Don't fret, lad,' Smythe said quickly. 'You've just got back. There's lots of times when we go out and find nothing.'

'You'll do better tomorrow,' Betsy insisted brightly. 'You just wait. Besides, you're not the only one who didn't have any luck today. I spent hours trying to make contact with Lilly Staggers, and she didn't so much as stick her nose out the door. But I'm not letting that stop me. I'm going right back out there tomorrow and trying again.' She turned her attention to the house-keeper. 'I also thought it would be a good idea if I went over to Eric Riley's neighborhood and see what I can learn about him. He's the one we know the least about, and he might have had a reason for wanting his uncle dead.'

'That's a good idea,' Mrs Jeffries replied. 'Smythe, did you have any luck today?'

'A bit,' he grinned. 'My source wasn't able to tell me where Jasper Claypool's luggage went; it seems to have disappeared into thin air. But I did have a bit of luck in another area. I got the names of a couple of people who were on the ship with Jasper Claypool.' He dug a piece of paper out of his pocket. 'There's a Mr Adam Spindler of number twelve Hobbs Lane in Chelmsford and a Miss Eudora Planter of Barslee Cottage in Richmond. We need to try to speak to either of these two right away. That's the only way we're goin' to find out why the vicar was returning to England unannounced.'

'But he wasn't unannounced,' Hatchet pointed out. 'According to what Lilly Staggers told Betsy, Eric Riley knew his uncle was in town. If he knew, maybe the others did as well.'

'I wasn't able to find out what was in that telegram the Rileys received on the day Claypool was killed,' Smythe said quickly. 'There were too many people hanging about the street when I nipped over there this morning. But I'll try again. Maybe *they* knew their uncle was coming to town too.'

'Let me have a go at finding out about that tele-gram,' Betsy insisted. 'Like I said, I'm going to talk to Lilly Staggers again, and if she doesn't know anything,

I'll try someone else at the Riley house. Surely someone snoops through the dustbin. And I'll try and find out if Lilly's been reporting to Eric Riley about her employers.'

'I'll see what I can learn about Eric's comings and goings on the day Claypool was killed,' Smythe volunteered.

'Excellent.' Then Mrs Jeffries said, 'Does anyone else have anything to report?'

'I've got a bit,' Luty tossed Hatchet a smug smile. He might have had a good idea, but she had some real information.

'I found out about Jasper Claypool's will. Feller hasn't changed it in ten years.' She gave them the rest of the details from her meeting with Josiah Williams. 'I know it's not much, but at least we know that he wasn't at his lawyer's changin' his will before he died.'

'That is useful to know,' Mrs Jeffries agreed. 'Do you think you can find out if he had contacted his solicitors? Perhaps he was killed to stop him going to see them.'

'My source had spoken to the clerk, and he claimed the firm hadn't heard from Claypool in ages. So that means if he was going to change his will, he hadn't mentioned it to his lawyers.' She shrugged. 'Anyways, that's it for me. Oh, wait a minute, I'm forgettin' something. I did find out something else. Seems that Horace Riley is in some fairly dire financial straits.'

'You mean the factory isn't doing well?' Betsy asked.

'The factory is doin' just fine. They've got more orders than they can fill, and as the general manager, Horace Riley makes a good salary,' Luty explained.

'But according to what I heard, his missus spends it faster than he can bring it in. They've got creditors hounding them all the time. One or two of 'em are threatening him with legal action.'

'So if his Uncle Jasper died and he inherited half of Claypool's estate,' Smythe murmured, 'that might help him out a bit.'

'More than a bit,' Luty replied. 'I'm still workin' on finding out how the Christophers are doin' financially. But I should have a report on them by tomorrow.'

'You've done very well, Luty,' Mrs Jeffries said. 'If everyone else is finished, I'll go next.' She paused for a moment and waited to see if anyone had additional information to contribute. But they were all looking at her expectantly. She told them about her visit to Finsbury Park and her meeting with the gardener at St Matthew's Church. 'I got the impression that Claypool wasn't just annoyed with his niece over how she lived, but over something specific in her life,' she concluded. 'It was really bad luck that the vicar choose that moment to interrupt us. We were having a very useful conversation. Of course, I've no idea if it has anything to do with our case.'

'So far we've no idea what has to do with our case,' Mrs Goodge muttered. 'But that's all by-the-by. From now on, I'm going to concentrate on learning what I can about the Christophers and the Rileys. At least they've got names and addresses.'

'And I'll have a go at finding out anything I can about the Christophers,' Wiggins added. 'Surely in a big house like theirs, someone will know something.'

'Perhaps I ought to try to learn what I can from the

178

other passengers,' Hatchet said. 'Perhaps one of them will know if Claypool cabled anyone from the ship. Perhaps that's how Eric Riley learned his uncle was coming home?'

'Can you go to Chelmsford and Richmond in the same day?' The housekeeper looked doubtful.

'I think I can do it,' he replied. 'There's an early train from Liverpool Street station. It should get me to Chelmsford by half past eight. If I can't get to Richmond by the afternoon, I can do it the following day. That'll be all right, won't it?'

'It should work very well. But do let us know if you need someone else to go see the lady in Richmond.' Mrs Jeffries smiled happily. This case was very confusing, but they weren't, as she'd feared, losing heart. 'And I'll have another go at Finsbury Park. I was going to speak to the people who live next door to the vicarage today, but I wasn't able to make contact with anyone. You'd think on a fine day someone would be outside, wouldn't you? Perhaps my luck will be better tomorrow. There's bound to be someone out and about. From what I heard from the St Matthew's gardener, family scandals for the Claypools and the Durants were common knowledge.'

Witherspoon was tired as a pup when he got home that evening. He was truly grateful that his housekeeper had a glass of sherry at the ready. 'This is heavenly.' He took a sip and sank back into the overstuffed chair. 'It's been quite a day, and I'm exhausted.'

'You look tired, sir.' Mrs Jeffries took her own chair. 'How is the case progressing, sir? Any new leads?'

The inspector sighed heavily. 'We did find out some new information. The trouble is, I'm not sure what it all means.'

'How so, sir?'

'We went to see Mr and Mrs Christopher again, and, well, I'm not certain, but it appears as if Mrs Christopher's twin sister, Edith Durant, might end up being our chief suspect.' He gave her all the details about their visit.

Mrs Jeffries listened carefully, occasionally nodding her head or asking a question. When he was finished, she said. 'So this Miss Durant is the only suspect you have so far that you know owns a weapon.'

'Correct, but that doesn't necessarily mean much. Just because the Christophers say they don't have a weapon doesn't make it true.'

'Did you speak to the staff, sir?'

'We did, but unfortunately,' he hesitated, 'I neglected to ask that question. Silly of me.'

'Not to worry, sir, you can always nip back in and have a word with the housekeeper tomorrow,' she smiled reassuringly. She knew how easily he lost confidence in his own abilities.

'I suppose I got a bit distracted by what the housekeeper told me,' he mused.

'And what was that, sir?'

He told her about the staff being given a surprise day out because of the painters, and then he told her about how the housekeeper was sure the Christophers were both lying. 'You see, they'd said they'd be leaving themselves, but then when she nipped back to get her coat, she overheard Mrs Christopher telling her husband they weren't going to leave. That they were going to stay no matter how long it took. That was rather peculiar, don't you think?'

'Indeed I do, sir.' Mrs Jeffries took a sip of her sherry.

'And then, of course, the woman went on to imply there was a bit of impropriety between Mr Carl Christopher and his sister-in-law.' He repeated to Mrs Jeffries exactly what the housekeeper had said. 'And of course, I was a bit confused, because according to Mrs Christopher, her sister wasn't even allowed in the house. You can see how very confusing it all is.'

'Indeed I can, sir.' Mrs Jeffries wasn't in the least confused, but then again, she had a much less innocent view of human nature than the inspector. She made a mental note to ask Betsy to find out what she could about a relationship between Carl Christopher and Edith Durant, 'But I'm sure you'll sort it out in the end. You always do. Is that it, sir or did you find out anything else?'

He drained the last of his sherry. 'We were able to track down one of the tenants from Dorland Place.' He told her about his visit to Mrs Mayberry and then rose to his feet. 'Now, of course, we've only her suspicion that the cottage was used for illicit purposes, but what I do find most odd is her assertion that the management of the factory knew about the situation and approved of it.' He started for the door.

She trailed after him. 'That should be an easy thing for you to confirm.' She and the others had already heard this gossip, she was glad that it had finally reached the inspector's ears.

He stopped and turned to her. 'Really? Do you think so?'

She realized he wasn't quite getting what she was saying. 'Of course, sir. All you have to do is find a few of the factory workers or office staff who were around ten years ago and ask them.'

'Do you think they'd know?' he asked curiously.

'I think there's a good possibility,' she replied. 'If the neighbors knew what was going on and that the company was looking the other way while it went on, then I think there's a good chance the staff knew about it as well.' She made a mental note to have Wiggins find out exactly who it was in the management who'd 'looked the other way', so to speak. It could only have been Horace, or perhaps Eric Riley.

He thought about it for a moment and then continued walking toward the dining room. 'I'll add that to my list of inquiries we need to make tomorrow.'

They spotted Betsy coming down the hall carrying the inspector's dinner tray. 'Good evening, sir. I hope you're hungry. Mrs Goodge has outdone herself tonight.' She smiled brightly and went into the dining room.

'It smells wonderful.' Witherspoon hurried after her. 'What have we got?'

Betsy put the tray down and lifted the cover off the dinner plate. 'Roast chicken, roast potatoes and carrots with butter sauce.'

'Excellent.' He took his seat and picked up his serviette. 'I must admit I'm very hungry.'

'Good, sir. There's a lovely rice pudding for dessert.' Betsy picked up the tray and started to leave.

'Oh, I forgot, sir. Wiggins is back,' Mrs Jeffries said quickly. From the corner of her eye, she saw the girl pause for an instant and then carry on.

'Did his grandfather get better?' Witherspoon speared a bite of chicken.

'Not really, sir,' Mrs Jeffries said. She wondered just how much about Wiggins's trip she ought to reveal. 'But he felt it best to come home. The old gentleman wasn't getting any worse, and he felt his presence was a bit disruptive for the household.'

Witherspoon nodded in understanding. 'Do tell the lad that if he needs to go back, it'll be quite all right. I suppose Fred will move back in with Wiggins for a while now.'

The dog was supposed to sleep on his rug in the kitchen. But everyone knew he slipped up to Wiggins's room as soon as the lights were out.

'Has he been sleeping in your room, sir?'

'Only since the lad's been gone,' Witherspoon said quickly. 'He came up that first night and scratched on my door. I didn't have the heart to send him back downstairs.'

'Yes, sir, well, we'll make sure your rug gets a good brushing, then.' She gave him a polite smile.

'Yes, and perhaps the bedspread as well.' He smiled sheepishly. 'He got up on the bed a time or two.'

Mrs Jeffries was fairly certain the hound had slept on the inspector's bed every night. 'I'll see to it, sir. Now, do you need anything from the kitchen?'

'No, I've got my dinner and my evening paper. I'll be fine.'

'I'll be up with your dessert in a few minutes, sir,'

she said as she withdrew. She hurried down the back stairs and into the warm kitchen. The others were all there. Betsy and Mrs Goodge were tidying up, Wiggins, with Fred dodging his heels, was pushing the huge wicker laundry basket out into the back hall, and Smythe was at the far end of the table oiling a door hinge.

'Everyone, come quick, 1 want to give you a report on what I've learned from the inspector.'

As soon as they were seated, she told them what the inspector had found out that day. 'So you see,' she finished, 'I think we'll have to do a bit more tomorrow than we'd planned. Smythe, do you think you can find the painters that were at the Christopher house?'

'The Christophers probably used one of the local commercial firms,' he said. 'I'm sure I can track it down. You want me to find out if Claypool was there that day.'

'Yes, and anything else that might be important.' She turned to Wiggins. 'You can get over to the factory and try to find out who in management told the neighbors to mind their own business.'

'You mean who was coverin' up for the dalliance?' A faint blush climbed his round cheeks. 'I'll see what I can suss out.'

'I can try and track down the gossip about Mr Christopher and his sister-in-law,' Betsy said. 'I should have plenty of time. Even if I can meet Lilly Staggers, what she has to say shouldn't take too long.'

'And she might be a good source of information about Carl Christopher and Edith,' Smythe added. 'You never know how far the gossip had spread.'

'I don't believe I'll be going to Finsbury Park after all,' Mrs Jeffries said. 'I think it would be best if I had a word with someone at the St John's Hotel. I want to find out just how often Edith Durant stays there and, more importantly, was she there on the day her uncle was murdered.' She looked at Wiggins. 'Before you go to Bermondsey, can you stop by Luty's? I think she'll need to use her international resources to find out if Edith Durant really has rooms at the Metropole Hotel in Paris.'

'Why is that important?' Betsy asked.

Mrs Jeffries couldn't say, hut something about the twins was nagging at the back of her mind. 'I'm not sure. But I think as Edith Durant is the only suspect who supposedly owns a weapon, we ought to find out everything we can about her.'

Betsy nodded. 'Should I find out if anyone at the Riley household owns a gun?'

'Yes, please,' the housekeeper replied.

'And what should I do?' Mrs Goodge demanded. Though they knew she wasn't going to leave the kitchen, she still didn't want to be left out.

Mrs Jeffries had a task for her at the ready. 'I want you to find out exactly when Hilda and Carl Christopher were married.'

CHAPTER NINE

Constable Barnes got down from the hansom carefully. His knee was giving him trouble today, but he was in far too good a mood to be bothered by something as petty as pain. On Mrs Jeffries's advice the day before, he'd sent some lads to question the local hansom cab drivers, and this morning, he'd gotten their reports. He was annoyed with himself, and if the truth be told, with the inspector as well, because neither of them had thought to do it earlier. It was shoddy police work, and he'd not make that mistake in the future. But at least now this case might start moving in the right direction. 'Do you want me to ask permission from either of the Mr Rileys before I start questioning the staff, sir?'

Witherspoon drew his coat tighter against the chill. 'No. Go on to the factory floor and speak to the foreman. Tell him we're making routine inquiries. If he is uncooperative, come back to the office and I'll ask one of the Mr Rileys to intervene.'

They started across the cobblestones toward the main entrance. 'Do you think either of them will tell us who was using the cottage, sir?' Barnes pulled the wrought iron gate open and they stepped inside.

'I don't know.' Witherspoon shrugged. 'But we must ask. We've got to find out. If the management knew what it was being used for and looked the other way, it means one of them must know who was using it.'

'They were protecting someone,' Barnes said softly, 'and knowing human nature as I do, I suspect someone around here must have a good idea who it was.'

When they stepped inside the front entrance, they went their separate ways. Witherspoon went down the hall to the executive offices, and Barnes went to see the factory foreman.

Witherspoon stuck his head inside the office and smiled at the two clerks. 'Excuse me, but is Mr Eric Riley available?' he asked the man closest to the door.

The clerk blinked in surprise. 'Mr Riley's out on the factory floor making his morning rounds, but he ought to be back soon.'

'Do you know if Mr Horace Riley is in yet?' Witherspoon asked.

'Yes, sir, he got in a few minutes ago.' The clerk rose to his feet. 'If you'll come this way, sir.'

Witherspoon followed the man to the office at the far end of the room and waited while the lad announced him. 'I'm sorry to barge in like this,' he said as he entered Horace Riley's office, 'but I've a few more questions for you.'

Horace had partially risen from his desk. 'Yes, uh, what is it?' He waved at an empty chair.

'This won't take long, sir,' the inspector said as he sat down. 'But I'd like to know if you own a weapon.'

'A weapon?' Horace repeated the word like he'd never heard it before. 'You mean like a sword or a gun?'

'We're actually more interested in whether or not you own a gun, and if so, what kind?'

His mouth opened in surprise. 'Of course I don't own a gun. Why would I? London is hardly the wild west.'

'You do realize, sir, that I'll be asking your servants this question.'

'Now see here, exactly what are you implying? I don't make it a habit to lie, Inspector.'

'I wasn't suggesting you did, sir,' Witherspoon replied. Though, of course, that was exactly what he'd done. 'However, it's sometimes possible that one forgets exactly what one does own. You have a very big house, sir. Are you sure that there isn't an old revolver or derringer tucked away somewhere?'

'Of course there isn't.' Horace's face flushed red. 'Well, at least, I don't think we've a gun. I don't recall ever buying one. But as you said, Inspector, it's a big house. It belonged to my wife's family. But I assure you, neither of us killed my uncle.'

'Where were you on the afternoon your uncle was killed?' Witherspoon asked.

'As I told you before, I was right here,' he shot back. 'You can ask my clerks.'

As he'd probably threatened the clerks with immediate dismissal if they said differently, the inspector didn't think they were a particularly good source for an alibi. 'Mr Riley, this morning we found out you left the office early on the afternoon the Reverend Claypool was murdered. Why did you think it necessary to lie to us? Why not tell us you'd left?'

Horace hesitated and then glanced toward the door. 'The truth is, I didn't want Eric to know I'd been gone,' he replied. 'I went home because I had a dreadful headache and I didn't want Eric to find out. He'll do anything to get control of this factory, and I didn't want him writing to Uncle Jasper with tales of my being ill all the time.'

Witherspoon looked over his shoulder at the open office door. You could see straight through to Eric Riley's office. 'Wouldn't he notice you weren't here?'

'Not if my door was closed,' Horace smiled slyly. 'I often close it when I don't want to be disturbed. All right, Inspector, I'll admit I should have told you the truth. But I had nothing to do with my uncle's death, and it was only a small lie . . .'

'Small lie,' Witherspoon interrupted. 'Excuse me, sir. But we're investigating a murder. There's no such thing as a small lie under those circumstances. Now, tell me the truth. I want to know exactly what time you left and exactly where you went. Please don't lie to me anymore. We know you took a cab that day to a street off the Lambeth Palace Road.'

Outside in the factory, Constable Barnes wasn't having much luck. 'I just need a list of people who worked here ten years ago,' he explained to the foreman. 'I'll not take up much of their time or keep them from their work.'

They were inside the foreman's office. The place was tiny with only a small table and a couple of rickety chairs. The walls were made of bare wood, most of which was streaked in small lines with paint of different colors. The floor was coated with what smelled like creosote, and the one tiny window was grimy with dirt. Empty paint tins were stacked waist-high in one corner, and in the opposite corner there was a peculiar-looking machine with nasty-looking hooks dangling from the edges.

Barnes and the foreman, a portly man with a florid complexion, black hair and truly awesome, bushy eyebrows, were standing opposite each other across the table.

The foreman's eyebrows drew together. 'Well, I suppose old Markle might be worth talking to. He's been here since the place opened.'

'Is he the only one?' Barnes asked incredulously.

'Oh no, we've a lot who've been here ten years or more,' the foreman replied. 'But they work the line and I can't pull 'em off. We'd have to stop the line, and I can't have that.'

Barnes sighed deeply. He could threaten the fellow or he could try to find a way around this problem. He decided to find a way around it. You generally got more information out of people when you didn't push them around as if they were nothing. 'How long have you been here, sir?'

The foreman's eyebrows shot straight up in surprise. 'Me? Oh, let's see now, it's been a good fifteen years since I came on.'

'Then can I ask you a few questions?' Barnes asked patiently.

'Me?' The foreman grinned. 'I suppose it'd be all right.' He nodded toward the rickety chair as he pulled out his own chair and sat down. 'Have a seat then, guv, and ask me anything you like.'

Hatchet opened the door of the first-class compartment and stepped on to the platform. Immediately, he turned and helped Luty out. 'I don't know why you felt it necessary to come along,' he said petulantly. 'I'm quite certain I can get Mr Spindler to speak to me,'

Luty snorted. 'If Spindler was ridin' first class from India to here, he's probably as toff-nosed as you are. He'd come closer to talkin' to me than you.' In truth, she'd tagged along because she couldn't think of anything else to do to help the case. Wiggins had come along early that morning and asked her to find out about Edith Durant's hotel room in Paris, but that hadn't taken long to do, just a couple of minutes to write out a telegram to a friend of hers at the Bank of Paris.

Hatchet shrugged. 'Much as I am loath to admit it, you do have a point. Besides, the story you've come up with is far better than the one I was going to use. Come along, then, madam. I believe there's a hansom stand just outside the station. If we're in luck, we'll soon have our answers.'

A few minutes later, they were in a cab and heading toward number twelve Hobbs Lane. Hatchet glanced at the fur muff in her lap. 'You didn't bring your gun, did you?'

Luty was very fond of her Colt .45. 'With a nervous nellie like you ridin' with me, of course not.'

'I am not a nervous nellie,' he protested. He often carried a small revolver of his own, especially when they were coming toward the end of a case. 'It's simply that you've no need of a weapon here. This isn't Colorado or San Francisco, where, I believe, one can have a gun pointed at one for no reason whatsoever excepting that someone doesn't like one's expression.'

'Fiddle-faddle.' Luty waved her arm dismissively. 'You're exaggeratin'. Anyways, I don't have my peacemaker so you can quit worryin'.' But she made a mental note to tuck it in her muff in the event things began to happen.

They argued amiably until the hansom pulled up in front of number twelve. Hatchet instructed the driver to wait and then helped Luty out onto the grass verge.

They stood in front of a huge, orange-red brick house with black trim around the roof and windows. The grounds were well-tended with an expansive lawn extending from the front to both the sides. Around the edges, a few tiny daffodils and shoots from bulbs burst out of the neatly dug flower beds.

'This ain't a poor man's house, that's for sure,' Luty muttered. 'Come on, let's get this show on the road.' She grabbed Hatchet's arm and practically dragged him up the stone walkway to the front stairs.

'Really, madam, do be careful, this is a new suit,' he protested when she gave his sleeve another yank.

'Sorry,' she said. They'd reached the front door. Hatchet reached for the ring-shaped brass knocker, lifted it and let it fall. A few moments later, a woman dressed in housekeepers' black opened the front door and stared out at them. 'Yes, may I help you?'

'Is this the residence of Mr Adam Spindler?' Hatchet asked.

'It is,' she replied.

'May we see him, please,' Luty asked meekly. She reached up and adjusted the veil of her sapphire-blue hat, holding her hand in such a way that the house-keeper couldn't fail to notice the diamond rings on her fingers. Luty didn't often flaunt her wealth, but she'd observed that people were far more likely to confide in you if they thought you were from the same class as themselves. She'd made it a habit to dress plainly when she was snooping amongst working people and to dress fancy when it was the upper crust. 'It's very important. I'm hoping he can help me find my long-lost brother.'

The housekeeper looked them up and down, assessing their wealth, background and probable class by the cut of their clothes and the size of their jewels. 'If you could give me your names, I'll see if Mr Spindler is receiving. He only arrived home late last night. Please step inside.'

'I'm Edward Hadleigh-Jones,' Hatchet whipped off his top hat as he entered the foyer. 'And this is my American cousin, Anna Hadleigh.'

The woman acknowledged the names by the slight inclination of her head, then she turned and went past the staircase down the hall.

The housekeeper returned a few moments later and led them into a sitting room. An elderly gentleman with wispy white hair rose from the settee. He smiled as they entered the room. 'Good day, madam, sir, I understand from my housekeeper that you're seeking my assistance?' His expression was curious.

Luty charged toward him with her hand extended. 'I'm Anna Hadleigh,' she introduced herself, 'and this is my cousin,' she gestured at Hatchet.

'Edward Hadleigh-Jones,' Hatchet said quickly as he extended his own hand.

'Adam Spindler.' The gentlemen shook with both of them and then turned his attention back to Luty. 'Do sit down, please.' He gestured toward the coral-colored settee. 'How may I be of assistance? My housekeeper mentioned a long-lost brother.'

They settled themselves into seats and Luty folded her hands demurely in her lap. 'Well, I know this is going to sound strange, but years ago, my younger brother ran off to India to do missionary work.' She sighed theatrically. 'Now understand, when he left England . . .'

'Excuse me, ma'am,' Spindler interrupted, 'but your accent doesn't sound very English.'

'I moved to America as a small child,' she replied quickly, 'and the longer you stay there, the more you sound like them. I only came back a few days ago. I'd gotten word from my cousin, here,' she jerked her head toward Hatchet, 'that Oliver might be coming back to England from India.'

'I see,' he nodded in understanding. 'Please go on with your narrative.'

'Like I was sayin', when my brother left here, he was a good Presbyterian. But for some reason, once he got out to India, he converted to the Anglican faith and joined that church. Well, my father was furious, and a number of letters were exchanged between the two of them. By then, we'd moved to Colorado, and Papa was first deacon at the Pueblo Presbyterian Church. Anyways, Papa finally got so angry he disowned Oliver and refused to allow Momma or any of us to get in contact with him.'

'How very sad. Exactly when did this happen?' Spindler asked.

'Oh, it was years ago, back when I was a girl.' Luty lifted her white lace handkerchief and dabbed at her eyes. 'You know what happens then, the years pass and we get on with our lives.' She sighed. 'But finally, I realized that I had to find my baby brother. That's where you come in. I understand you recently came back to England from India and that onboard that ship was a clergyman?'

'That's true.' Spindler cocked his head to one side and smiled slightly. 'But his name wasn't Oliver.'

'My brother's full name was Jasper Oliver,' she said quickly. 'And we think he might have been using my mother's maiden name because he got so angry at our Papa.'

Spindler nodded. 'Let me see if I understand you correctly. Your father disowned your brother because he became a member of the Church of England?'

'That's right,' Luty replied.

'And you think I might be able to help track this person down, is that correct?'

Luty had a sinking feeling in her stomach. By now, Spindler should have been so moved by her tale that he was spilling his guts about being on the same ship as Jasper Claypool. 'Uh, yes, that's right. We have it on reliable authority that a clergyman came in on a ship from India this past Monday. But as the poor fellow's disappeared, we were hoping you could help us.'

'We think this man might know where my cousin's brother lives in India,' Hatchet added. He didn't dare look at Luty. He'd suddenly realized there were a number of inconsistencies in their story and was doing the best he could to recover. 'You see, her dear brother retired in India and doesn't seem to have given anyone his address. We're hoping this other English clergyman might know where he lives.' He laughed confidentially. 'I imagine the English religious community is actually quite small, don't you?' He could feel Luty's eyes on him and knew she wasn't pleased.

'Yes,' Spindler said slowly. 'I imagine it is.'

'Well, do you think you could help us?' Luty asked. 'Did you talk to this here English preacher while you were on the ship together? Do you have any idea where I could find him?'

'The only place you'll find this poor man is at the cemetery,' Spindler replied sadly. 'He was murdered soon after he arrived in London. It was in the newspapers. Frankly, madam, I don't wish to be rude, but your tale is a complete fabrication that only a moron or an innocent would believe.'

Luty tried to look outraged, failed miserably and finally said, 'It was pretty bad, wasn't it?'

'It was absurd,' Spindler replied. 'To begin with, if he were your younger brother, then by the timeline you gave me and you'd moved to America when you were a small child, your brother must have gone to India as no more than a newborn. As mighty as our Lord is, he rarely sends babies out to make converts of all nations. Furthermore, for a Presbyterian to disown someone for becoming a member of the Church of England is ridiculous.'

'I told you to be an Anabaptist,' Hatchet hissed at her.

'You never said any such thing,' Luty shot back. 'You admitted my story was better than yours.'

'Only because mine was pathetic.'

'Excuse me,' Spindler interrupted, 'but would you mind telling me why you're here?' He no longer looked angry, merely curious and a bit sad.

Luty looked at Hatchet. He shrugged. 'We might as well tell him the truth. We're here to find out if you spoke to Jasper Claypool on the voyage out from India.'

'I spoke to him many times. As a matter of fact, he and I were very good friends in India. I was the one who encouraged him to come home.' Spindler's eyes filled with tears. 'I wish I hadn't, now. If he'd stayed in India, he wouldn't be dead.'

'I'm dreadfully sorry,' Hatchet said sincerely. 'You were obviously very good friends.'

'We were indeed.' Spindler turned away and looked out the window at the gray day.

'We're sorry he's dead too,' Luty said, 'and we aim to help find his killer.'

He jerked his head back and stared at Luty. 'Isn't that a task for the police?'

'Absolutely,' she replied. 'But sometimes they need a little help. Look, I'm goin' to tell you the truth now. I'm Luty Belle Crookshank and this here's Hatchet. He works for me.'

'I take it you weren't born in England?' Spindler queried with a smile.

'No, but my late husband was. Now I ain't goin' to waste your time with any more foolishness. But we're tryin' to help find out who killed the poor Reverend Claypool. Whatever information we get will make its way to Inspector Witherspoon, the policeman in charge of the case. You've got my word on that. I keep my word; you can check my references.' She rattled off an impressive list of London's best-known politicians, churchmen and financiers. She would have given him even more names, but he held up his hand.

'I believe you, Mrs Crookshank.' He got up and went to the bell-pull by the door. As a matter of fact, I was going to go to the police today and have a word with them. I'm fairly certain my information will be quite useful.'

Luty and Hatchet exchanged glances.

'If you don't mind my asking, sir,' Hatchet asked, 'What's taken you so long? Reverend Claypool has been dead for a good few days.'

'I didn't know he'd been murdered until late last night. My housekeeper told me when I arrived home. I was out of the country on an errand for Jasper.' Spindler sighed heavily. 'Let me ring for tea and we can discuss this matter like civilized people.'

'Thank you, sir,' Hatchet said softly. 'I do apologize for entering your home under false pretenses. But I assure you, we had the best of motives for our actions.'

'I'm sorry too,' Luty added. 'We shouldn't have lied to you.' She ignored the fact that they frequently lied to people when they were obtaining information.

'Oh, that's quite all right, ma'am. Sometimes the truth can be frightfully inconvenient.'

Betsy walked slowly past the Horace Riley house and tried to appear inconspicuous. But this was her third time down Canfield Lane, and if someone didn't come out soon, she'd have to move along. She got to the corner and crossed the street. Glancing over her shoulder, she saw a young woman coming out of the house from the side servant's entry. The girl stopped and fiddled with the neck of her brown jacket. She wasn't wearing a maid's cap, so Betsy thought it might be the girl's day out. The girl turned and headed off in the opposite direction from where Betsy stood.

Betsy was after her like a shot. She followed her for a long way, dodging in and out of traffic and trying to keep her in sight without being spotted. The girl turned into the railway station at Finchley, and Betsy ran to catch up with her.

She was lucky, the girl hadn't bought her ticket yet. She got in line right behind her and when she went up to the ticket agent, Betsy cocked her head and listened hard.

'Amersham, please, second-class return.' She handed over her money.

Betsy dug coins out of her pocket and saw that she had plenty enough for a ticket. When she reached the ticket clerk, she bought the same as her quarry. She raced on to the platform just in time to see the girl slip into a compartment at the far end of the train. Betsy managed to slip inside just as the conductor blew his whistle, and the train began to move.

'Thank goodness.' She smiled broadly as she sat down, 'I thought I was going to miss the train.'

The girl was in a seat by the window. She smiled timidly as Betsy flopped down next to her. 'You don't mind, do you?' she said brightly. 'I hate traveling on my own.'

'I don't mind,' the girl replied. 'But I'm not going far, just to Amersham.' She was a small young woman, very thin, with a long bony face, dark brown hair and deep-set hazel eyes.

'That's where I'm going.' Betsy grinned. 'Do you live there?'

'Wish I did.' She shook her head. 'I'm going to see my auntie, she works there. It's my day out. My name's Carrie Parker, what's yours?'

'Oh, I'm Betsy. Betsy Smith,' she lied. 'It's my day out as well. I'm going to visit a friend. Do you work for a nice household?' The use of the term, 'day out' identified both of them as servants.

'Not really,' she frowned. 'Mrs Riley generally only gives us an afternoon out once a week, but she told me I could go early today.'

'That was very kind of her,' Betsy said brightly.

The girl turned her head and stared out the window. Betsy noticed her hands were clenched so tightly together her knuckles were turning white.

'Are you all right?' she asked softly.

The girl jerked her head around and stared at Betsy. 'I'm fine.'

'I'm sorry, I didn't mean to be a nosy parker.' She smiled kindly and looked pointedly at Carrie's clenched hands. 'You just looked a bit nervous, that's all.'

Carrie looked down at her hands and slowly pulled her fingers apart. 'You're trying to be kind and I'm being nasty. I'm sorry. It's just that I am nervous and I've no idea what I ought to do.'

'About what?'

Carrie took a deep breath. 'Mrs Staggers, that's the

housekeeper, says she thinks Mrs Riley wants me gone all day in case the police come around.'

'Police?' Betsy repeated. 'Why would the police be coming around?'

Carrie shrugged. 'Some old uncle of Mr Riley's got himself killed Monday last.'

'How dreadful.' Betsy pretended shock. 'And your mistress doesn't want you talking to the police about it, is that it?'

'That's what Mrs Staggers says.' Carrie bit her lip. 'But honestly, I don't know what I could tell them.'

Betsy wasn't sure what to ask next, so she decided to plunge straight ahead. 'If you think you were given the morning off to get you out of the way, then you must know something.'

'Not really,' Carrie countered. 'Leastways I don't think I do. I didn't do nothin', you know. But Mrs Staggers and Mrs Riley, they saw me readin' that telegram before I burnt it, and Mrs Staggers says it's important and that Mrs Riley don't want me sayin' anything about it to the police.' She bit her lip and looked out the window again. 'I'm confused. That's why I'm going to see my auntie. Maybe she can tell me what to do. I don't want to lose my position. I'm not really very well trained, you know. Finding something else would be hard. But if the police ask me, I've got to tell them what I read. I don't want to go to jail, and that's where you go if you lie to police.'

'You're not going to go to jail.' Betsy could tell the girl was genuinely frightened. She reached over and touched her hand.

'How do you know?'

'Because I work for a policeman,' Betsy replied. 'He's ever so nice. He'll not let anyone put you in jail or hurt you.'

'I'm not scared of Mrs Riley hurtin' me,' Carrie cried, 'I'm scared of bein' on the streets. I've been there before, you see. It's horrible not to have a roof over your head.'

'I know exactly what it's like,' Betsy said firmly. She took both Carrie's hands in hers. 'I've been in that situation myself. But if murder's been done, you must tell what you know.'

The train was pulling into Edgeware Station. There wasn't much time left. Betsy had to get the girl's confidence before they got to Willesden Junction. They could change trains there for a train to Uxbridge Road. From there, they could walk to Upper Edmonton Gardens and the Ladbroke Grove Police Station. One thing was for certain – she didn't want to end up all the way out in Amersham with important information that might help solve the case.

'But that's just it,' Carrie cried, 'the telegram wasn't important.'

'Wasn't it from the murdered uncle?' Betsy charged. She forced herself to lower her voice. Shouting at the girl wasn't going to inspire much confidence.

'No, it was from Mr Riley, and all it said was that Mrs Riley was to hurry and meet him at the Bishops Head Restaurant by half past one. That's all. It didn't say a word about his soddin' old uncle.'

Mrs Jeffries smiled at the man behind the desk. 'I'm sorry, would you mind checking again? I'm sure my niece told me she was staying here. She always stays here.'

He sighed heavily and gave the open ledger page a cursory glance. 'I assure you madam, we all know Miss Durant quite well. She isn't here.'

'Did she go back to Paris?' Mrs Jeffries pressed. She wasn't certain what she hoped to find out, but she was finding out a few bits and pieces.

The desk clerk, a morose-looking man with an overly large mustache, shook his bald head. 'I'm afraid Miss Durant didn't disclose her plans when she was last here. Now if you'll excuse me . . .'

'That's nonsense. Surely she left an address so her mail could be forwarded.'

He glared at her. 'I assure you, ma'am, any mail that comes for Miss Durant is sent to a local address . . .'

'A local address,' Mrs Jeffries pretended outrage. 'Why haven't you given it to me? I must find my niece.'

'Madam, we're not in the habit of disclosing our clients' personal information.'

'But I'm a relation and I've something very important to tell her.'

'It's out of the question, madam.' He turned his attention to a man who'd just come up to the desk. 'Yes, sir, may I help you?'

Mrs Jeffries couldn't press any further. She couldn't risk any more of a scene than she'd already created. But she wanted that address. Where was Edith Durant's mail being sent? Find that address and she was one step closer to finding something useful about this case.

She walked out of the small but elegant lobby and turned the corner onto Ordnance Road. The traffic was heavy, and there were plenty of hansoms going past. But she decided to take the train. It was too late to get to Finsbury Park and back by teatime, so she might as well take a train home instead of a hansom or an omnibus. She had plenty of time. She went past the St John's Wood Barracks to Queens Road, thinking about the case as she walked.

On the one hand, things were beginning to move quickly, while on the other, she'd no idea if they were moving in the right direction. Eric Riley was the only one who supposedly knew his uncle was back in London, but she wasn't sure that was really true. There was some evidence that the others might have been aware of that fact as well. The Christophers had certainly behaved strangely that day, as had both Mr and Mrs Riley. But she needed proof that they knew, not just gossip that both households had been acting oddly.

She dodged around a vendor pushing a water cart. There were still so many other questions to be answered. Why had Jasper Claypool decided to come back to England at this particular time, especially as they knew he'd planned on retiring in India? Yet something had made him come back. What could it be? And where was his luggage?

By the time she reached the Marlborough Road Station, the only conclusion she'd come to was that she'd used the wrong approach at the hotel. Pretending to be Edith Durant's relative hadn't gotten her anywhere at all. She should have found a maid or a clerk and bribed them for information about the woman. Money always worked.

★ ★ ★

For once, everyone arrived for their afternoon meeting on time. 'I hope the rest of you have had better luck than I have,' Mrs Jeffries announced as she sat down. 'The only thing I learned is that Edith Durant's mail is sent to a local address when she's not at the St John's Hotel.'

'Which local address?' Mrs Goodge asked.

'There's the rub,' Mrs Jeffries sighed. 'I wasn't able to find out. As I said, it hasn't been a very useful day for me. Now, who would like to go first?'

'Mine shouldn't take long,' the cook said casually. But no one was fooled by her tone. 'I found out when Hilda and Carl Christopher were married: it was about a year before Jasper Claypool went to India. They were married in Claypool's old parish up at Finsbury Park. I found out something else, too,' she grinned. 'According-ing to the gossip, Carl was going to marry Edith until her sister Hilda inherited all their father's money.'

'He didn't have any money of his own?' Betsy asked.

Mrs Goodge shook her head. 'Not a cent. He's got good looks and aristocratic ancestors and that's about it. I don't think he expected that Edith would be vir-tually disinherited and that Hilda, the boring sister, would get it all.'

'Why would Hilda want to marry him?' Wiggins asked. 'If she and Edith Durant were identical, why didn't she get her own feller?'

'Apparently the sisters had a long history of coveting what one another had,' Mrs Goodge replied. 'Unlike most twins, these girls weren't best friends. If Edith had something, Hilda wanted it, and if Hilda had it, then Edith couldn't rest till it was hers. Supposedly,

Edith was the worst of the two. She was supposedly as bold as brass and always had been. Never afraid to try anything and always one step ahead of trouble, that's the gossip about Edith. Hilda was the quieter of the two. But despite their differences, they do try to see one another. Edith used to come visit Hilda quite a bit up until the last few years. Now she spends most of her time out of the country. Leastways, that's what the gossip says. That's all I found out.'

'You found out a lot more than me,' Wiggins announced glumly. 'I spent two hours tryin' to find someone from Eric Riley's house to talk to and I didn't 'ave any luck at all. His landlady was makin' the staff 'ave a spring clean. They went in and out, fetchin' and carryin' and bangin' on carpets, but every time I tried to get close enough to speak to one of the housemaids, the landlady would pop her head out and ruin it. You'd have thought with all them open windows and doors I'd 'a found out somethin'.'

'It happens that way sometimes,' Smythe told him. 'Don't take it so 'ard. You'll 'ave better luck tomorrow. I found out a bit today. I tracked down one of the painters who were at the Christophers' house on the day Claypool died. The other painter is doin' a job near Epping and I'm going to talk to him tomorrow. But the one I spoke to today told me that Mr and Mrs Christopher were both at the house all day.'

'What time did he leave that day?' Mrs Jeffries asked.

'They had the job done by four-thirty,' Smythe replied. 'But with cleanup and all, they didn't leave until a quarter to five that evening.'

'Then why did the Christophers let on to Mrs

Nimitz that they were going to Brighton for the day?' Luty demanded. 'That don't make sense.'

'Nothing about this case makes much sense,' Wiggins complained. 'I can't make hide nor hair of anything.'

'Perhaps they pretended they planned on leaving and then changed their minds?' Betsy suggested. 'People do change their minds.'

'Perhaps,' Mrs Jeffries grew thoughtful. 'Or maybe they received a telegram or a message that morning, something that made them change their minds?'

'I'll have a go at finding that out tomorrow,' Wiggins offered. 'I can check at the local telegraph exchange.'

'The painter didn't say anything about them receiving anything,' Smythe said. 'But he was down in the kitchen. I think the other one was doin' the back hall and the stairs. Tomorrow I'll ask his mate if he saw any messengers. That's it for me.'

'I found something out,' Betsy said. She told them about her meeting with Carrie Parker.

'And all the telegram said was for Mrs Riley to meet him at a restaurant?' Mrs Jeffries clarified.

Betsy nodded. 'That's right, and she'd no idea why it was important, but Lilly Staggers was sure it had something to do with Claypool's murder.'

'And supposedly, that's why Mrs Riley gave the girl the day out, to make sure she wasn't there if the police came back?' Hatchet asked.

'Yes, but Mrs Riley is in for a disappointment. I talked Carrie into coming back here and popping into the Ladbroke Grove Police Station. She's going to tell Inspector Witherspoon what she knows.'

'She know anything about whether or not Lilly

Staggers is working for Eric Riley?' the cook asked as she poured herself more tea.

'Carrie doesn't know anything about that,' Betsy admitted. 'But she did tell me that tomorrow morning, Lilly Staggers is to do the household shopping. I'm going to try and talk to her then.'

'Does the girl know if anyone in the house has a gun?' Mrs Jeffries asked. 'Or did you think to ask?'

'I asked,' Betsy said proudly. 'But she didn't know. She's not been at the house very long. That's all I found out.'

'You learned quite a lot, Betsy,' Mrs Jeffries replied. She was a firm believer in telling people when they'd done a good job. She smiled at them. 'All of you have.'

'We've got something to say,' Luty said. 'We found out where Jasper Claypool's luggage went.'

'Where?' Smythe asked eagerly.

'Adam Spindler's,' Hatchet said solemnly. 'Not only did Claypool's luggage go there, but apparently that's where Claypool was going to stay while he was in England.'

CHAPTER TEN

'Gracious, you did find out quite a bit,' Mrs Jeffries exclaimed.

'Wait till you hear,' Luty said excitedly. 'Claypool was goin' to stay with Adam Spindler and not one of his relatives.'

'Spindler was one of the people on the ship with Claypool, right?' Mrs Goodge asked. Sometimes she had a bit of trouble keeping everyone straight in her head.

'That's right.' Luty nodded. 'But that ain't the half of it. He and Claypool knew each other in India, he's the reason that Claypool came back when he did. Course he feels real bad about it, seeing as poor old Jasper ended up with a bullet in his head.'

'Really, madam,' Hatchet chided. 'Let's have a bit of respect here. Poor Mr Spindler is utterly devastated . . .'

'I didn't say he wasn't,' Luty defended herself. 'Oh, let's not pick at each other, let's just tell 'em what we found out. Go on, you take it from here. I don't want you claimin' I hogged the whole story for myself.'

'If you insist, madam,' he replied. He put down his teacup. 'As Madam has told you, we went to see Mr Spindler. The gentleman had only learned of Claypool's death last night.'

'But it's been in all the papers,' Wiggins pointed out.

'True, the English papers,' Hatchet replied. 'But Mr Spindler had been in France and only returned last night. He'd been on an errand for Jasper Claypool.'

'Let me guess, he was checking the Metropole Hotel for Edith Durant,' Mrs Jeffries said.

'That's right,' Luty interrupted. 'So now it don't matter whether my friend Mr Sauniere has any luck finding out about the woman. Adam Spindler's already done it.'

'Exactly what did he find out?' Smythe asked.

'Edith Durant rarely uses her rooms at the hotel. As a matter of fact, in the last few years, she's only been there a couple of times.'

'Does that mean she's here in England?' Betsy asked.

'We're not sure,' Hatchet responded before Luty could hog the floor again. 'But we think she might have a flat in Brighton. That's what the clerk at the Metropole told Mr Spindler.'

'Where do they send her mail?' Mrs Jeffries asked.

'That's another funny thing,' Hatchet said. 'When Spindler asked, he was told that they didn't forward it anywhere. On her instructions, Edith Durant's mail was picked up by a private messenger service every month.'

'It's almost like she doesn't want anyone to know where she is,' Betsy murmured.

Mrs Jeffries was beginning to have an idea of where

she was, but she would keep her opinion to herself until she had more proof. 'At least now we know a bit more about Claypool. But I still don't understand, why exactly did Spindler say Jasper Claypool had come home? He'd told his family he was going to retire in India.'

'And he'd even bought property,' Mrs Goodge reminded them.

'Supposedly, Jasper got a letter from one of his relations that upset him very much.' Hatchet took a quick sip of tea. 'The letter was from Eric Riley. He virtually accused his half-brother of embezzling money from the company. Eric claimed that Horace Riley is in desperate straits financially and that if Jasper wanted there to be anything left for the rest of them, he'd best come home and take care of Horace.'

'That's true,' Mrs Goodge agreed. 'We've already heard that his missus spends like a drunken sailor and that he's got creditors on his heels day and night.'

'Spindler was planning on returning home to England,' Hatchet continued, 'and he could see how upset his friend was over the letter, so he encouraged Claypool to come home with him.'

'Tell 'em the good part,' Luty insisted.

'In due time, madam.' Hatchet sighed in exasperation. 'As I was saying, Claypool decided to come to London, but he didn't want to give any of them advance notice of his plans. He didn't tell Mr Spindler why, but he was adamant it was to be a surprise visit. On the morning they arrived, he prevailed upon Mr Spindler to go on to Paris and ascertain the whereabouts of his niece, Edith. He told him he wanted to reconcile with

211

her. That same day, Spindler accompanied him to the telegraph office, and he sent messages to both Eric and Horace Riley, asking them to meet him. He was to meet Horace for luncheon at a restaurant near Lambeth Palace at half past one, and he was to meet Eric for tea at half past three. Spindler was quite sure of the times.'

'What about Hilda Christopher?' Mrs Jeffries said. 'Didn't he send her a message too?'

Hatchet shook his head. 'No, he didn't. He told Spindler he wanted to drop by their house unannounced. Apparently, there's been a bit of estrangement between him and Hilda Christopher for the past couple of years.'

'Did Spindler know why?' Mrs Jeffries asked.

'Supposedly, Horace and Eric had been pressing Claypool to sell those empty houses, but he'd promised Hilda he wouldn't. However, he'd decided that the houses should be sold, and he was going to prevail upon her to change her mind. He told Adam Spindler quite a few details.'

'But I thought it was Claypool who wanted those cottages left alone?' Mrs Goodge looked confused.

'It was, but only because Hilda wanted it that way. She'd asked her uncle to pretend he wanted them left alone. That way, her cousins wouldn't harass her over the issue.' Hatchet shrugged. 'After all, Claypool was thousands of miles away, so her cousins could only annoy him by mail. She was afraid if they knew it was her that wanted the property left undeveloped, they'd bother her constantly.'

'This is very confusing.' Betsy said what the rest of them were thinking.

'I know,' Hatchet smiled wearily. 'Even poor Mr

Spindler was confused. But he was quite adamant about everything he told us. Claypool and he had a long voyage together, and apparently the vicar confided in him completely.'

Wiggins reached for another bun. 'Why did Hilda Christopher want them left alone if the property's so valuable? Is she so rich she don't want any more money?'

'She told her uncle that she wanted them left alone as an investment, that she wanted to ensure there was something left for any children she might have one day. Her argument was actually quite sound. London property never goes down in value.'

Mrs Jeffries was trying hard to assimilate all the facts and assemble them into some semblance of order. But she wasn't being very successful in her attempt. She was as confused as the rest of them. 'Are you sure you can trust this Mr Spindler? He seems to know an awful lot.'

'We can trust him:' Luty answered. 'Leastways, I think so. He didn't act like he knew what all this information meant; it was more like Jasper Claypool had bent his ear about it all the way from India.'

'So it was Hilda Christopher who wanted the property left alone so her future children would have something?' Smythe's expression was clearly skeptical.

'That's what Claypool told Spindler,' Hatchet replied.

'But Hilda Christopher doesn't have any children,' Betsy pointed out.

'Right, and that's one of the reasons that Jasper came back. He wanted to get the issue settled once and for all. He didn't think it was fair to his nephews to let the property sit there empty, especially as Mrs Christopher wasn't producing any offspring,'

'So he came back to see if Horace was robbin' him and to settle this property issue.' Mrs Goodge reached for the teapot. 'Is that right?'

'And to reconcile with Edith,' Luty added. 'That's why he sent Spindler to Paris. He was takin' her a letter.'

'Is Spindler going to go to the inspector?' Mrs Jeffries asked.

'He's going to see him tomorrow morning,' Hatchet replied. He shrugged. 'I don't know what it all means, but at least now we know why he came home and, more importantly, that he saw his nephews and possibly his niece on the day he died.'

'I knew it,' Mrs Goodge said. 'The whole bunch is lying.'

'Yes,' Mrs Jeffries murmured. 'But which one of them killed him?'

They spent another half hour discussing the case, but no one came to any conclusions about what it all meant. 'I think we ought to meet again tomorrow morning,' Mrs Jeffries told them as the meeting began to break up.

'Why?' Mrs Goodge stared at her suspiciously. 'You have an idea about who the killer is?' The only time they met twice a day was generally when a case was coming to a head.

'I'm not sure,' she admitted honestly, 'but I've got a nagging feeling in the back of my mind.'

'A nagging feeling about what?' Betsy pressed. She

had great respect for Mrs Jeffries's 'feelings.' She wished she could grow some of her own.

The housekeeper shook her head in frustration. 'That's just it, I don't know. But something is bothering me, and I think we need to be "at the ready", so to speak.'

'That's good enough for me,' Luty announced. 'We'll be here at eight.'

As soon as Luty and Hatchet left, they went about their household chores. They wanted nothing left undone if they had to leap into action, so to speak.

Mrs Jeffries went upstairs and began to dust the staircase. Boring, mundane tasks tended to free her mind to think. But an hour later, when every speck of dust on three floors had been banished, she was still no closer to any conclusions. But she had realized one important thing: there was only one person with a real motive to want Jasper Claypool dead. Horace Riley. He was the only one with something to lose by his uncle's return. If Claypool received proof that Horace was embezzling cash from the firm to keep his creditors at bay, Claypool would probably fire him and put Eric in charge. He might also disinherit the man. He'd already disinherited a niece for immoral behaviour. Surely, to a clergyman, thievery was equally as wrong as adultery.

But something was still nagging her. She took the feather duster to the cupboard under the front stairs, opened the door and tossed it inside. The inspector would be home soon. Maybe he'd have more information, something tangible that would help her to see the pattern in these murders, the connection. There was always a pattern or a connection of some kind.

A few moments later, he was home and she had him cozily ensconced in the drawing room with a glass of sherry.

'This is wonderful.' He took a sip and sighed in pleasure.

'Have you had a good day, sir?' She watched him carefully as she took a sip from her own glass. He seemed in good spirits, and that generally meant he'd made progress on the case. She made a mental note to talk to Constable Barnes the next morning when he arrived to fetch the inspector. It was important that he hear what they'd learned, and she could take the opportunity to find out if he'd picked up any tidbits the inspector neglected to share with her.

On one of their previous cases, Barnes had admitted to her he'd figured out she and the others helped the inspector. But as his own career had benefited from their efforts, and as he had genuine respect and affection for Gerald Witherspoon, he'd kept their secret.

'We've made quite a bit of progress today,' Witherspoon said. 'Barnes sent some lads around the factory area to speak to the local cabbies, to see if either of the Rileys had left the premises on the afternoon Claypool was killed.' He paused and took another sip. 'Both of them had left.'

'So they were both lying about their whereabouts? Where had they gone?'

'Horace Riley would have lied about that as well,' Witherspoon said, 'but I told him the cabman remembered precisely where he'd taken him. So he finally told me the truth. He went to meet his Uncle Jasper at a restaurant on Paradise Street.'

'Gracious, so he did know his uncle was in London.'

'Right, as did Mr Eric Riley. He had tea with his Uncle Jasper later that very afternoon.' The inspector was still amazed at how often people lied to the police.

'But why did they lie about seeing Claypool in the first place?' Mrs Jeffries asked. 'Surely they must have realized you'd eventually catch them out. They were seen in public places with a clergyman who was later found murdered.'

'Ah, but both of those public places were frequented by lots of clergymen,' the inspector said easily. 'And they both hoped no one would notice them. They would have gotten away with it, as well, if they hadn't both been foolish enough to use a local hansom cab.'

'I don't understand, sir,' Mrs Jeffries admitted.

'Lambeth Palace, Mrs Jeffries,' Witherspoon explained. 'Home of the Archbishop of Canterbury and the seat of administration for the Church of England. Clergymen were the main customers for both the restaurant where Claypool met Horace and Eugenia Riley, and at the hotel lobby where he had tea with Eric Riley.'

'I see,' she said slowly. 'That's why no one came forward when his death was announced in the papers. No one at either place noticed him at all, why would they? He was just another old priest amongst dozens of them.'

'It's sad, but understandable,' Witherspoon said.

'Do either of the Rileys own a gun?' she asked. She decided to go right to the heart of the matter.

'Neither of them admitted to owning one,' he said. 'But we're going to talk to Horace Riley's servants again and see if one of them has ever seen a weapon at the house.'

'What about Eric Riley?' she asked.

'Constable Barnes and I are going to have a word with the woman who does his cleaning, and with his landlady. He rooms at a rather nice house in Bermondsey. If he has a gun, we're hoping one of them will have seen it.'

'You've had quite an interesting day, sir.' She gave him an encouraging smile. 'But then, you always find the killer in the end.'

'Thank you, Mrs Jeffries, but I'm afraid we've still a long way to go on this one. Constable Barnes tried to find out a bit more about our poor lady in the chimney but didn't get very far.' He finished his sherry. 'We know good and well that the management of the factory looked the other way while that cottage was being used by someone, but no one appears to have known about it but the neighbors.'

'You mean none of the factory staff knew what was going on?' She found that hard to believe.

'If they did, they'll not admit to it,' Witherspoon replied. 'Barnes spoke to the foreman today, and the fellow insists he'd no idea anyone but legitimate tenants used number seven. He claimed the workers had nothing to do with the cottages and for us to ask the Rileys.'

'Did you, sir?'

'They're sticking to their story, that the cottage simply hadn't been let and they'd no idea anyone ever used the place.' He put his glass down on the table and got up.

'Not to worry, sir.' She rose to her feet, picked up

his empty glass and gave him a broad smile. 'You'll sort it out, sir. You always do. Was that all that happened today?' she asked as he started for the door.

'Oh, we had a young woman come in with some information. One of the maids from Horace Riley's household. She confirmed what we'd already found out.' He took a deep sniff of the air. 'Something smells wonderful. I tell you, I could eat a horse tonight.'

Mrs Jeffries spent another night tossing and turning. In the wee hours she got up and made her way to her chair by the window. A strong wind had blown in from the west, leaving the night clear and clean, with no hint of smoke or fog. She stared at the gaslight across the road, focusing on the pale yellow flame and letting her mind go free. What was the motive for this murder? She had a feeling that was the key. But she'd no idea what that motive might be. Could it be plain old-fashioned greed? Could Horace Riley be so desperate to pay his creditors and hang onto his position that he'd murder his uncle? People had certainly been murdered for less. Perhaps it wasn't even Horace who'd done it. Perhaps Mrs Riley had decided she didn't wish to give up what was decidedly a lavish lifestyle. She came home that night after her husband. After lunching with Jasper Claypool, she could easily have followed him, frightened him into running and then chased him down and put a bullet in his brain. Mrs Jeffries knew better than anyone that the fairer sex could be deadlier than the male.

She sat up as another thought occurred to her. Why was Claypool killed where he was killed? St Paul's

Church on Dock Street wasn't near any of the suspects, nor was it near the Claypool factory. What was Claypool doing in the area? Did it have anything to do with his murder? Then she realized something. Dock Street was in the East End, near the railway stations that went to Chelmsford and Adam Spindler's house. That was probably why he'd been killed at that particular spot. He'd been on his way to his friend's house when his assailant caught up with him.

She sighed and shifted in the hard chair. What about Eric Riley? He was the one with the most to gain. But he could only benefit if Jasper Claypool remained alive. He needed Claypool to sack his half-brother and appoint Eric as general manager of Claypool Manufacturing. With Claypool dead, Eric would inherit half of Claypool's estate, but Horace would inherit the other half. They'd still be equals.

So who would be able to say how the company was going to be run? Obviously, whoever controlled both of the twins' shares. But who would that be? She thought back to what Luty had told them about Claypool's will. But she couldn't recall if that point had been discussed. All she remembered about the twins was that Edith Durant had been disinherited from Claypool's estate and that Hilda Christopher was going to get a set of books. Which meant that neither of them had a motive to murder their uncle.

By the time dawn was breaking and Mrs Jeffries went downstairs to the kitchen, her sleepless night hadn't brought her any closer to an answer.

'You're up early this morning.' Mrs Goodge gave her a cheerful smile.

'I didn't sleep well.' Mrs Jeffries poured herself a cup of tea. 'This case simply doesn't make any sense.' She told the cook some of the thoughts and ideas that had occurred to her in the wee hours of the morning.

Mrs Goodge listened carefully. Finally, when she was certain the housekeeper was finished, she said, 'Perhaps we're making this too hard. Maybe it's a lot simpler than we think.'

'But how could it be?' Mrs Jeffries wished that were true. 'Two murders, ten years apart, and the only thing that links them is an address in Jasper Claypool's dead hand.'

'Why'd he need to write the address down, anyway?' Mrs Goodge asked. 'Surely he knew where the place was.'

'Maybe not.' The housekeeper took a drink of tea. 'Except for his insistence on leaving the cottages alone, he seems to have had little to do with the factory or the cottages.'

'Do you think he might have been the one who killed the chimney lady?' Mrs Goodge grabbed a sack of flour from the counter and put it on the table. 'After all, we've only his word to Spindler that it was Hilda Christopher who insisted on keeping the cottages empty. Maybe it was him all along, and maybe he didn't want any builders in them because he knew Our Lady of the Broken Arm was stuck up in number seven.'

'Our Lady of the Broken Arm,' she repeated. She said nothing for a long moment, merely stared at the cook with a stunned look on her face.

Mrs Goodge blushed. 'Oh, sorry. I shouldn't have said it like that, it's just that's the way I've thought of her ever since Dr Bosworth told us she'd had a broken arm. I'm sorry, I didn't mean any disrespect . . .'

But Mrs Jeffries wasn't listening. She'd pushed back from the table, leapt to her feet and charged to the coat tree. 'Mrs Goodge, you're a genius.' She snatched her cloak down, swung it around her shoulders and reached for her hat.

'I am? Where are you goin'? The others will be here soon . . .'

'I'm going to Finsbury Park.' Mrs Jeffries felt in her cloak pocket and made sure her change purse was still inside. 'Tell Smythe to find that other painter today and find out for certain if anyone, a messenger or anyone else, came to the Christopher house that day. And send Wiggins along to the neighborhood as well. Have him find out if anyone saw a visitor go in or out of the Christopher house late that afternoon.'

'But . . . but . . . what about our meeting?' Mrs Goodge protested.

'You'll have to do it without me,' Mrs Jeffries cried. 'Oh, I'm dreadfully sorry to dash off like this, but it's urgent. You've just made me see what's been right under my nose all the time. Have Betsy get over to the St John's Hotel and find out how often Edith Durant has been here in the past few years and, more importantly, was she here when Claypool died. Have her bribe someone if she must.' With that, she dashed for the back door, leaving the cook staring after her.

When the others arrived, she told them what happened and gave them their instructions. 'But I've no idea what she found out from the inspector last night, because she was out of here too quick to tell me.'

'What's she up to?' Luty demanded. She was a bit put out, as Mrs Jeffries hadn't left any instructions for her to do something.

'I imagine she's got a reason for going to Finsbury Park,' Hatchet said. 'But I can't think what on earth it could be. None of the principals in our case have lived there in over ten years.'

'All I know is what she told me,' Mrs Goodge replied. 'But I've a feelin' you three,' she gestured at Wiggins, Smythe and Betsy, 'had best get crackin'. It'll not take her all day to get there and back.'

They all got up and started for the coat tree. Smythe grabbed Betsy's cloak and wrapped it around her shoulders. 'Stay warm,' he said. He handed Wiggins his jacket and then reached for his own coat. 'Right, then, we're off. Everyone, let's try to be back as quick as we can. I'm wantin' to find out what Mrs Jeffries has got up her sleeve.'

When they left, the other three looked at one another. 'What'll we do? I don't want to sit here twiddlin' my thumbs,' Luty complained.

Mrs Goodge had given the matter a bit of thought. 'I think you ought to snoop over at the Christopher house. I overheard the inspector tell Constable Barnes that they were going to see Eric Riley's landlady. So you'd best not go there. Then the constable happened to mention that he had some police constables talking to the servants at the Horace Riley household, so that's not a safe place to snoop either.'

Barnes had made sure Mrs Goodge had overheard these plans when she'd nipped upstairs during the inspector's breakfast and told the constable about Mrs

Jeffries's trip to Finsbury Park. The household had found a useful ally in the constable, and she wanted to make sure he was fully informed.

'Humph,' Luty snorted. 'I suppose it's better than nothing.'

'Now don't be downcast, madam,' Hatchet soothed. 'We could always go to Richmond and see the other passenger from the ship. Perhaps Jasper Claypool confided something in her.'

'Don't be a jackass, Hatchet.' Luty glared at her butler. 'Spindler already told us that Claypool barely spoke to the woman. Oh, fiddlesticks, I know what you're doin'.'

'I'm doing nothing, madam, except making a reasonable suggestion.'

'You're tryin' to rile me up so I won't feel bad about bein' left out.' Luty snorted again. 'But there's no need. I know that Hepzibah was in a hurry when she left this morning.' Hepzibah was Mrs Jeffries's Christian name.

'She didn't leave you out,' Mrs Goodge exclaimed. 'She knows you better than that. She knows you'll get out and keep snoopin', you don't need instructions from her to do your duty.'

'Precisely,' Luty grinned. She felt much better. 'We'll be back by teatime. Come on, Hatchet. Let's go snoop.'

Inspector Witherspoon and Constable Barnes stood outside the door to Eric Riley's room. His landlady, Mrs Davies, stood on the landing with them. She reached past them and knocked on the door. 'Mr Eric, there's some policemen here to see you.'

'Just a moment,' Eric Riley called. When the door

opened, he was in his shirtsleeves with a towel wrapped around his neck and a bit of shaving soap on his chin. He didn't look pleased to see the policemen. 'What are you doing here?'

'May we come inside, sir?' Witherspoon asked. He knew he had no legal right to force his way in without permission. They didn't have a warrant. But when they'd arrived that morning and spoken with the landlady, she'd mentioned that Mr Riley was still there. Witherspoon had decided to take the opportunity to ask him a few more questions.

Eric stepped back and motioned them inside. 'All right, but do make it quick. I've got to get to the factory. Uncle Jasper's lawyers are going to meet me there.'

'What about your half-brother, sir?' Barnes asked. 'Is he invited to the meeting?' The moment he'd stepped inside, he'd begun having a good look around the premises. He studied the line of the furniture along the floor, trying to see if any of the pieces had been moved recently.

'No, he isn't. Thank you, Mrs Davies,' he said as he closed his door.

The two policemen edged farther into the small, cluttered sitting room. But before they could ask any questions, Eric said, 'If you must know, I'm going to contest Uncle Jasper's will. I don't think he'd have liked his share going to an embezzler, and that's what Horace is.'

'That's a very serious charge, sir,' Witherspoon said softly. 'You told us this yesterday, but you never mentioned what evidence you had against your brother.'

'I'll show that to the solicitor,' he replied.

'Embezzling is a police matter,' Barnes reminded him. He noticed that the skirt of the fabric on the settee was jutting out slightly at the corner. Curious, he moved toward it.

'We're not a public company,' Eric replied. He frowned at the constable. 'Embezzling is only a crime if I or my cousins press charges, and we're not prepared to do that as yet. What are you doing, Constable?'

'Uh, yes Constable, what are you doing?' Witherspoon asked curiously.

Barnes had bent down next to the settee and was sticking his hand underneath it. 'I was just wondering why this bit of fabric was jutting out, sir. Oh goodness, what's this, then?' he pulled his hand back out and held up a small, dark object with a handle. It was a gun.

Eric Riley's jaw dropped. 'I've never seen that before in my life.'

Barnes sniffed the barrel of the weapon. 'It's been fired recently,' he said to Witherspoon. 'And according to Dr Bosworth, it's one of the type of guns that would leave a small hole in the victim.'

'I tell you, I've never seen that before in my life,' Eric wailed. He looked very frightened now. 'You can't think I killed my uncle. You can't.'

'Mr Riley, no one is accusing you of anything,' Witherspoon said. 'However, we will need for you to come with us to the station. If you like, you can send a message to your solicitors. As a matter of fact, I think contacting your solicitor is probably a very good idea.'

The others arrived back at Upper Edmonton Gardens by four o'clock. Mrs Goodge had tea laid on the table, but as the minutes went by, the head chair remained empty. By half past four, they were all anxious but trying hard not to let it show.

It was always in the back of their minds that they chased killers, people who had already proved themselves capable of taking a human life. When one of them didn't show up on time, the others tried their best not to think the worst.

'Where is she?' Luty demanded. 'I'm startin' to get worried.'

'Now, now, madam,' Hatchet soothed. 'Let's not allow our imaginations to run away with us. I'm sure Mrs Jeffries will be here momentarily.'

'She better be,' Wiggins exclaimed. 'It's raining out there now. Did she take her umbrella?'

'I don't think so,' Mrs Goodge said.

'I wonder what's keeping her?' Betsy looked at Smythe, who smiled reassuringly.

'Don't fret,' he said softly, leaning toward her. 'Mrs J knows how to take care of herself.'

'She was only going to Finsbury Park, right?' Hatchet directed the question to the cook. 'She wasn't going to confront any of our suspects?' He broke off as they heard the back door open. 'Wait a second, there she is.'

'I'm terribly sorry to be late,' Mrs Jeffries apologized as she raced into the room, taking off her cloak and shaking off the water. She tossed the garment onto the coat tree and hurried over to her place at the table.

'We were starting to worry,' Mrs Goodge said accusingly.

'How long does it take to get to Finsbury Park and

back?' Luty complained. 'We thought you'd fallen into a well and were about to come lookin' for you.'

She gave them an understanding smile. 'I'm so sorry, I didn't mean to worry anyone. But when I found out what I needed at Finsbury Park, I realized I had to stop by and see Dr Bosworth. It took me a good hour to track the man down. St Thomas's is quite a large hospital. Now, before I tell you anything, I have to know if you were successful?' She looked at Smythe.

'I had a word with the other painter,' Smythe said. 'And he 'ad seen somethin' more than 'is mate. He was workin' on the walls at the back stairs, so he was goin' up and down usin' the front door to bring in his equipment. His mate had the kitchen door blocked with a great ruddy ladder, so even though it was a bother, he had to use the front of the house.' He broke off and grinned. 'Lucky for us he did, too. Because he did see someone come to call and it weren't no messenger. It was Jasper Claypool himself.'

'Claypool was at the Christopher house?' Mrs Goodge was determined to keep everything straight in her mind.

'That's right. He showed up just before the painters was gettin' ready to leave,' Smythe replied. 'That's how come the fellow knew he was there, he'd come up the back stairs and was takin' the last of his paint tins outside. Just as he was walkin' down the hall, he sees this clergyman standing inside the drawing room starin' at Mrs Christopher. He kept on walkin' toward the front door, but he overheard what was bein' said. This clergyman was sayin' something like 'My God! What 'ave you done? Hilda! Hilda!'

Mrs Jeffries interrupted. 'Had Mr or Mrs Christopher seen the painter as he went down the hall?'

'No, he was moving real quiet. He said he always moved quiet when he wasn't usin' a servants door. Besides, he said the parson was making such a racket any one could have heard him. He thought the whole thing odd, but he's seen lots of odd things in houses where he's worked, so he went on about his business. Outside, he and his mate start loadin' their wagon with their equipment, and just then, the clergyman comes runnin' out like the devil himself was on his heels.'

'Then what happened?' Betsy asked.

'The painters pulled out into the traffic just as the old man made the corner and climbed into a hansom. But as they pulled their own wagon around the corner, John Collier, that's the name of the painter, happened to look behind him.' He paused and took a breath. 'He saw Carl Christopher flagging down a hansom, and, a second later, that hansom taking off in the direction Claypool's had gone.'

'Now that's very interesting,' Mrs Jeffries said. 'Anything else?'

'Not really. John said he and his mate talked about it for a bit but decided it weren't none of their affair,' Smythe replied. 'This is important, isn't it?'

'Oh yes,' she said. 'Very important. Wiggins, did you have any luck?'

'Sorry,' Wiggins said glumly. 'None of the servants in the neighborhood saw anything goin' on at the Christopher house. Absolutely nothing.'

'That's fine, Wiggins, I'm sure you did your best.' She glanced at Betsy.

'Edith Durant hasn't stayed at the St John's much at all in the past five years.' Betsy replied. 'But she was there on Monday night. But she just stayed for the one night.'

'Of course she was, and I imagine she arrived unexpectedly and quite late that night, didn't she?' Mrs Jeffries replied.

'That's right,' Betsy said. 'That's exactly what the maid told me.'

Mrs Jeffries sighed heavily. 'I don't quite know how we're going to do this, but I'm fairly sure I know who the killer is and more importantly, why the killing was done. But proving it is going to be difficult.'

'But not impossible,' Mrs Goodge said. 'Right?'

'Let's hope so,' she replied.

'Hey, don't anyone want to know what we found out?' Luty demanded.

'Of course we do,' Mrs Jeffries said quickly.

'Well, as you know, Hatchet and I didn't have much to do, so we went along to the Christopher neighborhood too.' She shot Wiggins a quick grin. 'You're gettin' good, boy, we didn't spot you anywhere.'

'That's nice to 'ear.' He smiled proudly.

'But we did see something else,' Hatchet interjected. 'A messenger from Thomas Cook's came to the house.'

'From Thomas Cook's? The travel people?' Mrs Goodge asked.

'That's right,' Hatchet replied with a nod. 'He brought Mr and Mrs Christopher train tickets. They're leaving for Paris tomorrow morning at ten o'clock.'

CHAPTER ELEVEN

Mrs Jeffries was silent for a long moment, then she said, 'Are you certain about this?'

'Course we are. I paid good money for that information. I bribed the messenger lad a half a guinea to tell me what he was bringing to the Christopher house.' Luty gave a half-embarrassed shrug. 'I oughtn't to be admittin' it, but sometimes it's easier just to put out a few coins, especially when you're in a hurry.'

'We've all done it,' Smythe agreed quickly. He was pleased to know he wasn't the only one who put out coin when the situation called for it. 'And it sounds like it was money well spent.' He looked at the house-keeper. 'Is them leavin' goin' to be a problem?'

'Oh, yes,' she replied. 'So we'll have to work fast. As a matter of fact, we'd best try and move things along tonight.' She fell silent, her expression thoughtful.

The room was so quiet the only sound was the faint ticking of the carriage clock. Finally, Mrs Jeffries said, 'It's a risk, but I think it'll work.'

'Who's the killer, Mrs Jeffries?' Wiggins asked eagerly. 'Can you tell us?'

She hesitated. 'Oh dear, I really don't want to say. You see, we're going to take an awful risk tonight, and if I'm wrong, I don't want the rest of you to have had anything to do with the whole process, if you get my meaning.'

They all stared at her suspiciously.

'Generally, Mrs Jeffries, you keep the name of the killer to yourself when you're not certain you've got the right person,' Hatchet said.

'I'm not certain,' she admitted. 'And if we act too quickly and I'm wrong, the inspector could look like a fool.'

'But you're usually right,' Betsy told her. 'You're good at figuring out these complicated cases.'

'But that's just it,' Mrs Jeffries interrupted. 'The case isn't complicated. It's very simple, and that's what frightens me. What if I'm wrong? What if we take action tonight and get the inspector involved and I'm absolutely one hundred percent wrong? It could ruin his career.'

'Seems to me 'e wouldn't 'ave a career if it 'adn't been for you,' Wiggins said softly.

'But he has one now,' Mrs Jeffries said, 'and I don't want to ruin it for him. But honestly, it's the only solution that makes sense. It really is.'

'But if you do nothing and the Christophers leave, you'll be letting a killer escape? Is that it?' Mrs Goodge pressed.

'That's right.'

'Then I say let's do it,' Betsy declared. 'Seems to me justice is more important than anything else. Especially for that poor woman that's been stuffed up a chimney for ten years.'

There was a general consensus of agreement around the table.

'Betsy's right,' Mrs Goodge said stoutly. 'We might be devoted to our inspector, but we do have a higher calling as well.'

'I agree,' Smythe murmured. He took Betsy's hand. 'We can't start bein' afraid at this point. We've got to do as we think best and not worry about the consequences.'

'Even if we're wrong about this case,' Luty said, 'the inspector could survive one blot on his record. Mind you, I don't think you're wrong at all.'

'You rarely are, Mrs Jeffries,' Hatchet added.

'But I haven't even told you my theory.'

'Doesn't matter,' Luty shrugged. 'We know you and we all know good and well that any idea you've come up with is based on fact.'

Touched by their faith, Mrs Jeffries blinked back tears. 'Right, then. We'll do it. We've got to work fast, though, and after everyone's done what's needed and come back here, I'll tell you my theory.' She began issuing orders like a general. 'Wiggins, get over to Ladbroke Grove Police Station and see if the inspector and Constable Barnes have returned for the day.'

Wiggins got up, and Fred immediately trotted over to him. 'Sorry, boy, you'll have to stay here. I can't risk you spotting the inspector. Should I get Constable Barnes to come back with me?'

'No, I don't want to risk compromising the constable. I just need to know where he is so we can put the plan into action.' She turned to Hatchet and Luty. 'I need one of you to find me someone who can act the part of an informant, and they'll need to do it tonight. Someone who will either walk into the police station or be willing to waylay Constable Barnes on his way home. Do you have anyone who might be willing to do that? I also need that person to then disappear. It would be awkward if he were summoned to give evidence in court.'

Luty looked doubtful. 'I know lots of people, but this is kind of short notice.'

Hatchet grinned broadly. 'I know just the right person,' he said.

'Who?' Luty demanded.

'Never you mind, madam. But take my word for it, it's someone who'll do anything for the right price.'

'I don't want you spending your money,' Mrs Jeffries exclaimed.

'He can spend mine,' Luty put in. 'I've got plenty of it and I ain't goin' to hear any arguments about it, neither. Better to spend money on something good like catchin' a killer than just lettin' it sit pilin' up in a vault and makin' my bankers rich. Now what do you want this here informant to say?'

Inspector Witherspoon had just settled into his chair with a glass of sherry. 'I'm sorry to be so late tonight,' he told Mrs Jeffries, 'but it was a very busy day. Then Constable Barnes got called away, and well, I hung around the station for a while waiting for him to return, but he never came back. I do hope everything is all right.'

'I'm sure he's fine, sir.' Mrs Jeffries took a sip from her own glass. She tried hard not to watch the clock, but if everything moved according to plan, Barnes should be on his way here at this very moment. 'Perhaps someone had some information for him, sir. I believe that happens sometimes. He's been on the force a long time and I imagine he has a number of informants that feed him bits and pieces from time to time.'

'Yes, I expect you're right.' He yawned. 'I suppose I ought to eat my supper, but . . .' He broke off at the sound of knocking on the front door.

'Gracious, I wonder who that can be?' Mrs Jeffries got to her feet and hurried out to the hall. Opening the door, she feigned surprise. 'Constable Barnes. What are you doing here at this time of night?'

He charged right past her. 'I've got to see the inspector, Mrs Jeffries. It's very important.'

'Of course. He's in the drawing room.' But he wasn't, he'd come out into the hall when he heard Barnes's voice.

'Constable.' Witherspoon stared at him in concern. 'Is everything all right?'

'No sir, it's not. We need to get to the Christopher house right away.'

'The Christopher house?' Witherspoon repeated. 'Now? Tonight?'

'Yes, sir. I've just heard from an informant. He's told me the strangest story.' Barnes gave a half-embarrassed shrug. 'At first I didn't believe the man, but he knew one or two details about the victim from the chimney, details that weren't in the news accounts. I had to take him seriously. We've got to get to St John's Wood tonight. The Christophers are leaving town tomorrow.'

Witherspoon was heading for the coat tree. He

grabbed his bowler and his heavy black coat. 'Right, then, you can give me the details on the way.'

'Shouldn't you send someone to the station for a few more police constables?' Mrs Jeffries asked. 'I mean, if you're making an arrest?'

'I really don't think we can take the time,' Barnes said. 'My informant was pretty adamant we get there as soon as possible, I had the impression that he was afraid they'd run for it tonight instead of tomorrow.'

'Should I send Wiggins to the station?' she pressed. She knew just how dangerous this killer could be. There were already two dead bodies. 'Perhaps he can ask them to send some lads around.'

'That's a good idea,' Witherspoon called over his shoulder. 'Have them send a couple of constables to number four Heather Street, St John's Wood. But tell Wiggins to have the sergeant have them wait outside the house. We'll use the whistle if we need them.'

As soon as they were gone, Mrs Jeffries raced down to the kitchen. 'Wiggins, get to the station. The inspector needs a couple of constables sent to the Christopher house.' She gave him the rest of the inspector's message.

'Right.' He was off like a shot.

Mrs Jeffries looked at Smythe. 'I think you'd best get over to the Christopher house as well. Stay out of sight but keep your eyes open.'

Smythe nodded. He knew she was asking him to watch out for their inspector. 'Right. I'll be back as soon as it's over.'

Betsy walked him to the back door. She put her arms around him and pulled him close in a fierce hug.

'Mind you take care, Smythe. I'll box your ears if you let anything bad happen to you.'

He chuckled and gave her a quick kiss. 'Now that we're together, lass, I'll not be taking any foolish chances. I'll just be keeping an eye out. Now that you've agreed to walk down the aisle with me, I'll not let any power on earth keep it from happening,'

'Are you sure your informant is reliable?' Witherspoon asked as the hansom pulled up in front of the Christopher home. Barnes's informant had given them the strangest sort of story.

Barnes sighed inwardly. He wasn't in the least sure about the man's reliability. As a matter of fact, the only thing he was positive about was that his informant probably was acting on instructions from the inspector's own household. But he appreciated the fact that they'd tried to protect him by sending him this information via an anonymous stranger rather than confronting him directly. At least now if they were wrong, the worst that could happen was a bit of embarrassment for the inspector and himself. On the other hand, if they were right, they'd be solving a double homicide. 'Actually, sir, I can't know for sure. But he certainly knew a lot of facts about this case.'

Witherspoon swung down from the hansom. 'Oh well, it can't hurt to have a look in and ask a few questions. Oh good, the lights are still on. At least we're not waking them.'

'It may be an odd story, sir.' Barnes handed the driver some coins. 'But it does make sense. It fits with all the facts.'

'Let's have at it, then.' Witherspoon hurried to the door and banged the knocker. 'I expect the worst that can happen is they'll show us the door.'

Blevins, the butler, opened the door and peered out at them. 'Inspector Witherspoon? Is that you, sir? What on earth are you doing here?'

'We'd like to see Mr and Mrs Christopher,' Witherspoon said. 'It's rather urgent.'

Blevins hesitated. 'I'm afraid it's not convenient, sir. The master and mistress are preparing to go away. The household is in a bit of disarray.'

'Yes, we know,' Barnes said calmly. 'That's why we've got to speak to them tonight.'

'Blevins,' Carl Christopher appeared behind the butler. 'Who is it? Good Lord, it's you lot. What do you want?'

Barnes elbowed the door lightly, forcing both of them to step back. 'We need to speak to you, sir. Please let us in.'

'Open the door,' Christoper instructed the butler. 'Come on, then. But it's most inconvenient.'

They followed their reluctant host into the drawing room, walking past trunks, carpet bags and cases stacked neatly in the hallway. Barnes noticed a small strongbox sitting on top of a stack of hatboxes.

Mrs Christopher was sitting at a small writing table next to the fireplace. Mrs Nimitz, the housekeeper, was standing next to her mistress with a ring of keys in her hand. Annoyed by the interruption, Hilda Christopher glared at the two policemen. 'What is the meaning of this'? How dare you barge in here.'

'We'd like a few moments of your time,' the

inspector began. 'We've had a very serious allegation made against you and your husband, and we thought it prudent to give you an opportunity to defend yourself.'

Mrs Christopher reached for the key ring. 'You may go, Mrs Nimitz. We'll continue this later.'

The housekeeper bobbed a quick curtsey. 'Yes ma'am.'

'Just a moment.' Witherspoon stopped the woman when she would have left. 'I've a question for you.'

'This is outrageous,' Carl Christopher snapped.

The inspector ignored him. 'Mrs Nimitz, please answer this question truthfully.'

'I always tell the truth, sir,' she replied as she cast a nervous glance at her mistress. 'Always.'

'In the last ten years, have you ever seen Mrs Christopher with her sister, Miss Durant?'

Hilda Christopher gasped. She got to her feet. 'How dare you! I'm sending Blevins for our solicitor! Nimitz, you don't have to answer these absurd questions.'

But Mrs Nimitz ignored her mistress. 'I've seen Miss Durant in the house, sir, and I've heard them together in the drawing room when Miss Durant used to visit.'

'But did you actually see them together in the drawing room'?' he pressed. 'Or did you only hear them?'

She thought for a moment. 'I only heard them, sir. And that was several years ago, Inspector. Miss Durant hasn't been here in ages.'

'Now see here, Inspector,' Carl Christopher stepped toward his wife. He went to put his arm around her waist, but she brushed him aside.

'How old were you when you broke your arm?' Witherspoon addressed the question to Mrs Christopher.

'I don't have to answer to you,' she snarled. Her beautiful eyes blazed with fury. She whirled around, turning her back on the policemen.

'Hilda, darling,' Carl soothed. 'Don't lose your temper, dear. I'm sure this can all be sorted out.'

Hilda ignored him and started for the drawing-room door. 'You can talk to these fools if you want. But I don't have to answer these ridiculous questions.'

'I'm afraid you do, ma'am.' Barnes hoped those constables would get there soon. He knew something was going to happen, and better yet, he knew they were on the right track. These two weren't in the least mystified by the questions, only angry. 'Unless, of course, you'd rather accompany us to the station.'

But Hilda wasn't listening; she'd stormed out of the room and slammed the double oak doors shut with a resounding bang. A moment later, they heard a faint click.

'Good Lord,' Carl Christoper muttered. He looked completely stunned. 'She's locked the door.' He ran to the door. 'Hilda? Hilda, come back. Don't leave me here. Hilda!'

Then they heard the front door slam.

Barnes raced to the window and tossed back the curtains. 'She's running, sir,' he called to Witherspoon. He saw her racing down the street with a small, square box in her hands. Barnes guessed it was the strongbox.

The inspector was already on the move. He pushed Carl aside and banged his fist against the heavy wood. 'Hello, hello, Mrs Nimitz. We're locked in here. Mrs Nimitz, can you hear us?' He kept banging as he spoke.

Barnes was struggling with the window, but he couldn't get it to budge. 'It's painted shut, sir.'

Carl Christopher stumbled backward, his gaze still fixed on the door. He had a dazed, uncomprehending expression on his handsome face. 'She left me here. She's gone. I don't believe this. She left me here.'

Witherspoon was still banging. 'Mrs Nimitz, anyone. Can you hear me?'

'Just a moment, sir,' the housekeeper's voice came through the wood. 'I'm trying to get the ruddy thing open, but it's locked. Blevins, get out of the way.'

Barnes dashed to the other window and tried opening that one. 'It won't budge either,' he muttered in disgust. He turned to look at Christoper and saw that the man had sat down on the settee and was staring blankly ahead. 'Do you know where your wife has gone, sir?'

Christopher gave a faint shrug. 'My wife? She's gone. She's left me here. Somehow I always knew it would end like this. I knew it.'

Barnes didn't like the man's color. His skin had gone from white to ashen. 'Are you all right, sir? Do you need anything?'

'All right?' he repeated dazedly. 'Why would I be? She's gone and she's left me to face it on my own. She knows I can't do without her. She knows how much I need her. But she's gone. She always goes when she gets bored, but this time, she won't be back.'

The inspector banged on the door again. 'Mrs Nimitz, are you still there?'

'Yes sir, I'm trying to get it open, but it won't move.'

'Have you got a spare key?' Witherspoon shouted.

'I've sent Blevins downstairs to have a look in the butler's pantry. It'll be just a minute, sir.'

But in fact, it took them twenty minutes to free the three men, and of course, by that time, Mrs Christopher had disappeared without a trace.

'Sit down, Betsy,' Mrs Jeffries told the maid. 'It might be hours before they're back.'

Hatchet poured himself another cup of tea. 'I'm glad to hear that my friend was able to convince Constable Barnes of the truth of our tale.'

'Are you goin' to tell me who this feller was?' Luty demanded.

Hatchet thought about teasing her a bit, but he could see that the others were equally curious. 'His name is Michael Pargenter and he's an actor friend of mine. This was just another job for him, only instead of pretending to be King Lear, he played the role of a disreputable informant with a grudge against Carl Christopher.'

'That's quite a good touch,' Mrs Jeffries said. 'I'm glad you thought of it.'

Hatchet shrugged modestly. 'I had to give our mysterious informant a reason for going to the police. I thought an old grudge against Christopher would be just the thing. But he did say he had a rather hard time convincing the constable the story was true.'

'Let's hope it is true,' Betsy murmured. 'Otherwise there's going to be lots of red faces around here.'

'And mine will be the reddest.' Mrs Jeffries sincerely hoped the sequence of events for both murders was correct. Otherwise they'd have gone to a great deal of trouble over nothing. But the others had agreed with her that as farfetched as it appeared, it made sense.

They heard the back door open, and Betsy leapt up from the table. But before she could get down the hall, Smythe came charging into the room. 'She's done a run for it,' he announced. 'And they've lost her completely.'

'What?' Mrs Jeffries rose as well. 'Who's run for it?' She hoped it was the right person.

'Hilda Christopher.' Smythe plopped down in the chair next to Betsy. 'I was standing across the street, keepin' an eye on the place, when all of a sudden, she comes racing out the front door. At first I thought something 'ad gone 'orribly wrong and she was lookin' for help of some sort. But then she took off running like the devil 'imself was chasin' her. I didn't know what to do. I was afraid if I took off after her that the inspector might be in trouble, but then I heard all this shoutin' comin' from the house. Blow me if a minute later I didn't see Constable Barnes at the window. He was tryin' to get the ruddy thing open and I could hear shoutin' from inside. It was the inspector. I realized he was all right, so I hot-footed it after Hilda Christopher. But she had too much of a lead on me and I couldn't catch up with her.'

'What happened then?' Luty asked eagerly.

'Then I got as close to the house as I dared and I heard more shoutin' comin' from the drawing room. I think they were locked in.'

'Locked in the drawing room?' Mrs Goodge asked, her expression incredulous.

'That's right. I think Hilda Christopher had locked

all of them, including her husband, in the room, and run for it.'

'He's not her husband,' Mrs Jeffries said slowly. 'And she isn't Hilda Christopher. She's Edith Durant.'

It was almost dawn by the time the inspector arrived home. He went straight down to the kitchen. 'Ah,' he smiled as he saw his entire staff gathered around the table. 'I suspected you'd all still be awake. It's not necessary, you know. I don't expect you to wait up for me when I get called out on a case.'

'We know it's not necessary, sir,' Mrs Jeffries replied. She'd relinquished the chair at the head of the table. 'But none of us could sleep until we knew you were safely home. What happened, sir? Did you make an arrest?'

Witherspoon slipped into her chair at the head of the table, and she handed him a cup of tea. 'Well, yes, we arrested Carl Christopher. But I'm afraid his . . . er . . . well, she's not really his wife, she got away. We're watching all the train depots and docks, but so far, she's not to be found.'

'Carl Christopher, sir? Is he your killer?' Mrs Jeffries prodded. They were all well aware of most of the facts of the case.

'He killed Jasper Claypool.' Witherspoon took a quick sip. 'But he claims that Edith Durant did the other killing. That's right, Edith Durant.' He closed his eyes briefly. 'It's quite an ugly story. But at least now it makes some sort of sense.'

'Did you find out who the woman in the chimney was?' Wiggins asked. Mrs Jeffries had told them they had to ask questions, that they had to let him tell them what had happened.

'Yes.' Witherspoon sighed heavily. 'And that's part of what makes it such a sordid tale. The woman was Hilda Christopher. She was murdered ten years ago by her own sister.'

'Gracious, that's shocking,' Mrs Goodge pursed her lips.

'Oh, that's terrible,' Betsy cried.

'How dreadful,' Mrs Jeffries said softly. She was pleased to see that none of them were overacting too much.

'It is a dreadful tale,' Witherspoon said, 'and unfortunately, very true.'

'How did you figure it out, sir?' Betsy asked.

'I didn't really. An informant flat-out told Constable Barnes that the woman living as Hilda Christopher was really Edith Durant. He said they'd killed Jasper Claypool because he'd come back to England unexpectedly and he could expose their charade.' The inspector shrugged. 'As the informant also said the Christophers were getting ready to flee the country, we had to go round there straightaway. When we got there, I started asking the servants if they'd ever seen the two sisters together. You see, we had no proof of any of this, so I was trying to get some circumstantial evidence, so to speak. When all of a sudden, Mrs Christopher runs out and locks all of us, including Carl Christopher, in the drawing room. I suppose I ought to be glad she made such a precipitous move, because if she hadn't we'd not have had a hope of a successful prosecution. But luckily, when

Carl Christopher realized she'd abandoned him, he started talking.'

'He confessed?' Smythe asked. 'That's a bit of luck.'

'Yes, wasn't it?' Witherspoon said. 'He insisted on telling us everything.'

'But how on earth did they get away with it?' Mrs Goodge asked. 'You can't pretend to be someone else for ten years.'

'But you can,' the inspector said. 'The girls were identical twins and the only one who could ever tell them apart was Jasper Claypool.'

'If Carl Christopher was in love with Edith Durant, why did he marry Hilda?' Betsy asked.

'Hilda inherited all her father's money.' Witherspoon took another swig of tea. 'He and Edith continued seeing one another after he married Hilda. Then, when Jasper announced he was going to India, they saw their chance. Jasper was literally the only person who could tell the girls apart. Once he was gone, Edith could take Hilda's place, live with her lover and do whatever she pleased. They lured poor Hilda to the cottage they'd been using for their assignations, and then Edith strangled her with a scarf.'

'But why put her body in a chimney, sir?' Mrs Jeffries poured herself more tea.

'The ground was too wet for them to bury her,' Witherspoon replied. 'And of course, once they'd murdered her, Edith had to come up with a tale to keep everyone, including builders, out of the cottages, so they convinced Jasper to leave them alone as a sort of future investment for Hilda's future children.' Disgusted, he shook his head. 'Carl claimed

246

they always meant to come back and get her, but they never did it.'

'So they murdered that poor man just because he could tell them apart?' Wiggins pretended great shock.

'Awful, isn't it.' Witherspoon sighed. He talked about the case for another few minutes, answering their questions, making comments and generally telling them every little detail about the encounter. Then he yawned and got up. 'Since you waited up for me, I insist that you take the day off tomorrow. We can get our meals from a restaurant and everyone can have a nice, long rest tomorrow morning.'

They protested, but their inspector insisted. Then, after giving Fred a final pat on the head, he went upstairs to his bed.

As soon as he was gone, Betsy said, 'But I don't understand how they could have been so sure they'd get away with it.'

'They were sure because they knew that very few people knew Jasper was coming home,' Mrs Jeffries replied. 'They got very lucky when both the Rileys lied to the police as well.'

'But why did they lie?' Wiggins asked. 'Why not tell the inspector they knew he was in town and 'ad seen 'im?'

'Horace Riley lied because if he'd said anything, the whole issue of why Jasper came back to England would have come out.' Mrs Jeffries shrugged faintly. 'He wasn't going to admit his uncle had come home to fire him for embezzlement.'

'But what about Eric?' Mrs Goodge asked. 'Why didn't he say anything? He'd not stolen or murdered anyone.'

'No,' Mrs Jeffries agreed, 'he hadn't. But I expect it was Eric who knew that Edith and Carl were using the cottage. Once that body was discovered in the chimney, I suspect Eric had a very good idea who it was. He wanted control of the factory. To get it, he needed his own share of the company and control of both the twins' shares. Once Jasper was dead, I think he decided he was going to blackmail Edith and Carl. They had plenty of money. They didn't need the factory income.'

'How'd you suss it out?' Smythe grinned at her. 'Come on, tell us.'

'I wouldn't have if Mrs Goodge hadn't mentioned the chimney victim's broken arm. Then I remembered something Arthur Benning had told me. When the cousins were all children, Edith had pulled a prank that resulted in broken bones for Horace and Hilda. She'd rushed out in front of a pony cart and they'd all been thrown.' Mrs Jeffries smiled faintly. 'That's why I went back to Finsbury Park. I needed confirmation that it was Hilda's arm that had been broken. Benning said it was her right arm that had been broken all those years ago. He remembered because there had been so much gossip about the incident. Then I stopped by to see Dr Bosworth, and he confirmed that our chimney victim's broken arm was the right one.'

'Then it was just a matter of puttin' two and two together,' Wiggins supplied. 'I mean, the clues was all there, right under our noses so to speak.'

'Absolutely,' she agreed. 'Edith Durant had no known address but was seen occasionally in Brighton. I suspect that everytime "Hilda" got a bit bored with

248

Carl, she took off and pretended she was Edith. She went to Paris or to Brighton or someplace else and made sure people saw her. And, of course, the fact that she'd been doing it less and less in recent years proved that they thought they'd gotten away with it. It must have been an awful shock when they opened the front door and saw Jasper Claypool.'

'Why were they acting so strange with their staff on the day Claypool showed up? Why pretend they were going to Brighton?' Mrs Goodge picked at a few crumbs that had fallen on the table.

'Because I think that when the staff was to return that evening, "Edith Durant," would show up unexpectedly and demand to see her sister. As the staff thought the Christophers were gone, they'd never suspect the subterfuge. I suspect that the Christophers used those kinds of opportunities to keep up their charade.'

'Why do you think she left him? Carl, I mean. Why do you think she ran off and left him to face it on his own?' Betsy asked softly. She glanced at Smythe. Nothing would ever make her leave him.

'Because as soon as the inspector started asking questions, she knew the game was over. I don't think she planned to run, it was simply convenient. Providence had placed the key to the drawing room in her hand, the strongbox was sitting in the hall, and she knew her only hope was to get away. Once the police started looking, the charade was sure to be exposed.'

'And she knew Carl was weak,' Smythe said. 'From what the inspector said, it was Edith that was the stronger of the two.'

'And the smarter.' Betsy grinned.

'I don't understand why Jasper Claypool had the address of the cottage in his pocket,' Wiggins said.

'I thought about that as well and I must admit I'm a bit perplexed. As we all know, Claypool knew where the cottage was so he wouldn't have needed the address,' Mrs Jeffries replied. 'Perhaps it's one of those things which will remain a mystery.'

'I know why,' Mrs Goodge said. 'I've done it myself a time or two. Claypool wrote it down because he was an old man. He was probably planning on taking a hansom cab to that address and he didn't want to forget it when he had to tell the driver where he wanted to go.' She smiled sheepishly. 'Sometimes when you're older, you forget the silliest things. It can be very embarrassing.'

'That's probably exactly what happened,' Mrs Jeffries said quickly. 'It certainly sounds logical.'

'Do you think they'll ever catch her?' Mrs Goodge asked. She was irritated that the woman had gotten away.

'I'm sure they will,' Mrs Jeffries replied. But she wasn't, not really. She suspected that Edith Durant had planned some sort of escape route long before. The woman probably had money stashed all over Europe and the Americas in a whole variety of names. Apparently, she was quite good at pretending to be someone she wasn't. 'Let's keep our fingers crossed that they get her.' She yawned and got up.

The others started to clean off the tea things, but she stopped them. 'Go on up to bed. We can take care of this later.'

The others left for their rest, except for Wiggins.

He'd picked up the big brown teapot and was taking it to the sink. 'It's no trouble, Mrs Jeffries,' he said. He looked past her, making sure the rest of them were gone.

'What's wrong, Wiggins?' she asked.

'Uh, if it's all the same to you, I think I'd like to go back and check on my grandfather.' He gave an embarrassed shrug. 'I'd like to make up with my cousin, too. I don't want them thinkin' the worst of me, and leavin' like I did, well, it's bothered my conscience something fierce.'

'I think that's a very good idea,' she replied.

'You don't think the inspector will mind, do you?'

'He'll not mind in the least, Wiggins. Not in the least.'